PRAISE FOR KATE RHODES

'A classy, edge-of-the-seat thriller which will keep you guessing throughout!' B.A. Paris

'An absolute master of pace, plotting and character' Elly Griffiths

'Rhodes does a superb job of balancing a portrayal of a tiny community oppressed by secrets with an uplifting evocation of setting' *Sunday Express*

'Dark, intense, and expertly crafted' Rachel Abbott

'Beautifully written and expertly plotted, this is a masterclass' *Guardian*

'Kate Rhodes directs her cast of suspects with consummate skill, keeping us guessing right to the heartbreaking end' Louise Candlish

'A vividly realised protagonist whose complex and harrowing history rivals the central crime storyline' Sophie Hannah

'Expertly weaves a sense of place and character into a tense and intriguing story' *Metro*

'The whole book tingles with tension. I hope it does for the Scilly Isles what Ann Cleeves did for Shetland' Mel McGrath

'Evocative, immersive, twisty' Sarah Vaughan

'Gripping, clever and impossible to put down' Erin Kelly

'A twenty-first-century Agatha Christie' Julia Crouch

‘Chillingly compelling and expertly assembled’ B.P. Walter

‘Terrifying and tense, as unpredictable as it is compelling’
Lesley Kara

‘Kate Rhodes is approaching pole position in the crime writing stakes with her beautifully plotted and elegantly written thrillers’
Financial Times

‘Terrifying’ *Crime Monthly*

‘Tense and properly chilling’ *Fabulous* magazine

‘Clever, atmospheric and compelling’ *Woman’s Weekly*

ABOUT THE AUTHOR

Kate Rhodes is an acclaimed crime novelist and an award-winning poet, selected by Val McDermid's New Blood panel at Theakston Old Peculier Crime Writing Festival for her debut, *Crossbones Yard*. She has been nominated twice for the prestigious CWA Dagger in the Library award, and is one of the founders of the Killer Women writing group. She lives in Cambridge with her husband, the writer and film-maker Dave Pescod, and visited the Scilly Isles every year as a child, which gave her the idea for the critically acclaimed Isles of Scilly Mysteries series.

Follow Kate on X @K_RhodesWriter, Instagram @katerhodes-writer, on facebook.com/katerhodesauthor and her website: katerhodesbooks.co.uk/.

deadman's pool

KATE RHODES

Orenda Books
16 Carson Road
West Dulwich
London SE21 8HU
www.orendabooks.co.uk

First published in the UK by Orenda Books, 2025

A catalogue record for this book is available from the British Library.

B-format paperback ISBN 978-1-916788-66-4
eISBN 978-1-916788-67-1

Typeset in Garamond and Muli by typesetter.org.uk
Printed and bound by Clays Ltd, Elcograf S.p.A

For sales and distribution, please contact *info@orendabooks.co.uk* or visit *www.orendabooks.co.uk*.

deadman's pool

In memory of Thomas Ford – 'Fordie' – a special young man, remembered with love by his family, friends, and colleagues in the lifeboat crew

'Our dead are never dead to us, until we have forgotten them.'
—George Elliot

PART 1

1

Monday, 8th January

Lao is gone. Mai has been without him for two days, and his absence makes her whole body ache.

The freezing basement where she's trapped has been her world for so long, every object is carved into her memory, like the Vietnamese relatives she's determined not to forget. The room is four metres long and two metres wide, containing only a few pieces of shabby furniture. Her single bed frame is covered in nicks and scratches. Mould blossoms from the walls in powdery black circles, and a broken radio lies on the floor by her bed. If she climbs onto the table in the corner, it's possible to glimpse the garden outside. She stands there often in summer, longing to see birds and flowers in bloom, beyond the confines of her prison. The window is obscured now by brambles running wild, despite the winter chill.

She used to scream for hours, praying someone would hear, but that ended years ago, when she realised it was pointless. Her cell has few comforts. There's a toilet and sink with cracked enamel, and hooks on the wall for the second-hand clothes she hates. The man only provides dresses suitable for a child, even though she's turned sixteen. They bring her little sister Tuyet to mind. She lived with Mai from the day of their capture – until six months ago, when the younger girl vanished in the middle of the night. Mai doesn't know where Tuyet was taken, but still thinks of her every day.

Life is harder than before. The man used to bring them food every night, and even taught them English from a book, if they behaved well. Now the heater is broken, and she's always cold.

Mai has only been allowed to leave her cell a handful of times. The man made her lie on the backseat of his car, covered in blankets, late at night. When she emerged, she was surrounded by trees. The fresh air against her skin felt like a miracle. She could hear night birds calling and smell rain on the dry earth. The wind seemed to call her name as it rushed through the trees. Suddenly the lure of freedom was overwhelming, and her need to find Tuyet. Mai ran away, racing through the dark woods, until she tripped and fell. The man caught her and dragged her back to his car. He's punished her ever since, for abusing his trust.

When she fell pregnant in April, he was furious, even though it was his child. The beating he gave her left bruises all over her body. Mai was half-starved by the time he finally returned, yet the baby kept on growing. She lay in bed at night, smiling whenever it stirred. The baby moved restlessly, like it was desperate to escape into a bigger world.

Mai's labour was terrifying. She delivered her child alone, in agony, but when she held him for the first time, the bond was instant. She called him Lao, in honour of her father. It was easy to ignore the man's curses when he delivered nappies and a Moses basket. But he turned away whenever she breastfed Lao, like it disgusted him to watch.

The Moses basket is empty now, yet Lao's scent of soap and innocence remains. Mai touches the padding, where his body has left a hollow. She can still trace it with her fingertips. Lao was less than a fortnight old when the man took him, two nights ago. What if he never returns, like Tuyet? How will she survive? When Mai closes her eyes she's forgotten how to cry; her tear ducts are empty. Even her mind feels numb, emotions cauterised. She stares at the wall instead, remembering how it felt to cradle her son in her arms.

2

The sea is behaving itself when I reach Hugh Town harbour this morning, which is rare in mid-winter. A fresh storm is already gathering on the horizon. That black ridge of cloud will attack Scilly's beaches soon, before spinning west to create havoc at sea. My wolfdog, Shadow, is in his element. He races down the steps from the quay, through clumps of seaweed, then over sand exposed by the ebbtide, his fur ruffled by the harsh breeze. Town Beach on St Mary's is one of his favourite places to explore. He loves hunting for old lobster pots to chew or rancid fish to dig up, until he returns smelling foul.

'Get back here, you filthy mongrel,' I yell out.

Shadow pauses a hundred metres away to look back. He releases one contemptuous bark, then continues running. Soon he's just a pale-grey streak, vanishing into the distance.

'No respect whatsoever,' I mutter.

The police launch is moored among the crab boats at the end of the quay. My first duty of the day will be to deliver Scilly's only Roman Catholic priest, Father Michael Kerrigan, to St Helen's. It's an uninhabited island, two miles away by sea. He's going on his annual pilgrimage. When I heard he was planning to sail his ancient boat there alone in storm season, I volunteered to ferry him across. My job as deputy chief of police in the Isles of Scilly includes many unusual duties, but the most important one is keeping the population safe, even if that means providing a taxi service occasionally.

I'd hate to spoil Michael's view of St Helen's as a sacred place, but the trip will help me check for signs of smuggling too. Most people think the trade died out here centuries ago, yet it's alive and well, and winter is peak time for bringing contraband drugs, booze and cigarettes through the islands. My team has been working with the Maritime and Coastguard Agency all year to try and bring landings on the off-islands under control. But a few night-time patrols won't stop packages being dropped or collected from Scilly's quietest corners, unless we're vigilant. The ocean is a paradise for small, unlit boats. Our lifeboat even had to rescue an inflatable dinghy with three terrified young women on board last year. They were Albanian nationals, too afraid to name the traffickers who left them drifting on the open sea. The mainland police ferried them to the nearest immigration centre. I'd like to believe they stand a better chance in the UK, but their fate is uncertain. They often wait months for their applications to be processed.

Michael's voyage is much less risky. The prospect has put a smile on his face, like he can't wait to get closer to his God. He won't be getting a luxury ride on our police launch, but at least it runs well. The twenty-five-foot fibreglass hull is covered in scrapes, from bumps against the harbour wall and collisions with unlicensed boats. The dayglow letters announcing that it belongs to the Isles of Scilly Constabulary have almost worn away, but our pathetic budget means it won't be replaced anytime soon.

The priest is approaching when I jump on deck, feeling the vessel shift under my weight. He's small and wiry by comparison, dressed in waterproofs and trainers, his grey hair cropped short. Michael's brisk pace proves that he's in good shape for a man in his fifties – a result of refereeing local football matches. His passion for sport is almost as profound as his faith. He looks expectant today, like he can't wait to leave harbour. I'm surprised to see he's only carrying a small rucksack for his trip to St Helen's.

'No other luggage, Michael?'

He steps onboard. 'I'm only going for two days. Thanks for the lift, by the way. My boat's knackered. I need Ray to fix the engine, again.'

'What about food, and a sleeping bag?'

'It's a pilgrimage, Ben, not a spa break. It's meant to be challenging.' He sounds amused. 'St Elidius lived there without any creature comforts for decades. It won't hurt me to rough it for a while.'

The man's grit is impressive. I like camping too, but not in freezing weather, without food or access to a hot shower. There's nothing on St Helen's apart from ancient ruins, kittiwakes and wild seagrass.

I'm about to call for Shadow when he leaps onboard, panting for breath, just as I release the mooring rope. I gave up trying to second-guess how he reads my mind long ago. He rarely follows orders, but his loyalty is rock solid, so I can't complain. Shadow forms his own opinions about the islanders. He's grown fond of Michael, after a bumpy start, and settles by his side as we leave the quay.

I've always loved boats, so it's no hardship to steer north, leaving the harbour's protection behind, with brine misting my skin. If we travel fast, I'll get back well before the storm hits. The islands lie scattered across the sea, their black outlines afloat on the gunmetal tide. Sailing is a fact of life in Scilly, where everyone learns to navigate as a child. It's a different matter for strangers on these waters. I've seen too many summer visitors being rescued by the lifeboat after damaging the hulls of their yachts. Every season they fall prey to the hidden mountaintops lying just beneath the surface, but I don't need GPS to steer safely round Tresco's eastern coast, provided I keep my distance.

Father Michael looks pleased when St Helen's appears on the horizon. There's little point in talking over the engine's drone, as the boat scuds over low waves. I try to imagine myself in his shoes. He'll spend forty-eight hours alone on a wind-ravaged island that was last inhabited three centuries ago. The idea carries little appeal. My son Noah is one year old, with my wife Nina and I juggling childcare between us. I never enjoy leaving them behind, despite being bug-eyed from sleep deprivation most days.

We're drawing level with Tresco's Pentle Bay, where the arc of white sand looks inviting, even in winter. The North Islands lie directly ahead, the wind dropping suddenly when St Martin's hilly profile looms over us.

Michael turns to me as we approach our destination. 'Have you visited St Helen's much, Ben?'

'Just a few times in my teens, but not since. The council don't like visitors because of the birds' nests, do they?'

'It's okay if you avoid the cliffs. That whole area's protected.'

'Someone told me it's full of burial sites.'

He nods. 'You can't dig there, in case you disturb a monk's unmarked grave. Do you know the island's history?'

'Only that it had a hospital and a church, back in the day.'

'Take a look while you're here, the place is extraordinary.'

'Why, exactly?'

'I can't define it. You'll feel the atmosphere for yourself.'

'You won't convert me, Michael. I'm a diehard sceptic.'

'So was I, until this happened.' He taps his dog collar, grinning. 'Keep an open mind, my friend. God might be waiting for you.'

'I'm past saving.'

'No one's a hopeless cause, believe me.'

The priest goes on teasing me as we cross the calm waters of St Helen's Pool, with the island filling the horizon. It's always tranquil here, unless there's a force-nine gale, the waters protected from east and west by the stony ridges of Tean and Northwethel. I can't explain why I feel edgy as we moor on the quay. Maybe it's the air pressure changing with the coming storm, but my heart rate quickens.

The island looks innocent enough, with its southern coast edged by white sand that glitters with mica, and granite boulders strewn along the shore. It's shrunk over the years, thanks to rising sea levels. High tides have rearranged the coastline, drowning more of its beaches every winter. Cairns stand tall on the rise, like a family of giants. No one knows who created those landmarks from thousands of hand-sized rocks, but they appear to be on guard duty, prepared to defend St Helen's from invaders.

When I glance back at the sea, I spot a motor cruiser departing at top speed. It must have been visiting St Helen's, because there's nothing between the island and the USA's eastern coast. It's too small to identify, so I take a photo with my phone, planning to enlarge it back at the station, in case it's a smuggler.

Michael seems happy now we've arrived. His smile is peaceful when he turns to me, but I'm still unsettled.

'Otherworldly, isn't it, Ben?'

'It's lucky I don't believe in ghosts.'

'Christians call these places "thin". The gap between us and the spiritual world is narrower here than any shrine I know, even Lourdes. It was hallowed ground for centuries.'

'It still feels haunted.' The sky overhead is boiling with clouds. 'I'd better get back, before the rain hits.'

'Do a quick tour with me first, please. It's part of your heritage.'

He strides inland before I can reply, appointing himself as my guide. It's lucky that St Helen's is less than half a mile long. We take just five minutes to march over hard sand to the ruins of the eighteenth-century plague hospital, known as the Pest House. The low granite structure is smaller than my cottage. Its chimney stone is still intact, even though the roof and windows gave way decades ago. I've known of its existence since I was a boy, but never stood inside its ruins.

Michael explains that sailors were forced to quarantine here, instead of infecting the islanders with diseases caught on distant voyages. Men languished in grim conditions until they either recovered from cholera, typhus or the plague, or died of their illness. It must have been terrifying, knowing the pendulum could swing either way. The building would have been packed to the rafters with dying men, more like a prison than a hospital. Many of them never made it home. The graveyard outside is full, with headstones poking up from the weeds. Shadow seems spooked by the place too, barking at top volume.

'Show some respect,' I hiss.

He continues making his infernal noise, jumping up repeatedly. I see now that my dog's pale-blue gaze seems to be asking for something specific, so I pay more attention. He only acts this way when he's sure something's wrong.

'What is it, Shadow?'

He chases across the beach, then looks back, expecting me to follow. It could just be the unfamiliar territory that's excited him, but there's no time for games. I should be leaving, yet Michael seems determined to complete his history lesson. We cross two hundred metres of shore to reach the site where the religious community built their church a thousand years ago.

I notice something much less spiritual, close to the ruined buildings. It's the remains of a campfire, with food wrappers and half a dozen beer cans scattered across the sand. Michael shakes his head. Part of his reason for coming here is to keep the island pristine. Last year he filled three binbags with plastic and ruined fishing nets, washed up by the tide. He explains that St Elidius built the circular prayer oratory alone, in the eighth century, and lived there as a hermit. His bones were interred beneath the altar as relics. The religious community he founded remained here for three hundred years. I can see the foundations of the monk's cells, still standing beside the oratory's granite walls.

Shadow's behaviour distracts me as I absorb the information. He's barking at the top of his lungs now, shattering the island's peace, then he starts digging at a frantic pace. Soon he's created a hole so deep his body disappears into the sand. I try to ignore his antics.

'How did the monks survive here, Michael?'

'It tested them, but hardship was part of their calling. People say they grew crops, sold holy water, and kept bees for honey. The brothers charged passing ships taxes too, in exchange for blessings, or a pilot to give them safe passage to St Mary's.'

We're still talking when Shadow puts his head back and howls.

'Something's upset him, hasn't it?' Michael says.

'He's just being a drama queen.'

Rain is starting to spit when I walk over to check why my dog's so excited. I see a fragment of black plastic at the bottom of the hole, but Shadow is still digging. His frantic movements kick sand into my face, until I pull him away, then kneel down to see what he's found. It looks like a smuggler's cache. They often bury contraband on our beaches, leaving markers behind so runners can find them. This one's parcelled up neatly, with gaffer tape, like all the rest.

I was hoping to save Michael from the grubbier side of island life, but I can't just leave it here. It might contain cannabis resin, or heroin. The smugglers probably lit a fire and drank a few beers before sailing away, leaving their toxic goods behind.

'What kind of philistine leaves rubbish on a holy island?' the priest mutters.

'Let's find out.'

I tug at the plastic, but it's lodged deep in the sand. Shadow seems eager to discover what's inside too, whining softly as my hands fumble in the cold, piercing the wrapping with a key. Someone has wrapped the contents in soft blue fabric, instead of the usual bubble wrap.

'What on earth is it?' Michael asks.

A lock of ink-black hair spills across my hand. Instinct makes my eyes blink shut, but when they open again, I see part of a human face, blanched white, like marble. Is it male or female? The jawline's so narrow, it could even be a child. My hands shake as I cover those ruined features with fabric again. The body lying in the hole is partly decomposed, the skin breaking down.

Shock keeps me frozen in place. Why would anyone kill such a young victim, then bury them under a metre of sand? Maybe it's collateral damage after a drug deal went wrong? Or we're facing a new menace: people smugglers, trading in human lives, like they're just another commodity.

Father Michael is on his knees as I pull out my phone. His

hands are gripped tight in front of his chest, and he's murmuring a stream of Latin words. He appears to be calling for divine intervention, but it won't help. I bet the victim cried out to their God too, and the howling wind was the last sound they heard.

3

The storm chooses the worst time to attack us. Rain pelts my skin, as if someone is flinging chips of ice at my face. I should get Michael under shelter, yet it feels wrong to leave the grave unguarded. I'm struggling to believe that someone sailed here for a winter barbecue, drank some beer, then buried a corpse, ten metres away. But we can't just stand here, getting drenched. Shadow stays close, and he's smart enough not to disturb the crime scene. He behaves the same with my son, standing guard for hours, alert to any potential threat, while Noah learns to crawl. I lean down to feed Shadow some treats; he's performed better than many search-and-rescue dogs, his sense of smell incredibly acute. My biggest concern is the priest, whose glassy stare has drifted out of focus as shock takes hold.

Michael doesn't reply when I ask if he's okay. He must have seen death many times, when he delivers last rites, but nothing prepares you for a life snuffed out, then discarded so casually. There's something contradictory about the burial. The killer cared enough about the victim to wrap their body in a shroud then use plastic sheeting to protect it from the elements. The shifting sand may have left it nearer the surface than when the grave was originally dug. But why would anyone sail to a remote island in mid-winter, when they could have cast the body into the sea? It reminds me of the Albanian women, left to drift last summer, at the mercy of the tides. Traffickers don't just cross the Channel by the shortest route anymore – the trade is getting more sophisticated. Large boats reach obscure parts of the British coastline, sometimes offloading dinghies full of terrified victims if the coastguard get too close, to avoid getting caught.

I need evidence bags and sterile material to keep the site free of contaminants, but I'll have to improvise until help arrives. There's a danger of corrupting the scene, so all I can do is take photos, then cover the victim's face once more, weighing the plastic down with stones to prevent further damage.

'Where can we shelter, Michael?'

His eyes are still glazed. 'Only the Pest House.'

'Let's go, before the storm gets worse.'

The plague hospital won't provide much cover, without a roof, but it's our best chance of escaping the biting wind. It also removes Michael from the scene, before his shock deepens. We run together, back to the Pest House, where the building's empty windows gaze out to sea. Round Island lies just five hundred metres away. Its shape looks oddly celebratory; it resembles a child's birthday cake, with a lighthouse flickering at the centre like a candle, flaring every ten seconds, night and day. The sight warms me, even though rain is coursing down the back of my neck. It's a reminder that the storm may be vicious, but most of humanity is well intentioned. There are safeguards in place to protect mariners from the sea's worst moods.

The priest's face is pale when we crouch behind the building's ancient stone walls. I search my pockets for food, but all I have are treats for Shadow and a single energy bar. Nina buys boxloads of the things, to counteract my tendency to skip meals then come home bad-tempered.

'Eat this, for the shock, Michael. Don't go fainting on me.'

He remains motionless until I give him a gentle nudge, then obeys my instruction, like a child following a teacher's order. I peer out to sea. No help will arrive until conditions improve. St Helen's Pool looks calm enough, but breakers are cresting in the distance, ten feet high as the swell gathers strength. Great conditions for deep-water surfing, but not for sailing over miles of rough Atlantic. My suspicions are confirmed when my deputy, Sergeant Eddie Nickell, sends me a text. He's arranged for the islands' pathologist to be ferried over once the storm subsides.

I'm beginning to understand the sailors' bleak existence when they lay in the Pest House, fighting for their lives. The outside world must have seemed far out of reach, even though the sick men survived on basic provisions dropped by islanders on the landing quay. Only the brave would make that journey, terrified of carrying a fatal disease back home, from air-borne infection.

When I check my phone again, the signal is weak. We're at the outer limits of communication here, twenty-eight miles from the mainland, with the nearest mast a half-hour sail away. But I manage to contact the Coastguard Agency, asking them to check if their patrol boats have spotted any uncertified vessels landing on St Helen's recently.

It takes me three attempts to reach DCI Madron, but I can't leave him in the dark. He insists on being the first to hear important news. My boss must be outside when he picks up, the wind keening in the distance.

'I'm off duty, Kitto. What is it?'

'We've got a major incident, on St Helen's. I thought you should know.'

'Are you incapable of doing your job unsupervised?'

'Listen to me, sir, please. It's a body, buried in the sand.'

I hear him drag in a breath. 'Stay there. Don't touch anything without my permission.'

'But I should—'

'Follow my orders, for once in your life.' Madron hangs up, or the connection fails, but the effect is the same. My hands are tied until he gets here. I can't even comb the area for clues.

There's only white noise now at the end of the line. The breeze steals my curses, as my frustration builds. Madron has watched me like a hawk for the past five years, questioning all my decisions and refusing to modernise our systems. The DCI expects updates twice a day on every case I lead. He's obsessed by formal protocols, even in a crisis, when investigations should move like lightning.

Shadow is giving me more practical assistance than Madron ever does. He's lying beside Michael, resting his muzzle on his thigh, providing warmth and a calming influence. The priest's gaze is slowly coming back into focus while he strokes Shadow's fur.

'Help won't arrive for a while, Michael,' I say. 'You can sail the launch straight home, once the wind drops.'

'I'm not leaving you to deal with this alone. Sorry I lost it back there, but I couldn't believe it. Who'd bury someone, right next to a shrine?'

'There's been smuggling on the off-islands lately. Maybe they came here to trade, and a deal went wrong. But it's odd the victim's so young.' I could mention the Albanians we found, too terrified to betray their captors, but the priest is already shaken.

'It doesn't make sense.' His voice is muted, but he seems calmer than before.

'Stay out of the wind, for now. I'll check if anyone's sailed here recently.'

Shadow rises to follow me, but I motion for him to stay behind. The breeze batters my face again as I leave the shelter. I used to love gales as a kid, when storm-force winds blew so hard, it felt like they could lift me off my feet. There's no chance of that now, at six and a half feet, built like a rugby full-back, with a battered face to match, yet the gusts still feel savage as I reach the brow of the island. The ground is covered in scrub grass, heather and bracken, even though only a thin coat of soil covers the stone. People once scrambled up here to perform sky burials, but the landscape feels tainted now. The local topography has changed completely since then. Maybe the killer believed the beaches would all be claimed by the sea one day, their crime undetected.

When I reach the eastern cliffs, there's a sheer thirty-yard drop where the land plummets into the water. I peer down at breakers hitting the rock-strewn beach, and suddenly the air swarms with birds, screaming out warnings. Herring gulls wing high into the air, defending their nests; they flap against the breeze then hover above my head, releasing harsh cries. On a normal day I'd stop and admire them, despite the ugly sound. I can see kittiwakes too, on the ledges below, sheltering from the wind.

There's no way a boat could land on this side of the island, and whoever visited hasn't left me any evidence. All I can see is rough grass at my feet, tangled with native figwort and hogweed. I retreat from the cliff's edge, and the gulls fall quiet. I've never felt more out of place. This island belongs to nature, not humanity. It's hard to believe that people ever lived here, gathering rainwater when their well ran dry, reliant on crops raised from stony ground.

My old boss's words return to me as I head west across the island. She ran London's Hammersmith force with an iron fist, and her advice on murder investigations was simple: act fast, using specialists and all available officers, to get the job done. Evidence degrades in minutes, not hours. I've got no idea how long that body has lain under the sand, but the only resources at my disposal are an intelligent dog and a priest who can't believe that a holy site has been defiled.

It takes me just fifteen minutes to circle the island's shores, looking for clues. I hate the sea on days like this, for its cruel sense of humour. It plays pranks just when help is most needed. I stand still for a minute, watching waves hitting the shore with force, throwing out clouds of spume. The noise may have calmed the sick and dying patients in the Pest House, but it sounds like a cracked record today, repeating the same angry message.

It's early afternoon when help finally arrives. I see my uncle Ray's converted fishing boat rising and falling as it navigates choppy waves then cuts across the flat water of St Helen's Pool. He's the ideal ferryman for the journey. My uncle spent years in the merchant navy and knows the local sea conditions better than anyone. Ray raises his hand in greeting but remains on deck, always happiest with his own company. His passengers look much less comfortable, particularly the islands' only pathologist, Gareth Keillor. His face is greenish-white from the rough journey. DCI Madron is on the prow with Sergeant Eddie Nickell. Eddie casts his gaze over me and Michael, checking we're unhurt. He was a novice when we started working together, but now he's married with two kids, a friend as well as a colleague, with several murder cases under his belt. He no longer looks like a raw recruit. His blond hair is cropped short, his blue eyes solemn.

Madron is first to disembark. His expression's sour as waves lap over his polished shoes. He's wearing a smart black raincoat and looks more like a stockbroker than a cop, his movements stiff with tension. Keillor leaps onto the wet sand next, clutching his medical bag. He's sixty-plus, like Madron, but much more agile. The man's given me dozens of golf lessons over the years, tolerating my hopeless swing. His persona's different today, his sense of fun hidden from view. Eddie leaps clear of the waves last of all. It's proof that he can still perform acrobatics at the drop of a hat, like he did at school.

The DCI marches towards me, but something's changed. He's normally straight-backed, like a sergeant major, but today he looks frail. He tells me to act as SIO, then mutters something about bad timing, as if the body in the sand is a personal mistake. I focus on Keillor instead. His eyes appear owlish when he peers up at me through thick tortoiseshell glasses.

'Where is it, Ben?'

'By the church ruins; there's picnic rubbish right by the grave.'

He shakes his head. 'You'd better show me, before the next shower.'

Eddie looks unsettled too. He's great at the social side of policing, able to put anyone at ease, but much less comfortable around death or injury. I advise him to head straight for the Pest House to look after Father Michael until Keillor has completed his examination. It's easier to witness death in a photograph instead of eye to eye. Why give him nightmares too, if it can be avoided?

'Take photos of the barbecue site first, Eddie. The rain's probably destroyed any DNA, but try not to contaminate anything. We'll need gloves to pack the rubbish in evidence bags.'

Eddie stands his ground. 'Can I see the victim first, boss? It'll help me understand.'

He approaches the crime scene slowly, his shoulders rigid. Keillor is kneeling beside the hole Shadow dug, wearing sterile gloves. I watch him pull back the plastic from the victim's face and observe those ruined eyes for the first time. Madron looks shaken, which is a first. He's normally so guarded it's impossible to judge his reaction, unlike Eddie. My deputy makes an odd choking sound under his breath. It sounds like a protest, as if he'd gladly punch whoever left this stranger to suffocate. I expect him to reel away then spew his breakfast onto the sand. That's how he's reacted when we've confronted corpses in the past, but this time he doesn't flinch. It's another reminder that he's ready for everything policing can chuck at him these days. His face blanches, but he remains on his feet, his gaze steady.

Keillor is too immersed to notice our reactions. He gets to work fast, always the consummate professional, his movements quick and precise. I listen while he phones Liz Gannick, Cornwall's chief forensics officer. I can hear her barking at him from five metres away. The woman's communication style is caustic at the best of times, but her advice is sound. The body must be exhumed and taken back to St Mary's immediately, before its condition degrades, now it's been exposed to fresh air. Eddie is already taking photos, then helping to scoop sand away from the body. We must be gentle, trying not to disturb the black plastic sheet encasing it. Madron keeps his distance. He stands three metres away, sheltering under his umbrella, mouth downturned.

It takes us twenty minutes to expose the grave fully. I'm even more convinced now that the victim was young because the body is tiny. I bet the killer thinks they've committed the perfect crime – a burial on an island where people are forbidden to dig or remove items from the beach, but the tides have revealed the secret. Winter's relentless waves have shifted the sand further north, bringing the body closer to the surface.

Keillor takes his own photos for the coroner's report, focussing on the exposed face. There's curiosity in his eyes when he looks up at me.

'It's a juvenile, Ben, a female adolescent most likely, based on size. The cold's preserved her, but you can see the soft tissue's breaking down.'

'Has she been here long?'

Keillor stares down at the body. 'Three to six months, I'd say. I'll need tissue analysis to be sure, but it's clear she was in poor health. Her teeth are in a dreadful state. That's odd, at her age.'

I crouch down to study the victim's face more closely. There's nothing inside the eye sockets except blackened hollows, but her exposed jaw catches my attention. Most of her teeth are intact, but several are blackened by decay. It's unusual these days, when most kids obsess over their teeth, bleaching them to a perfect white.

Madron only approaches once the remains are placed in a body bag, still wrapped in cloth and plastic. My boss's face looks pinched with cold, his grey eyes matching the overcast sky. He thanks the pathologist for his work on an unpleasant day. His formality seems out of step with such an ugly crime scene, but politeness is Madron's default whenever he meets a professional equal. The DCI saves his scorn for the rest of us.

Eddie finishes packing away the beer cans, spent matches and foil wrappers in evidence bags. Then he stands beside me, absorbing details. His resilience is part of the reason we're friends as well as colleagues. He never shies away from things that scare him, and I try to do the same. The only difference between us is that I'm ten years older, with a stronger stomach.

'Why here?' Eddie asks.

'People smugglers had a death onboard, maybe, or some islander's got a warped idea of heaven. St Helen's is like a churchyard, isn't it? The ground was consecrated for centuries.'

'This place gives me the creeps.' Eddie shivers as the wind picks up then nods at the sea. 'You know what sailors used to call that stretch of water, don't you?'

'Deadman's Pool.'

He gives a slow nod. 'They threw plague victims in there to avoid digging more graves in this rocky soil. Lead weights were sewn into their shrouds to carry them straight to the ocean floor.'

The fact that we're standing beside a vast underwater cemetery unnerves me as we lift the corpse from its shallow grave, leaving the scene intact. It feels almost weightless, a child's body, not a full-grown adult. Keillor instructs us to take care as we lift it from the sand. My gaze returns to the sea as we carry it to the boat. It's changing every minute. The clouds have dispersed, and the water has faded to a guileless blue, in the blink of an eye, proving it can never be trusted. We'll have to sail back to St Mary's over a drowned graveyard, carrying the smallest murder victim I've ever seen.

4

Mai jumps to her feet when footsteps sound overhead. She waits in silence, her mouth dry with fear. The man treats her better when she wears a smile, but that's not an option today. Mai listens while someone prowls around upstairs. Is it him, or a stranger? The building above remains a mystery. It seems to stand empty most days, until he pays his night-time visits, but for the first time ever, she's eager to see him. Maybe he took Lao to a doctor to find out why he was crying so much? She's praying that today her baby will be returned to her arms, no longer in pain.

The door finally creaks open, and a food package is shoved through the gap. It slams shut again before she can reach it.

Mai lapses into Vietnamese when she calls out, too upset to remember foreign words. Pleas babble from her mouth like a fast-flowing river, but all she can hear is the key twisting in the lock. The man is leaving already. He may not return for days.

Mai wants to release the tears welling in her eyes, but what would be the point? She opens the plastic bag instead. It contains an orange, a can of Coke and a few sandwiches wrapped in foil. The bread smells stale and unpleasant. Why bother to eat or drink if her one reason for living has been taken?

She rests on her bed, exhausted. Mai remembers her mother in Vietnam leaving their cabin at dawn to take a bus to the city to clean the homes of wealthy families, while her father toiled on building sites. Her parents were well educated but took any work available to feed Mai and her sister Kim. They never complained. Their example taught her that family matters above all. She must stay strong to nurse Lao, when the man brings him back. Mai forces down bites of the sandwich. It tastes sour and the texture's dry, but she makes herself swallow it. She must accept every scrap of food she's given, for Lao's sake, if not her own.

5

Ray raises his hand in a brief salute before heading back to Bryher, taking Shadow with him, leaving me to pilot the police launch to St Mary's. It's a typically lowkey gesture from my uncle, who never makes a fuss about anything, even though he braved foul weather to help us out. I feel bad about neglecting him recently. He stepped into my father's shoes after his death, when I was fourteen. The least I can do is get him a bottle of his favourite Irish whiskey as a thank-you gift. Shadow will be glad to return home with Ray. He deserves a chance to dry off in front of the fire instead of waiting hours for me at the police station.

Father Michael hurries onto the police boat, once we've carried the victim's body onboard. He looks eager to escape St Helen's now his pilgrimage has been derailed. His expression is sombre when he drops onto the bench in the wheelhouse, followed by Gareth Keillor, Eddie and DCI Madron. There's frustration in the set of my boss's jaw, a muscle ticking in his cheek. I've never seen him express a personal emotion at work, but something about the case seems to have riled him. I know that he's a churchgoer, so part of it could be anger that a pilgrimage site has been defiled.

All five of us remain silent as we pass Tean's ragged outline, then sail south to St Mary's. The sky is summer-holiday blue, with no clouds overhead, as the sun drops towards the horizon. It feels like the storm was a figment of my imagination. If the temperature was a few degrees warmer I could take a dip, to rinse away memories of the victim's skin, bluish white, like broken porcelain.

The quay is empty when we moor. It's normally a popular hangout on St Mary's, with a coffee shop and benches for people to sit and watch the fishing fleet unload their catch, but the cold wind is keeping them at home. The island's only ambulance is waiting for us, to place the victim's body inside. Keillor remains calm as he nods goodbye, then climbs into the passenger seat, heading for the hospital's mortuary at the top of the hill. I know he'll get to work immediately and examine the body in sterile conditions. He's always quick to act, driven by curiosity as well as professionalism.

When we reach the police station on Garrison Lane, the front door stands open and the place looks welcoming. The building may be covered in ugly grey pebbledash, but Sergeant Lawrie Deane is always a calming influence. The man didn't complain about having to cancel his day off. He's busy preparing hot drinks. Deane isn't blessed with good looks, his greying hair shaved close to his skull, with acne-scarred skin that remains pale all year round, yet he's a sight for sore eyes this afternoon, hovering with his tea tray. The only officer missing from our team is Constable Isla Tremayne. Our newest recruit has been patrolling the island all day, despite the rough weather.

'Get Isla back here, can you, Lawrie?' Madron says. 'We need a team briefing immediately.'

Deane grabs his phone, leaving me and Eddie to help ourselves to the cakes on offer. I can't explain why witnessing death always leaves me hungry. Maybe it's a primal reaction, to remain strong after seeing another life wasted. I cram half a scone into my mouth before checking the photo I took of the boat leaving St Helen's. When I enlarge it to the maximum setting it's a hopeless blur; all I can tell is that it's white and medium-sized, with a fishing platform on the back. Half of the privately owned boats on Scilly look identical. I have to push my disappointment aside. The case has only just begun, and the boat may have no link to the girl's death. There will be many more pointers leading us to the killer, provided we work hard.

Madron has refused a hot drink. Through a crack in his door I catch sight of him bowed over his polished mahogany desk. He looks weakened by today's events, but his office has few comforts. The only personal items on display are some framed photos of his wife, and their daughter's wedding day. There are no other clues to unlock the man's chilly personality, except the neatly catalogued files on his shelves, even though most police paperwork is online these days. It demonstrates the DCI's love of ancient policing methods, while I try to keep up to date. He's spent most of his working life behind that desk, keeping his shoes clean, which suits me fine. I get cabin fever if I'm stuck indoors for more than an hour.

I forget about the DCI while I move around the team room, printing out photos of the crime scene. When I look up from the computer screen again, PC Isla Tremayne is parking the force's motorbike outside the station, her movements deft as she removes her helmet then hurries indoors. She's a twenty-six-year-old graduate, a native islander and as smart as a whip, with a no-nonsense manner and a passion for sea swimming. She joined our team three years ago and seems to enjoy every aspect of her job. I can't judge whether her enthusiasm will survive seeing our latest victim.

Madron emerges five minutes later. The team room is packed with desks, where we all huddle in winter, while the DCI enjoys his privacy. Eddie balances his laptop on his knee, ready to take notes for the incident log, while Lawrie and Isla gaze at our boss like he's their new guru.

'I was hoping we'd get through winter without another major incident,' Madron says. 'We need this wrapped up fast. Listen carefully, all of you, to my instructions.'

Madron addresses us in a sharp tone, like he's reprimanding a gang of naughty kids. He starts by giving an overview of the crime scene. Deane's face reddens when he hears that the victim may be a teenager. His world revolves around his two grandsons, who live near him, here on St Mary's. Death makes him squeamish, even though he tries to hide it. Isla's mind is much more forensic. Her gaze remains glued to Madron's face while she absorbs the details.

'We need information about boats seen visiting St Helen's in the past six months,' the DCI says. 'We've found asylum seekers on Deadman's Pool before now, so this could be connected to trafficking. Contact the Coastguard Agency today. I want photos from their night patrols.'

'I've already requested them, sir,' I say.

He ignores my comment. 'A passing cruiser could have buried the victim in the sand then sailed away, unseen, but there's an outside chance the coastguard can help. We know human trafficking is getting worse in the UK, but the last case here was a year ago.'

'Surely they'd have thrown her into the sea and sailed away? It could be a local who knows the islands inside out,' I say.

'Think before you speak, Kitto, for God's sake. No one's been reported missing, have they?' He stares back at me unblinking, but I won't back down.

'Everyone in Scilly knows St Helen's was once a holy island. Few visitors go there, except the odd pilgrim, or birdwatcher. It's pure fluke that we found the grave, thanks to Shadow. Whoever left that body believed it would never be found.'

'Or maybe the killer was a visitor who's done some research.' Eddie catches my eye. 'Thousands of families come here each summer. The crime may have been committed then.'

'Why bury the body in sand?' Isla asks. 'It was asking for trouble.'

'Stick to the facts, all of you.' The DCI raps the table with his knuckles, silencing us. 'St Helen's is pure granite, with just a thin layer of topsoil. The ground there's too hard to dig. The only exception is the area by the pest house, which is full of ancient graves. Our man was in a hurry, and we need to know why.' He scans each of our faces in turn. 'Kitto will deal with operational details. Find out all you can from the community about passing boats. Our victim may have been involved in smuggling activity.'

I keep quiet, but his point doesn't convince me, and the look on Eddie's face shows he feels the same. Why would a teenager die in a fight between smugglers, unless they're dealing with human cargo, which normally happens on the mainland? But the

DCI seems in no mood for professional argument. He's already moving on to logistics.

'Find a venue for our public meeting tomorrow morning in Hugh Town, please, Isla, before this gets leaked. The church hall's closed, so find an alternative, then announce it on local radio. Inform the Island Council too, so they can spread the word. I want the incident log and timeline completed today. The body was found at ten-fifteen this morning.'

'Shouldn't we be guarding the crime scene, sir?' Deane asks.

'No one will sail there on a rough sea. We'll wait for forensics before disturbing the ground.' Madron rises to his feet, then glances at me. 'I'll ring Gannick and give her an update. No time-wasting, please, Kitto.' He glowers at me, then disappears back into his lair.

'Can we see your photos of the scene, boss?' Isla's voice is muted.

'Of course, but nothing on the incident board. Okay?'

Isla studies the photos first, while Lawrie Deane peers over her shoulder, his expression horrified. It's not surprising. There's nothing in that ravaged face to offer us hope. The sergeant is always reliable, but his aversion to violence is well known. A sensitive soul must be lurking in there somewhere, behind his bluster and common sense.

All three members of my team look numb as they return to their desks. The victim may have been killed by an islander or a passing sailor. At times like this, the Atlantic seems much too wide to reveal a buried truth. We've never begun a case with so little evidence at our disposal and the weather against us. A fresh band of rain lashes the window, hard, as we set to work in silence.

6

Eddie's face is lit with curiosity when we set off for the hospital at 6.00 pm. His shock seems to have worn off, leaving his appetite for work intact.

'Why do you think she was buried there, boss?'

'God knows, but only a psychopath would fire up a barbecue straight after burying a child.'

He studies me again. 'I used to sail to St Helen's with mates for a bit of freedom. Teenagers still do it now.'

'Not in mid-winter, surely?'

'The cold didn't touch us back then. We just wanted to get drunk and chase girls.' The memory makes him smile, until the subject darkens again. 'This will stir up all the conspiracy crap the schoolkids are on about, won't it?'

'How do you mean?'

'Well, according to my nephew, some mad theory's going round about rich islanders committing dark deeds for money, like child trafficking. Maybe this place seems too safe and boring, so they're making stuff up. It's spreading like wildfire.'

'Just what we need.'

'Did you see many cases like this in London, with young victims?'

'It's rare, thank God. I read a Scotland Yard report on murder fatalities a few weeks back. It said that less than eighty teenagers are killed in a typical year.'

'Just our luck it's happened here. The DCI's in a state about it, isn't he?'

'Madron can't stand anything bad happening on his patch, that's why.'

Eddie gives a slow nod. 'You've got way more experience of murder cases. How come he patronises you?'

'Maybe it's just his manner.'

'Or he sees you as a threat? Anyway, it's wrong, in my view. I know the boss is a hundred percent dedicated to his job, but you're committed to the islands too. He should be grateful.'

'It's his problem, not ours, Eddie.'

I appreciate his support, but when he falls silent, his tiredness shows. Eddie wears the stunned look that's common among most parents of small children. I see it on my own face whenever I brush my teeth: a mixture of exhaustion and contentment. Noah has turned my life inside out, yet I wouldn't change a thing. Maybe someone just like us is grieving for their daughter. I still can't believe that anyone on the islands could kill a child then sail out to a remote island to bury her, all without being seen. It would be easy in a city, but not on a tiny archipelago with less than two thousand souls. Some islanders must know why the victim met such a lonely death. We'll need to find out who's been visiting the island recently, and anything they've witnessed.

Gareth Keillor is in his office beside the mortuary when we arrive, peering at his laptop, already dressed in scrubs.

His voice is muted. 'Bad news, I'm afraid. The coroner won't consent to a post-mortem yet. The laws have tightened on child pathology since the Alder Hey scandal; she'll need strong evidence to agree without parental consent.'

'Even though one of the parents may be the killer?'

Keillor gives a slow nod. 'There's plenty I can do in the meantime. My examination won't give us as much as a full autopsy, but it's a start. I've removed the shroud and bagged everything for forensics.'

Eddie and I put on sterile overalls. They stop any fibre, hair or dirt from transferring to the victim's body, but I've always hated their smell of old rubber and the way the neoprene clings to my skin. It's an odd sensation to confront the body again when I step into the theatre, inhaling a lungful of disinfectant and the stink of decay. The corpse lies on a gurney, covered by a white sheet. Eddie makes a tutting sound under his breath when it's drawn back, but he remains upright.

The victim's tangled black hair falls past her shoulders. I can see she's female, but her body's a mess, with welts of exposed flesh. Her limbs are bird-like, with bones poking through her skin. Is it a child, or a woman with a petite build? I've seen more murder victims than I care to remember, but this one strikes a nerve. Her size made her an easy target, and no one protected her. The anger swilling around my gut feels raw. I need to know exactly what happened or her image will stain my memory forever.

'What happened to you?' Keillor mutters to the corpse.

The pathologist is in the zone already. I see it in his rapid movements as he yanks a surgical light down from the ceiling, a microphone beside it. Then he circles the gurney, dictating technical phases I don't fully understand.

'Butyric fermentation, left tibia compound fracture. Corpse wax on torso.'

He pores over the body, touching each limb, before focussing on her hands.

'Compound fracture to left ulna and radius, confirmatory X-ray needed.'

Keillor straightens up suddenly, like he's touched a raw fuse. He switches off the microphone, then gazes at us.

'I can see how she died. Come and look for yourselves.'

Eddie remains a few paces behind me. I can only see the girl's ruined body, with claw-like fists still curled in the defensive position that failed to save her life, until Keillor redirects the light. It almost blinds me with its fierce ray, but it does the trick. The set of her head looks wrong, announcing her injury.

'Her neck was broken?'

He nods rapidly. 'It takes force to break someone's spine. I imagine this child was thrown against a wall or pushed down some stairs.'

'Slow down, Gareth, please. Why are you so sure?'

'There are more broken bones, in her hand and left arm. She would have died fast from the primary injury – paralysed from the neck down. Victims of hanging die the same way. The only other possibility is that she was beaten with a blunt instrument like a sledgehammer, then strung from a rafter.'

'Jesus,' Eddie mutters. 'What a way to go.'

'It tells us plenty about the killer,' I say. 'They enjoyed using force on a young girl. Maybe they've done it before.'

Keillor is still gazing at the victim. 'I'll do X-rays to check her age, but I'd say she was thirteen or fourteen, from the size of her bones.'

The announcement leaves me groping for answers. It's possible the murderer is still on the islands, and we'll find evidence on their phone or computer. They must be well organised, to complete the crime without being seen. I still don't understand why no one's reported the girl missing. She must have parents or siblings, desperate for her to come home.

'Have you finished here, Gareth?'

'Lord, no. This is just the start,' he says, his expression dogged. 'I'll take tissue samples for the lab to check her general health. Those rotten teeth need explaining. I'll ask for a DEXA scan to prove it, but I bet her bone density's poor. The lab should deliver results in three days, with luck.'

'Can you tell if the abuse was sexual?'

'It's unlikely with decomposition this far gone, but I'll take samples anyway.'

'We're checking boats seen in local waters from the past six months with the coastguard and port authorities, but plenty of foreign boats go under the radar. Can I have a genealogy test too, to get an idea if she's a UK national?'

'It'll take days, I'm afraid. That lot pride themselves on being slow.'

'Better late than never. I'm hoping Liz Gannick gets here soon to check the scene for us.'

He nods rapidly. 'She's promising to come tomorrow, if she can dodge the next storm. We'll need her input to make the coroner play ball. Be warned, she sounded tetchy on the phone.'

'That's her on a good day.'

We've all worked closely with Professor Liz Gannick, Cornwall's chief forensics officer, in the past. Keillor is one of the few people she respects. I've experienced her temper plenty of times, but she's a genuine expert, so I take the rough with the smooth.

Keillor is poring over the body again, and I spot the evidence bag from the crime scene on his steel table. It contains the fabric and plastic sheeting the corpse was wrapped in when Shadow discovered it. Gannick won't be thrilled, but I need to look inside. I may have missed vital clues while the rain lashed down.

I pull on surgical gloves before emptying the bag onto a plastic sheet. Eddie's gaze is laser-focussed as I unfold the materials, scanning for evidence. They don't reveal much about the killer at first sight, except their thoroughness. Grey gaffer tape was applied in neat parallel lines to seal the package shut. It doesn't match the sloppiness of leaving barbecue rubbish on the beach, but the two scenes may not even be connected. Littering is something teenagers do when they're too pissed or stoned to care about the environment. That's a world away from committing a well-planned murder.

The killer took pains to wrap the girl's body respectfully. I unfold the dark-blue shroud and see that it's a shawl, stained and crusted with sand. There's an exotic yellow flower at the centre. An orchid, maybe? The material appears to be fine wool that's worn thin in places. When I pick up a corner, an object falls onto the table, no bigger than my thumb. Eddie holds it up to the light. It's a turtle, carved in a semi-transparent green stone that could be jade. I think it's a good-luck charm. What kind of monster beats a girl to death then leaves a talisman in her grave? You'd have to be sentimental, or mad, to believe that one kind gesture could negate such terrible violence.

Eddie takes photos of each item with his phone, then I return them to the evidence bag. By the time I've finished Gareth Keillor is placing the corpse in a zipped body bag, his movements tentative, like he's handling a Ming vase. I help him lower it back into a refrigerated drawer that pulls out from the wall. Now his work is done, I notice his bleak expression.

'My oldest granddaughter's her age, Ben. She's twice the size of that poor kid.'

I should offer to buy Keillor a drink, to dilute the ugliness we've seen, but words stick in my throat. It's been a day full of surprises, with few concrete leads to chase. I can't wait to get back to my family and forget the case for a while. Eddie must feel the same. He disappears soon after I tell him to go home.

I bump into one of the island's nurses hurrying into the building as I leave. Pete Harcourt is an islander I've known all my life. He's heavyset with greying hair, about ten years older than me, wearing his blue nursing uniform. He's helped me plenty of times, including putting my shoulder bone back in place after I dislocated it once, playing rugby. I've got to know him better on a professional level this year, through Noah's regular health checks. There's nothing remarkable about Harcourt's face except a crescent-shaped scar that's left his jaw slightly misshapen, a silver line cutting through his stubble. I know about his injury, because there are few secrets out here. A dog attacked him when he was a boy. The creature had to be put down, and Harcourt needed reconstructive surgery on the mainland, to mend his face. His physical scars are almost imperceptible today, but I'm glad Shadow's not with me. An attack like that would put anyone off dogs for life.

'Everything okay, Ben? You look tired,' Harcourt says.

'Just a long day,' I reply, 'plus sleep deprivation.'

'You have my sympathy. My daughter never shut her eyes for the first year. How's Noah doing?'

'Great, thanks, Pete. He's almost walking.'

'That's quick. He'll be a strong character, I bet.'

Harcourt smiles, then hurries away to his consulting room. His manner is always kind, even though he's dealt with personal tragedy, losing his wife just last year. There's no time to offload today's events anyway, and details of the murder must stay confidential until the public meeting tomorrow.

Lawrie Deane has left me a voice message. The crime file is up to date, and he's making calls to find out who's been seen sailing out to St Helen's in recent months. Isla has set up tomorrow's public meeting for the morning, just as Madron asked. My team have worked hard, but I'm still not satisfied. When I gaze downhill from the hospital, the islands look too pure for the type of evil I've witnessed today. They're strewn across the dark ocean, with their lights twinkling like distant stars.

My walk back to the harbour takes me past DCI Madron's cul-de-sac. His front garden is immaculate, even in mid-winter, with borders cut into a lawn that's so flat and weedless the grass looks artificial. Madron's car is parked on the drive. I wish we had the kind of relationship where I could drop by for some professional advice, one to one, but that would take a miracle. He hates impromptu visits, especially from colleagues. Today's events must have shaken him too, yet our chances of an honest chat between equals are non-existent.

7

The sea is flat calm when I sail home to Bryher with the night air chilling my face. My daily commute from St Mary's can be bumpy in winter, with the bowrider I built in Ray's workshop chopping through every swell, but it helps to distance me from work. Sea mist flavours my mouth with salt as I sail into the headwind, the journey calming my thoughts. Fifteen minutes pass before Bryher's lights glitter on the horizon. My uncle aways leaves a lantern burning outside his boatyard. It's a legacy from his years at sea, when a well-lit coastline could mean the difference between life and death, before GPS made navigation far less hazardous.

Ray's still working, at 8.00 pm, the whine of his circular saw reaching me on the quay. When I peer through the window, he's hunched over his bench, cutting strakes of wood for a new lobster boat, so I leave him to it. The man's passion for his craft is still strong, after decades as Bryher's only master boat builder. Ray's one concession to getting older is the apprentice he recruited last year. Sam Austell's making good progress, but the lad's got enough sense to go home every afternoon at five, while my uncle often toils until bedtime, purely for the love of it.

Shadow appears out of the dark as I head inland. He leaps up to greet me, desperate to lick my face. His tail wags like a windscreen wiper at top speed when I stroke him.

'Good effort today,' I tell him. 'You love outsmarting me, don't you?'

He gives a single bark of agreement then races away. I break into a jog for the half-mile journey home. Time for exercise has been limited since Noah arrived, so my lungs need a workout. The house my grandfather built hunkers among the dunes on Hell Bay, with little to protect it from westerly storms except marram grass and seakale. I stop to gather my breath and watch the sea rolling inland. The next landmass is Bishop's Rock, three miles away, savaged year-round by vicious tides.

My house is lit up like a beacon. I'm expecting to find Nina stretched out on the sofa, poleaxed by caring for our boisterous one-year-old, but another woman steps into my arms when the door flings open. Zoe Morrow is almost forty, but could be in her late twenties, a tall version of Marilyn Monroe, with short peroxide-blonde hair and an electric smile. She was my closest friend growing up, and that won't change. I can still read her like a book, and vice versa. She's been fragile since coming home from her teaching job in a street school in India, leaving her marriage behind. Nina looks amused when Zoe keeps her arm locked tight around my waist. My wife doesn't have a jealous bone in her body, which is part of her appeal. Plenty of former girlfriends assumed there was more to me and Zoe than history, but they were wrong. She's always been more like a sister than a friend.

'What's the news, Big Man?' Zoe says. 'Rumours are flying about dark secrets on St Helen's.'

'You know I can't say.'

'When did you get so boring? You used to be fun.'

'It happens when you hit forty. You'll soon be knitting and watching the history channel.' There's an empty wine bottle on the coffee table, explaining why my two favourite women are so relaxed. 'I'll take a look at Noah first, then give me food and alcohol.'

Zoe releases me to check on my son. The muscles in my chest unlock for the first time today when I peer inside our small nursery. Noah lies inside the cot Ray built for him from offcuts of oak. It's a beautiful crib, with the island's native agapanthus lilies carved on each side. My son is completely at ease, shifting position as I watch. He's restless even in sleep, always hungry for action, while my own body feels lax with tiredness.

Nina and Zoe are in the kitchen when I return to the adult world, the air filled with garlic, oregano and red wine.

'There's lasagne in the oven,' Nina says. 'Finish it if you like.'

'Great, I'm starving.'

'As usual.' Zoe rolls her eyes.

I heap food on the biggest plate I can find and take my time opening a fresh bottle of wine, hoping they will have forgotten about St Helen's in my absence. But they both inspect me as I pile into my dinner.

'Spill the beans then, for God's sake,' Zoe says.

'Believe me, it's not a great story.'

'You're not usually this secretive.' My wife's amber stare is hard to avoid.

I have good reasons to keep quiet, professional as well as personal, but by morning it will be common knowledge. Maybe it's best they hear it from me instead of the islands' grapevine, which often gets things wrong.

'This is confidential, until tomorrow. Okay?' They nod in unison. 'Michael Kerrigan needed a lift this morning to St Helen's, but Shadow found something in the sand, by the church ruins.'

'Was it pirates' gold, Big Man?' Zoe asks.

'Nothing good, I'm afraid.'

'You're stringing this out for the drama. What was inside?'

I swallow a breath before replying. 'A young girl's body.'

'A child, you mean?' Her smile vanishes.

'No one's reported her missing, that's the weird thing. And they took a lot of trouble wrapping her up and burying her there.'

Zoe stands up so fast her chair clatters to the floor. She's already wrenching the back door open as I reach for her arm.

'Stay here, Zoe,' I call out. 'Don't just leave.'

I watch her running away through the open doorway. She hares across the beach with the same loping stride she had when we were young, helping her to win every race between us. I know there's no point in chasing after her. When Nina appears at my side, she takes my hand, her fingers slipping between mine.

'That went well, didn't it?' I say.

'Anything to do with kids upsets her right now. Give her time to process it.'

Zoe's outline is shrinking as she sprints towards the hotel where she grew up, on the far side of the bay. She's endured four miscarriages in the past few years, as repeated cycles of IVF have failed. I should have found a way to explain today's events more gently, without triggering her sadness. I hate leaving her alone in her family's hotel, which always stands empty until the tourist season starts at Easter, and Shadow won't follow her, even though Zoe is one of his favourites. When I try leading him outside, he snarls at me, then slinks away.

'Maybe he's tired,' Nina says.

'You're right, he's worked hard today.'

'So have you, from the sound of it.' She puts her arms around my neck. 'Want to talk it out?'

I lean down to kiss her. 'You'd have bad dreams.'

'Share some of it, at least. Anyone would be traumatised.'

I follow her back to the kitchen. 'We've been dealing with smugglers on the off-islands all year. Bags of dope or crates of booze for runners to collect at night. It could be connected to the girl's body, but it's hard to believe human trafficking goes on here, even though it's a problem on the mainland.'

'Finding that body must have shocked you.'

I give a slow nod. 'Whoever killed her took time wrapping her body in this shawl with this big yellow flower at the centre.'

'Because she mattered to them in some way. If she didn't, they'd have just thrown her into a pit without thinking, wouldn't they?'

I nod in reply. 'Madron's uptight, as usual, questioning everything I say. Eddie's noticed, and I bet the others have too. It happens whenever he's stressed.'

'You should complain to his senior officer.'

'I'd have to be really pissed off to go over his head, in such a small team.'

'I'm happy to listen. Why not let me help?'

'You do all the time, just by being here with Noah. Without you, I'm screwed.'

'That sounds romantic, Ben.' Her eyes shine back at me, their colour a warm amber. 'Pure poetry.'

'I'll try again. How about my love for you will last for all eternity?'

'Shakespeare must be turning in his grave,' she says, laughing. 'Stick to plain English. How about just saying I love you?'

'You know I do.'

'Same here, that's why I came back.'

Our relationship started slowly. We met when Nina travelled here for a break, still grieving for her first husband. I fell for her straight away, but she went back to the mainland for a whole year, giving herself time to recover, before flying back. Nina does everything at her own pace, but it's a trait we share, so I can't complain. It's a joke between us that talking about my feelings doesn't come easily. Maybe it's because the people I love tend to disappear – my parents and my closest work colleague in London, all gone before their time. Nina has none of my superstitions. She works part-time at the island hospital as a counsellor, yet rarely seems stressed herself. Her skill at separating work from home life is unparalleled, but it feels wrong to offload on her until I've got positive news to share.

There's a bigger conversation waiting to happen. Nina wants another baby soon, to give Noah a sibling, but the subject's on hold because we never agree. I can't face her risking another pregnancy, after her illness last time. The doctors say she's fine now, but I'd rather not take the risk. The topic keeps resurfacing, but not tonight, thank God. We sit in companionable silence while I finish my meal, then go through to the living room, where the fire is reduced to embers. I throw a log onto the grate and watch the flames rekindle.

'Do you ever wonder if we're doing the right thing, raising Noah here?' Nina asks.

'It didn't do me any harm.'

'Cities are great too. I loved Bristol as a kid. I joined an orchestra, and went to art galleries and theatres all the time. Kids should experience these things, shouldn't they?'

'He'll grow up in nature here. We can teach him to sail, swim and fish. Or are you yearning for filthy air, overcrowded schools and traffic jams?'

'Interesting that you get so defensive,' she says, smiling. 'Determined to stay in Scilly forever, are you?'

'Why not, if it suits us?'

'You know I love it here – we're surrounded by friends – but my parents hardly get to see Noah. Dad'll be seventy next month. I don't want them to miss out, that's all. Noah loves spending time with them too.'

'So let's visit them more. Anyway, the islands are great for kids.'

'But there's a bigger world out there, waiting for him.'

I don't reply. The truth is, I can't imagine abandoning the islands again, even though Nina's talking sense. The ten years I spent in London felt much too long.

'Maybe we could stay till he reaches primary-school age, then try a year on the mainland?' She studies me again, her gaze gentle. 'You're tired, let's talk about it another day. Want me to play some music?'

'Only if you feel like it.'

'I always do, but I'm rusty. Stop me if it sounds bad.'

Nina takes her violin case down from the shelf, handling her violin with care. It's a hundred and fifty years old, the sounding board faded to a dark gold. She draws the bow across the strings once, checking for pitch, then releases a soft melody, guaranteed not to wake Noah. She went to music school, a long time ago, but still plays well. Tonight's tune is elegant and slow. It rolls between a dozen notes, repeating the same delicate rise and fall. It's a soft refrain, like waves retreating from the land in summer, yet my thoughts won't settle.

I can still feel the girl's cold weight in my hands, when we lifted her from the sand, and see her blue-white skin. I have to find the monster who put her there, or she'll be in my head forever. When I open my eyes again, Nina is returning her violin to its case, and it's time we slept, before Noah wakes us again at dawn.

Shadow's reason for staying at home becomes clear when I enter the hallway. He's lying outside the nursery, blocking the entrance. His grey eyes are so alert, I can tell he's put himself on guard duty. Memories could be troubling him as well, the sight of that dead girl affecting his mood.

'It's not your problem,' I say, stroking his back. 'We'll take care of Noah. Go and sleep by the fire.'

Shadow dismisses my suggestion by turning his head away. It's the canine version of total contempt, leaving me powerless. He remains in place, determined to watch over my son all night in the cold.

8

Mai stares at the thick winter darkness in her room. She's unable to sleep, so she recalls her old life, to bring morning closer. Her childhood was happy, until that day she was walking Tuyet and their cousin Kim to school in the next village. A van drew up by the side of the road, then two men got out and bundled all three of them inside.

That started a terrifying journey. The three girls were held in a cabin for months then forced into a lorry with a dozen younger kids. She was ten years old, but Tuyet and Kim were even younger. Caring for them kept Mai sane. Years have passed since she left her homeland, but she still remembers her fear when they were forced onto a dinghy then cut adrift. She was terrified they would all drown but couldn't let it show, afraid of panicking the younger ones. That was when the man came in his boat. He plucked her from the dinghy, with Tuyet clinging to her side. She has no idea if the other children survived.

Losing Tuyet hurt even more than giving birth to Lao, it rekindled her longing for home, making it keener than ever. If the man doesn't return her baby soon, her mind will shatter.

She beats her fists on the locked door, longing for someone to come. When Mai runs out of strength she screws her eyes shut and remembers her father's quiet dignity. He was so proud when she won a school prize for her prowess in English, promising that studying hard would lead to a better future for them all. Mai keeps thinking of her family, but misery drowns her memories. She was a child when the man locked her and Tuyet in this bare cell, too small to fight back. He claims to love her, but that's a lie. He raped her for the first time two years ago, while Tuyet cried in the corner. The pain and humiliation made her hate him with every atom in her body, yet she can never reveal her feelings.

There must be a way to escape and hunt for Tuyet and Lao, but the man is too strong. She could never win a physical battle between them, so she abandons the idea. To reach freedom she must use her mind as a weapon, not her body. Her parents taught her about *kien*, when she was small. The word means strength and resilience, the ability to survive disasters. Her father said, 'Remember you have *kien* in your soul, Mai. It burns in you like a candle's flame.'

He must have been right, because she's survived this long, but now it feels like her spirit is dying. The night's darkness is slow to lift. A narrow beam shines down from the window above, but it's better than no light at all. She can only pray that it's a hopeful omen.

9

Tuesday, 9th January

My morning begins at 6.00 am, when Shadow enters our bedroom. It irritates the hell out of me, because I fitted a doorknob last week that promised to be dog-proof. It took him five minutes to master how to twist it with both paws, then push, allowing him to slink inside. His pale-blue stare always wakes me, even though he stands in the corner, not making a sound. Nina is still fast asleep when I haul myself upright to hiss at him.

'If you're that bloody clever, why not open the sodding front door as well?'

Shadow ignores my irritation, his tail wagging at top speed. He sprints away once I free him, heading across the bay towards the hotel. My anger soon fades, despite the icy breeze. My dog's zest for life often puts me to shame.

I only remember the first photo I took on St Helen's yesterday when I spot my phone on the hall table. I carry it through to the office to download the image. I enlarge the boat's outline to the maximum setting, but the image collapses into pixels. It's only when I reduce it slightly that the fishing platform becomes recognisable. I can identify the shape, even though it's out of focus. The boat is unique in Scilly.

My uncle built it years ago for Alan Madron. The DCI is a keen sea fisherman in his downtime, like Lawrie Deane. But what made him sail out to St Helen's when he was off duty, then turn tail when he spotted our launch? And why on earth didn't he mention it when I summoned him to the murder scene soon after? Madron's failure to explain why he sailed to St Helen's strikes me as odd but not incriminating. The girl's body may have been left there months ago. There must be a logical explanation for my boss's presence nearby, even though, right now, I can't imagine one.

I find Nina in the nursery with our son on her lap. She looks tired but gorgeous, with chocolate brown hair falling in a sleek line to her shoulder. Noah is gulping milk from his plastic cup like he's been starved for days.

'Did he wake you?' I ask.

She shakes her head. 'Just a bad dream about that girl on St Helen's.'

'I shouldn't have told you.'

'I'd have heard anyway, at your meeting. I'm cadging a lift from Ray so I can be there. Remember, I could help on the case, if you want a counsellor's view.'

'You don't normally volunteer your services.'

'Mental illness causes murders, Ben, especially when the victim's a child. But you already know that.'

'It's the risk level I don't get. The killer could have been spotted sailing over to St Helen's, even at night, yet they went anyway. And why hasn't the girl been reported missing? She could have died on a smuggler's boat, but they'd have just tossed her overboard. They wouldn't care about leaving a victim on sacred ground.'

Nina is watching my reactions. She's observant enough to assess anyone's state of mind from a brief conversation. I know her interpretation of events could unlock the truth for me, but there's so little proof to analyse.

'I think it's an islander,' she says. 'The location's symbolic in some way.'

'More than one person could be involved. The girl was wrapped up like a gift, with a tiny jade carving in her shroud. Whoever left barbecue rubbish close by is much less respectful.'

'Unless they panicked?'

I remember the dead sailors centuries ago with lead weights wrapped in their shrouds, their bodies abandoned in Deadman's Pool. St Helen's is still special to people in Scilly, a calm resting place for generations of monks and mariners, the place haunted now by thousands of birds.

I'm still mulling the idea over when Noah gives a blood-curdling scream. Maybe he's picked up on the dark theme of our conversation, or he's drained his cup, his milk supply suddenly gone.

'Want me to get him dressed?' I ask.

'Thanks. I need to wash my hair.' Nina drops a kiss on my cheek. 'Maybe marrying you wasn't such a big mistake after all.'

'You got lucky, sweetheart. Girls were queuing up for me.'

My wife sniggers. 'Invisible ones, you mean?'

The tragic state of my love life before she arrived always amuses Nina. I've never worked out why a string of relationships fizzled out. Maybe it came down to a lack of effort on my part, but she changed my thinking. Her intelligence and clear-eyed calm still draw me like a magnet, and Noah appears to feel the same. His body is rigid with fury when she passes him to me. I have to wedge him into the crook of my arm, legs thrashing, while he bawls in protest.

'Stop shrieking, mate,' I tell him. 'You're like a bloody foghorn.'

Noah's voice fades to a grumble as he bounces on my hip, and I mash up a banana with a fork. His thatch of black hair needs cutting, like mine. I'm feeding him with his favourite red plastic spoon when I notice the weather outside. Rain lashes our windows, driven by gusts of wind that rattle the glass. Sailing to work will be impossible until it lifts, which frustrates me. My concern about the dead girl has deepened overnight. The news will hit our community hard until we know exactly what happened. But at least the banana has sweetened my son's mood. He beams at me when I wrestle him into a T-shirt and a pair of miniature jeans.

It's 7.30 am by the time I leave him with Nina and cross the island. I used to love squally weather, but today it's a nuisance, making sea journeys hazardous. I scan Shipman Head Down, looking for Shadow. He's missing for once, probably keeping warm with Zoe at the hotel, or anyone that offers him food. My dog's loyalty towards me and my family is rock solid, but he's easily distracted by a free meal.

I'm hit by harsh conditions when my bowrider leaves the protection of New Grimsby Sound. The motor strains as it fights the headwind then labours through ridges of choppy waves. I've crossed the mile-long strait to St Mary's so often, I've seen all the Atlantic's moods and faced worse conditions, but my hair is dripping by the time I reach Hugh Town, just before 8.00 am. It's lucky I don't have far to go. My walk to the station takes five minutes at a brisk pace, with the streets empty, apart from the postman delivering letters. I stop for a brief chat, because civility matters in a place this small, and he's an old schoolmate. There's no escaping familiar faces in Scilly, but these days I welcome it. Tight communities offer you protection, unless you have something to hide.

Rain is still dripping down the back of my neck when I reach the station, which stands empty and unlit. Madron is usually first to arrive, and I was hoping to learn about his boat trip, but he may have gone straight to the quay to prepare for our public meeting.

I only notice the cardboard box left on the steps as I unlock the front door. It's bound to contain food. People often leave us food as a goodwill gesture and I can tell that someone's been extra generous, because the box is a sold weight in my hands, weighing three or four pounds. Fruit cake, most likely. I dump it on Lawrie's desk for him to sort out. He's responsible for the constant supply of refreshments stacked by the kettle, making his waistline expand a little every year. I'm heading for Madron's office when hunger nags at me. I've forgotten how it feels to enjoy a leisurely breakfast, but cake is better than nothing, so I open the box, expecting to see a Tupperware container or biscuit tin. Instead, I see it's packed with a yellow blanket.

Surprise takes hold the moment I lift it. A doll has been placed inside, swaddled in fabric. Maybe it's someone's idea of a joke? But when I look more closely my breath catches.

My hands are trembling when I pull back the fabric and my fears are confirmed. I'm looking down at the corpse of a real-life baby. The horror of it sends my brain into freefall, my guts twisting into knots. The boy is naked under the covering, and tiny compared to Noah. His face is ashen, with eyes sealed shut.

Instinct makes me reach for him, but his skin feels much too cold. How did he die when there's no outward sign of damage? This child was only a few weeks old. I'm trying to control my panic when his eyes suddenly fly open, black pupils fixed on my face, then he releases a thin scream.

'Thank Christ for that,' I say, almost choking.

First a child's death, now an abandoned infant. I can't tell if this baby spent all night outside, or just a few minutes. I'm still motionless with shock when Lawrie Deane arrives, cradling the baby in my arms.

Deane's whistling, as usual, when he hangs up his coat. 'Babysitting today, are you, boss?' he asks.

'Not this time, Lawrie. Someone left this boy on our doorstep.'

'Are you kidding me?' Deane's smile is replaced by surprise when he gazes down at the infant.

But we can't both stand here, gawping like fools. The baby's minute hands are freezing. Why would a mother abandon their child on a small island, when it will only take minutes to track her down?

'Can you hold him?' I ask. 'He needs warming up.'

'Give him here. I'll try not to drop him.'

I can tell it's been years since Deane held a baby. He looks comical, a big man in full police uniform, with a severe haircut, a tiny infant clutched against his chest, but he's doing well. Deane handles him gently, while I make phone calls. Madron doesn't pick up, so I leave him a voicemail then ring the hospital. Dr Ginny Tremayne, the chief medic, soon answers my call.

'I need your help, Ginny. A baby's been left here,' I say. 'He's tiny, just a few weeks old.'

There's a moment of silence, then her words are hesitant. 'That doesn't make sense. The last child born in Scilly was three months ago. I'd know if another baby was due, unless the mother concealed the pregnancy and gave birth alone.'

'Can you come and check him over?'

'I'll cancel my appointments; give me five minutes.'

When I put down the phone, Lawrie is doing his best to make the baby comfortable. He's wrapped him in a clean towel from the station's bathroom and he's turned up the radiators. It strikes me that the parents must want this boy to survive. The box is insulated with newspaper as well as the blanket. I look for clues, but find nothing else inside it, until a slip of paper flutters onto the desk. I recognise the logo printed on it immediately. It shows a white sailboat in front of an island, rising from a line of pure blue sea. It's the logo of Five Islands Academy, the only secondary school in Scilly. It may have been left there deliberately, or it was already inside the box. The mother could be a schoolgirl, too afraid to reveal her pregnancy to anyone.

The timing seems odd, just one day after finding the girl's corpse. Something about the methodical care taken in protecting it from the elements makes me believe that the same person has left us the baby. But why allow him to survive and not the girl? The person cares about the baby's welfare enough to risk being spotted. He looks fragile but clean, without a single bruise, even though he's emaciated. All his ribs are visible under his blue-white skin.

Deane is still caring for the child, blowing on his hands to warm them and rubbing his feet, when Dr Ginny Tremayne appears in the doorway. She's mother to Isla, our youngest recruit. Ginny runs a small team at the hospital, including part-time nurses, who travel between the islands, taking care of everyone's aches and pains. I'm glad she's come herself instead of sending a staff member. She drops her umbrella by the entrance then hurries inside, her grey hair flying loose from its ponytail.

Ginny's concern shows when she examines the boy. His cheekbones look gaunt, dark eyes huge when he protests at being exposed to the air. She rests her stethoscope on his chest, then shines a light into his eyes. Her movements are so deft when she wraps him again, I can tell she's cared for hundreds of newborns in her long career.

'He's got a chest infection. I want him on antibiotics straight away. Where did you find him, exactly?'

'On our doorstep, just now, in a cardboard box.'

She shakes her head. 'He's malnourished but clean. Someone's tried to look after him. We need to find the mum fast, to check she's okay.'

'You're certain it's no one you've treated?'

'Positive. Most women go to the mainland for delivery, unless they're premature. Some poor girl will have given birth in secret, too ashamed to ask for help. That's happened here once or twice in the past.'

'We'll find her, don't worry.'

The rain has stopped when Ginny carries the baby out to the police van, tucked inside her coat to keep him warm. Then I drive them the short distance uphill to the hospital. The boy continues his quiet protests all the way, like he knows that he's been abandoned. I feel relieved when Ginny hurries away through the hospital doors. The boy is her responsibility for the time being, and she'll do everything in her power to help him recover.

When I gaze downhill, people are disembarking from a ferry arriving from the off-islands. A group are already waiting outside the Inn on the Quay, where Isla and Eddie are setting up our meeting. I can see all the way to Round Island, where the lighthouse is sending out white threads of light every half-minute. Fresh clouds are gathering on the horizon. The pressure on the back of my neck feels heavier, but my curiosity is increasing about the secrets this landscape holds. A killer and a brand-new mother are hiding somewhere, just out of reach.

10

I drive straight to the harbour then head for On the Quay, hoping to see Madron before our meeting. The restaurant is an ideal location for it, because it's easy to reach. Ferries drop their passengers right outside, and it's a popular haunt with islanders, serving fresh local seafood, and big enough to accommodate a hundred. I keep my head up when I march towards the entrance, to avoid being waylaid. It's one of the benefits of being built like a brick wall, with hefty shoulders. I can muscle through crowds of people in no time at all.

Eddie and Isla are preparing the space when I jog upstairs, but there's no sign of our boss. Madron loves any opportunity to perform, so he'll be planning a big entrance, just when I need to hear about his voyage to St Helen's. The space is airy with tall windows, giving a fine view over Town harbour, where half a dozen lobster boats tug at their moorings, jostled by the high tide. My two officers have already heard about the baby at the station, but neither can guess who left it there. I'm helping them set out chairs when Lawrie arrives, clutching a projector, his expression flustered.

'Liz Gannick's stuck at Land's End. She bawled me out on the phone, like the bad weather's down to me.'

'She'll want collecting from the airport on time or she'll go nuts,' Eddie says.

No one volunteers to pick up our forensics guru, so it'll be my responsibility, if there's a break in the storm. Lawrie keeps his head down, famously allergic to conflict. Professor Gannick can be a diva at the best of times; delays and inconvenience turn her into a toxic force.

'One of you needs to ring the counsellor at Five Islands. We can start there, looking for the baby's mother, if she doesn't come forward. It's likely to be a youngster. We need a list of girls who could have concealed a pregnancy and given birth alone.' I glance at the closed doorway ahead. 'Has anyone seen the boss?'

The DCI is still absent, and we only have time for a brief update before people flock inside. If Madron doesn't arrive soon, I'll have to start without him. The islands are quiet in winter, so an emergency police meeting always draws people from the off-islands, even in poor weather. By the time I've set up my laptop to project images on the blank end wall, the place is heaving.

The DCI marches through the doors just before the meeting's due to start. He's dressed in full uniform, with epaulette studs shining and his cap pulled low over his forehead, yet it's clear something's wrong. He's seemed uneasy since we found the body, his posture tense as he mounts the stage. The entire population of Hugh Town appears to be assembled here, so it's standing room only. Most of the Island Council are sitting in the front row. They work as volunteers, and most are retirees keen to help the community after long professional careers. Lawrie Deane is a member too, the only police representative.

Emma Angarrack is St Mary's newly appointed mayor and the Island Council's youngest member. She's dressed in an expensive coat, with jet-black hair framing her face. She juggles her role as mayor with running a successful giftshop here in Hugh Town. Her husband, Steve, is sitting beside her, looking equally smart. He's the headteacher at Five Islands Academy. He was a few years senior to me at school and he's a member of the lifeboat crew too, so our paths often cross. He's gone from being a head boy to a pillar of the community without a single glitch. There's a messianic glint in his eye. He's won the entire community's respect by turning the academy into a high-achieving school after years of poor results. I'm glad they've both turned up. We need the support of the islands' power-holders, or policing becomes much harder in a small community.

Madron waits until everyone's settled then rises to his feet. His voice is solemn when he speaks at last.

'Thanks, everyone, for risking life and limb to get here. I'm afraid there's been a fatality. You should prepare yourselves for some unpleasant details.' A hiss of shock travels around the room. 'A body was found on St Helen's yesterday morning, buried in the sand. A young girl in her early teens. We believe she was killed, then someone sailed out to St Helen's to bury her by the ruined church.'

There's a babble of voices, tinged with panic. I keep my gaze on the crowd. It's possible that the killer is among us right now. Their reactions could leave them exposed.

'I want to reassure you that we'll work round the clock to find out what happened. The girl may have been a foreign national, and the Coastguard Agency will help us find out if she was abandoned by a passing boat. We need to know about any boats seen landing on the island. I urge you to come forward at the end of the meeting and give my officers any information you have about this girl's tragic death.'

The DCI answers a few questions from the crowd before letting me take over. I must look a mess beside him, but neatness isn't my forte. I'm dressed in jeans, walking boots and a shirt that's still wet from my journey, my hair dishevelled by the breeze. It's lucky that my giant build seems to command respect. Everyone pays attention when I scan the packed restaurant, where every face is familiar. Ray is standing by the exit with Nina, who's carrying Noah in one of the canvas slings we use to cart him around. I wish there was just one piece of news to deliver, but we need to find the baby's mother too.

'I'm going to show you two items from the crime scene. Take a close look, please. They may belong to someone here. The first is a piece of fabric, and the next is a figurine, just a few inches high.'

My photos appear on the wall, blown up so large you can see snags in the blue fabric and grains of sand on the turtle's back. There's a sudden commotion as someone breaks through the crowd then barges towards the exit. I see it's a young girl but can't identify her before she vanishes. Shock waves are rippling through the crowd. We've had murders in Scilly before but always driven by identifiable motives, like jealousy, marital breakdown or a business deal turned sour. This time it's different. There's no reason on earth for the cold-blooded murder of a child.

I wait for a minute before focussing everyone's attention back on the shawl. I explain that it was used as a shroud, with the keepsake wrapped inside. My uncle's apprentice, Sam Austell, is first to raise his hand. Austell has found a better path after a stretch in prison for drug dealing, and I owe him a big personal debt. He saved me from drowning last year. I could have met the same fate as my father if he hadn't hauled me from the sea in time.

'That flower's a Vietnamese symbol,' Austell says. 'The orchid means eternal health and good luck over there.' Sam turns his phone in my direction, and I glimpse the same blue background with a yellow flower at the centre.

'Thanks, Sam, that could help us. Has anyone seen it before? Maybe it belongs to someone who's been travelling?' My questions are met by silence. 'Let us know if you've seen anyone sailing over to St Helen's in the past few months too. They may have witnessed something important. It's clear people have spent time there. We found the remains of a barbecue, and some beer cans, near where the child was buried.'

I reassure the crowd that someone must know if a neighbour or friend's been making solitary trips to St Helen's. The crowd are talking among themselves, when I call for their attention again and make my second announcement, about the baby I found at the station this morning, fragile, but alive.

'A woman or young girl on the islands may have hidden her pregnancy and the child's birth from everyone. We have to find her soon. She could be in serious need of medical care. If you know anything at all, please stay behind.'

When I glance around, people's faces look blank. The death of a child and an abandoned baby have provided more drama than we've seen all year. I'm hoping a queue of helpers will approach us, ready to share information, yet the place soon empties. It doesn't surprise me that so few members of the public are willing to talk. We're well liked here, on an individual basis, but not as police officers. The islands' mindset of rugged individualism doesn't sit well with law and order. It's a pity, with so few leads to follow. The mayor and her husband have already left. Madron has gone too, leaving my questions unanswered. He must have slipped through the fire escape while I spoke to the crowd, able to disappear fast, like Scotch mist.

Phillip Warleggan is the only person waiting to see me when the meeting ends. He's been a member of the Island Council ever since retiring from his job as a bank manager in St Mary's. The man looks like an old war hero, troubled by bad memories. The wrinkles on his brow have carved deep furrows into his skin. He's wearing a cravat and double-breasted coat, his grey hair combed neatly to conceal his bald spot. Warleggan has lived in Scilly for thirty years. He fought a long campaign to keep the last remaining bank open in Hugh Town, but headquarters claimed the branch was losing money and shut it a few years ago. Warleggan has acted as a walking Citizens' Advice Bureau ever since, giving free advice on pensions, savings and debt to many island families. I even spoke to him myself, recently, about raising a new mortgage to build an extension.

Warleggan's expression is grave. 'This is dreadful news, Ben. I can't believe anyone would be so brutal.'

'We'll soon know what happened, if people share information.'

He nods rapidly. 'I visited Vietnam years ago. The lotus on that prayer shawl is their national symbol, Buddhists see it as a sign of eternal life. The flowers close at night, then reopen each morning, dying and coming back to life. People wear shawls just like it in the temples.' Warleggan delivers his speech in a slow baritone.

'That makes it an odd shroud for a murdered child. Did you notice anything else?'

'Only that Sinead Harcourt was crying when she ran off earlier. I assume that something she heard upset her badly. I hope she's okay.'

'You're very observant, Phillip. Maybe you should quit your voluntary work and join us?'

'My working days are over, thank goodness.' He smiles, then studies me more closely. 'Finding that grave upset you, I can tell, and it's not surprising. You've got a young one at home yourself, haven't you?'

'Noah's just turned one, almost walking, already headstrong.'

'He sounds like a force of nature. Do contact me if I can help you. I'm on your volunteer list.'

'Thanks. I appreciate your support.'

Warleggan bends slightly from his waist to say goodbye, like he's taking a bow. It's odd that although he lives at the heart of our community, I know little about him, except that he speaks like a vicar, delivering good news and bad in the same even tone.

When I turn round, I see that the restaurant has almost emptied. Just two islanders are left talking to Eddie and Isla, while my oldest team member stares at the lotus flower, still projected on the wall, like he's mesmerised.

'Have you spotted something, Lawrie?'

'I've seen that flower before on the islands, but can't remember where, for the life of me.' He rubs his temple hard, like he's freeing a trapped thought. 'My memory's crap these days, when I'm tired. Those photos from St Helen's kept me awake last night.'

'Me too. It's her age that bothers me.'

'Do you want me to cancel my leave till the killer's found?'

'Thanks. I'll be doing the same.' Deane starts to turn away, but then I stop him. 'You're the anchor in this team, Lawrie. The way you've mentored Eddie and Isla is brilliant. I should have thanked you before now.'

He gives an awkward smile, a flush appearing on his pit-marked skin. 'It's the best part of my job. I like seeing them develop.'

'They benefit from your support every day.'

Deane appears shocked by the unexpected praise, but I mean it. His slowness irritates me sometimes, but he's the ballast that keeps us on an even keel. It would be wrong to underestimate the guy. His father was in the armed forces, so he's lived all over the world and learned several languages along the way, making his world view wider than mine. Deane's smile is slowly returning, but he still looks relieved when our conversation returns to professional duties.

'Do you know the Harcourt family well, Lawrie?'

He nods. 'They're friends, as well as neighbours. I'm Sinead's godfather. Me and Pete go to the pub most weekends for a game of pool. Sometimes she tags along.'

'What do you think upset her?'

Deane blinks at me. 'She's been edgy since Gail died last year. It was a bad time to lose her mum, at fifteen. It's unsettled her badly, but anyone can see she's turning pretty. Her dad keeps an eye on her round the clock these days.'

'You think she ran off because the meeting reminded her of losing her mum?'

'Sinead's got some odd ideas. She believes in ghosts, and the conspiracy thing's got to her too,' Deane says. 'The schoolkids say there's some evil network running the islands, involved in smuggling everything under the sun, including children, with big amounts of cash changing hands.'

I nod. 'Eddie mentioned that yesterday. Do you know how it started?'

'Probably some rubbish on TikTok, but Sinead thinks it's true. Once she latches on to an idea, there's no changing it.'

'Eddie and Isla will handle things here. Can you come with me to check Sinead's okay?'

Isla normally accompanies me on visits like this. She's got great interpersonal skills, and it helps to have a woman present, but Deane's position as a trusted family friend could help. He looks glad to have a duty to fulfil as we hurry outside to the police van.

I check my phone on the way. Madron has called while my phone was on silent. His message is delivered in a strident monotone:

'Keep the case file up to date, Kitto. I expect a full write-up of today's meeting. I'll be keeping a close eye on you, so don't be slapdash. I want this case closed fast.'

The man rings off immediately, giving no hint about his own movements yesterday morning. I shove the phone back into my pocket with teeth gritted. My boss delights in criticising me, and my chat with Eddie revealed that the whole team has noticed. I've tolerated it for years, but loyalty isn't a given. It has to be won. My patience is wearing thin, now he's the one keeping secrets. One more rebuke and I'll pay him a home visit and tell him to back off.

11

The Harcourts' place lies in an isolated position a mile outside Hugh Town. I study the winter landscape as Lawrie drives north along the Strand – Town Beach is empty this morning, apart from a few dog walkers braving the elements in raincoats and wellingtons. We soon reach open country, where small fields are seamed together by drystone walls. The farmland is colourful all year round, with wheat turning it gold in summer, followed by the winter flowers these islands have traded in for over a century. Most are grown on St Martin's but they thrive here too. I can see acres of lilies, pinks and daffodils rolling away, waiting for pickers to begin the harvest.

'Is Sinead still at school, Lawrie?' I ask.

'It's her last year. Pete worries about her finding a job when she leaves.'

Deane looks content as we pass his house on Telegraph Hill. The place is his pride and joy, a typical stone-built cottage, small and neat. The front door gleams with fresh blue paint, and it's equally smart inside. He invited me and Eddie round recently to admire the kitchen he's just fitted. Deane has three main passions in life: DIY, sea fishing and spoiling his grandkids rotten.

We swing down a farm track fifty metres beyond his home, the mud rutted with deep grooves left by tractors, passing a house that was abandoned years ago. Its front door is boarded up, the land around it running wild. That happens too often in Scilly. Visitors buy up old properties, planning to use them as holiday homes, but never find time to fix them up, until they become ruins. Deane shrugs when I ask who owns the place.

'Some development company on the mainland, probably. There's asbestos in the walls, so the council put shutters over the windows, in case kids went in to play. Want me to check the deeds?'

'No need. It's just a waste, when youngsters can't afford to buy here.'

'Tell me about it. My grandkids will have to live on the mainland at this rate. Who's going to run things when we're old?'

Everyone in Scilly accepts that our property laws need to change, with petitions being raised every year. The only other house on the track is the Harcourts' at the end of the lane. It's a detached red-brick building surrounded by high fences, like it's trying to keep the world at bay.

The path to the front door is overgrown, with brambles snagging my clothes as I follow it. No one answers the doorbell, but there's an old Ford Fiesta on the drive, so I bide my time.

Harcourt's welcoming smile when he opens the door soon vanishes, like he's primed for bad news.

'Sorry to bother you, Pete,' Deane says. 'Have you got a minute?'

'Is something wrong?' Harcourt's gaze flits in my direction.

'We're after Sinead, if she's at home.'

'No, she's not, and she's not answering my calls. I expected her back hours ago.'

'Can we come in anyway, for a quick chat?' Lawrie keeps his voice low.

Harcourt ushers us inside, muttering an apology. Hospitality is so engrained in Scilly, neighbours always welcome you if you're passing. I only know the man in his professional capacity as a nurse, but his reticence proves that his life hasn't been easy. Someone told me once that his peers called him Scarface when he was young, with the casual cruelty of bored teenagers. His manner seems designed to deflect attention, and even his taste in music is lowkey. The radio on his work surface is playing an orchestral melody, the tempo slow and restful. Harcourt offers us coffee but remains silent otherwise. It's only when he joins us at his kitchen table that I notice his hands trembling.

'Sinead's not in any trouble, is she?'

Lawrie reassures him again, then updates him about our grim find on St Helen's yesterday, while I glance around the kitchen. It's in better condition than his garden, and there's an old photo on the wall of his wife Gail, holding their new daughter in her lap. I remember her as a pretty, upbeat woman with an infectious laugh. The place must echo without her around these days.

Harcourt's frown deepens when he learns about Sinead fleeing from our meeting, visibly upset. 'She's been fretting about something all week.'

'Do you know why?' I ask.

'Anything bad happening on St Helen's would throw her. She sees it as sacred ground where she's always safe. She's lost faith in the world since her mum died.'

'I'm sorry she's having a hard time.' My gaze continues to scan his kitchen. A sensation like an electric current travels down my spine when I spot a small green charm on one of the shelves. It's identical to the one from the crime scene. 'Where did you get that piece of jade, Pete?'

He glances at it. 'Emma Angarrack's shop. I bought a couple for Sinead's birthday. She thinks they bring good luck.'

'We found a similar one at the crime scene. Has she been collecting them long?'

'A few months.' Harcourt blinks his eyes as the idea registers. 'But Sinead's got nothing to do with that girl dying.'

'Of course not; we're just looking for information.'

'People assume that Sinead's trouble because she's different to other kids. She's curious by nature, always discovering things. What's wrong with that?'

'Nothing at all. I was the same.'

I've never seen Harcourt angry until now, red-faced, with a vein throbbing in his neck. But I'm more interested in why his daughter got so upset. Sinead Harcourt sounds like the kind of teenager that a predatory abuser might target, vulnerable after losing her mum. She could have concealed her pregnancy, even from her dad, then struggled to cope with the baby's arrival, abandoning him out of panic. Harcourt still looks furious when I ask if Sinead ever hangs out with older friends.

'She's got a few long-term mates around her own age. They all want to go off to college together, then come back here to live. Sinead would hate leaving them behind.'

I keep my voice low. 'You said she sees St Helen's as sacred ground. Why is that, exactly?'

Harcourt pulls in a breath. 'We scattered Gail's ashes there, last year. We sail over every few weeks. Sinead thinks the place is full of spirits.'

'When's the last time you visited?'

His back stiffens. 'Sunday, to leave flowers for Gail's birthday. My wife always said St Helen's was magical too.'

'It's got a unique atmosphere, that's for sure. Can I take a quick look in Sinead's room, please, before we go?'

'Don't you need a warrant?'

'Not with your permission, Pete. I wouldn't disturb anything, if you agree, and you can be present the whole time.'

Harcourt gives a grudging nod, then leads me upstairs, with Deane trailing behind. I can tell he's reluctant to upset his friend, but I have to find out why his daughter fled from our meeting in tears.

When I enter her room, the atmosphere is gloomy. The walls are charcoal grey, with ghostly shapes chalked across them. Even the ceiling is painted black, making the room feel cave-like. The shelves contain books about witchcraft, hauntings and conspiracies. The girl seems fascinated by the idea of evil existing in our midst, and I can see why. Grief can turn your world dark overnight. I experienced it myself at fourteen, when my father drowned.

Sinead's wardrobe is full of long dresses, in black and grey, that only a Goth would choose. The shapeless garments would have concealed her changing shape, if the baby was hers. My concerns increase when I spot more jade charms arranged on her bedside table, identical to the one from the child's grave.

There's a photo of Sinead's mother smiling down at me. It hangs beside her bed and must be the last thing she sees before she goes to sleep. I'm getting a sense of how the girl's life has changed. She would have felt completely secure here, until catastrophic loss rocked her foundations. Someone could easily manipulate her in that broken state, forcing her to keep secrets, even from her dad.

Harcourt remains in the doorway. His expression's blank, when I finish my search, as if he can't believe what's happening.

'Sinead's had a tough year,' he says. 'But at least she got time to say goodbye. That's the only good thing about cancer.'

'It must have been a hard time for you too.'

'My nursing background helped. And life goes on, doesn't it?'

The man's bravado is typical of the island mentality, where people pride themselves on resilience. I think about Nina's counselling work with traumatised children, but it's the wrong time to suggest professional support for Sinead. Harcourt will have considered it already, given his profession.

'Did you stay long on St Helen's on Sunday, Pete?'

Harcourt shakes his head. 'An hour or so. We took a walk, then came back on the ebb tide.'

'See anyone else there?'

'Not a soul, but there were the remains of a picnic and the embers of a fire burning on the sand, by the old church. We chucked some driftwood on it and stood there for a while.' He's already pulling out his phone. 'Sorry, but I have to find Sinead. She must be upset.'

I catch Deane's eye. 'Stay here with Pete, please, Lawrie. I'll take the van. Call me when Sinead gets home.'

Deane is quick to offer comfort as I leave. The last thing I hear is the sergeant volunteering to ring Sinead's friends to track her down.

The visit stays with me as I drive to the airport to meet Liz

Gannick's flight. Harcourt and his daughter are bound to be close, after their loss, but I still need to know why she rushed out of our meeting. If Harcourt was correct about there being a bonfire still smouldering on St Helen's on Sunday, someone must have been there just hours before, even though no right-minded person would choose such a haunted place for a mid-winter barbecue. I need to know why Madron sailed there too, but he's still not answering my calls.

I'm about to get into the van when Sinead Harcourt appears on the lane, twenty metres ahead, dressed in black from head to toe. The girl is striking, even in funereal clothes. She's got one of those perfectly symmetrical faces you see on TV, but her pallor and dark eye makeup make her look ghostly. Some man on the islands may have been drawn by that ethereal face, exploiting her lack of trust in the adult world. She seems to be weighing up whether I'm a threat. I raise my hand to wave, but the gesture startles her. Sinead leaps through the hedgerow beside the road, then hares away across a ploughed field, with her black hair flying in the breeze.

12

Mai hears a vehicle drive past in the distance. Voices reached her a moment ago through the thick walls. They were so faint, it could have been imaginary, her mind letting her down. She silences her instinct to scream for help. The man punishes her if she yells, with a beating or denying her food. His unpredictability is terrifying. Sometimes he's kind, promising that one day he'll take her abroad to start a new life together. Other times he uses only his fists to communicate.

She remembers the *kien* her father saw in her as a girl. It helps her to stay strong, when all she can think about is being reunited with Lao and her sister. She gazes round the cramped room, looking for a weapon to set her free. Mai runs her fingertips over the bare concrete floor. There's nothing except dust, and cobwebs in the corners of the room, but she doesn't give up. She examines her bed with its battered frame. The wood is old and worn. When she runs her finger along its surface, there's a place where the wood feels rough. It's a splinter as wide as her forefinger, hidden from view by her dirty mattress. She tries to pull it away, hoping to use it as a tool, but it crumbles in her hands.

Mai examines every inch of her living space. At last she finds a piece of metal, jammed in the grate below her sink. It's a nail, rusted and blunt, three inches long. It takes her ages to work it loose with her fingernails. She feels elated when it finally drops into her palm; the steel feels cold against her skin. Mai crouches down to rub it over the rough floor in slow, rhythmic strokes. Then she examines it again. There's no change yet, but the point will sharpen over time. The idea of killing the man makes her hands shake, but maybe the time has come to fight back, even though he's far stronger?

The girl's movements are tentative, her arm swinging in a slow rhythm, using the floor for a whetstone. Almost an hour passes before she rises to her feet again, to press her ear to the door. The silence sounds eternal. Mai keeps praying to hear Lao's thin cry, or any sign that someone knows she's trapped below ground, but there's only the tap of rain, as a fresh downfall pelts her window.

13

It's midday when the Skybus carrying Liz Gannick, Cornwall's chief forensics officer, finally drops from the sky. The flight to Scilly is not for the faint-hearted, especially in storm season, when the islands' twelve-seater planes are buffeted by the breeze. They fly so low over the sea, it feels like any high wave could claim them. The landing tests passengers' courage too. Planes set down on one of the shortest runways in the UK. It takes skill to land with such precision, and the stakes are high, because the runway ends on a cliff edge. If the brakes fail, the pilot and everyone onboard would crash onto St Mary's allotment site, thirty metres below.

I'm braced for verbal abuse when the passenger door opens. Gannick levers herself down the metal steps on her crutches at breakneck speed. She bellows a greeting in her broad northern accent, but the frown on her elfin face looks permanent. The woman could still be a teenager, with a tiny frame, despite being in her forties. Her hair is a different colour each time we meet, a few electric-blue streaks framing her face.

'What horrors have you got in store for me this time?' she asks.

'It's the worst yet, Liz. Thanks for coming over.'

'This is my job, remember? I don't do it for kicks.' Her tone's caustic. 'Let's get moving. The bloody weather's cost us a whole day.'

'Give me a minute, I'll fetch your kit.'

Gannick always comes prepared, with huge boxes on castors, containing her mobile lab and the tools she uses in situ.

'Send the big one to my hotel. I only need the small one today.'

The woman's definition of small is a metal box that weighs a ton when I push it over the concourse. Gannick complains bitterly about travelling through foul weather then throws her crutches into the van. It's only when she swings herself into the passenger seat that she falls silent.

'You've gone quiet on me, Liz. Should I be worried?'

Her eyes glitter. 'You screwed up, big time, exposing that body to the elements.'

'I wasn't expecting a murder scene. We've been dealing with smugglers all year; I thought it was a cache of drugs, not a grave.'

'Let's hope the rest of your investigation goes better.' She glances across at me. 'Where's Madron, anyway? He normally runs the welcome party.'

'You've got me this time. We've booked rooms for you at Tregarthen's Hotel.'

'That's a decent start. Where's that bloody dog of yours?'

'On Bryher, taking a day off.'

'You should leave him there for good.'

'Come on, Liz. Shadow's helped us in the past, and he found the body. I'm still thinking of getting him trained for search and rescue.'

'Forget it. He's wayward, like his master.' Gannick pretends to hate Shadow with a passion, but often slips him treats when no one's watching. 'Tell me the full story. Don't miss anything out.'

'We've got a potential witness. A teenage girl reacted badly to the news about the murder, then ran away from me, just now. Her mother's ashes were scattered on St Helen's. It's possible she's made trips there and saw what happened to the victim.' I pass on details of the infant left at the station this morning, as I drive downhill to Hugh Town, less than five minutes away. Gannick's face is lit with curiosity by the time we arrive.

'How could anyone conceal a pregnancy in a place this small?'

'Maybe she had no choice, if there's danger at home,' I reply. 'It could be a young girl, or someone trapped in a bad relationship.'

Gannick's gaze shifts to the sea as I haul her kit down the concrete steps from the quay to the police launch, exercising muscles that have lain dormant for months. The chief SOCO seems glad to be in Scilly again, despite the hard breeze coming off the water as we leave harbour. She looks content for once, observing the islands scattered along the horizon like pebbles flung into the sea. Storm petrels are keeping pace with us overhead. They must be hoping we'll trawl for fish, providing them with a free meal.

I feel uncomfortable when my boat enters the calm of Deadman's Pool. The buried child lingers in my head, and the air's chill is biting as I drag Gannick's kit box down the jetty on St Helen's, towards the crime scene. The strange atmosphere seems to leave her unaffected. If she can sense the hardships the monks endured, or the decades of suffering at the Pest House, there's no outward sign.

She hands me a white Tyvek suit. 'Put this on before you come any closer. The scene's already contaminated.'

I do as she says but she's far quicker than me. It only takes her a few minutes to get kitted up then cross the beach to the oratory, where yellow crime-scene tape billows in the breeze. The area where Shadow dug up the sand is covered with plastic sheeting, weighed down by stones. Gannick is on her knees already, pointing a blue-beamed torch at the surrounding area, looking for blood traces underneath rocks. Her gaze is laser-sharp when she studies me again.

'Have you done a fingertip search?'

'Not yet, I was waiting for you.'

'Seriously?' Her voice is shrill with outrage. 'You just sat here, doing fuck all?'

'It was pissing down. I had a civilian in shock, and Madron ordered me not to touch anything.'

'You should have ignored him; you know the protocol by now,' she hisses. 'Don't just stand there. Get on with the bloody job.'

I'm tempted to argue, but it would only slow my investigation down.

'Where do I start?'

'Circle the crime scene, behind me. Widen your parameter each time. Use the flags in the kit box to mark what you find, but don't touch anything. You'll need magnifying goggles. Fibres from clothes, or even a single hair could give us a result. Don't fuck up my search.'

Gannick's rudeness is oddly reassuring. It's the one thing that never changes in an uncertain world. The woman's contempt slips from my mind when I see her work ethic. She's already scooping samples into plastic vials, hands flying, while we crawl over the sand. The goggles I've found in her toolkit increase the scale of my vision tenfold. I can see a dune chafer staging a vicious war with a sand beetle among grains of sand. Insects fascinated me as a kid, but I ignore the wildlife today, hunting for anything a killer may have left behind.

The forensics chief drags herself along, using a metal fork to rake the sand. Gannick doesn't bother to look up, but I see she's found something, her lips forming a brief victory smile.

'Stop rushing, for Christ's sake,' she barks out. 'You'll miss something vital.'

I take off my goggles to assess the scene. We've examined every grain of sand in a five-metre radius of the grave; there's just one marker flag showing an item that could have fallen from the killer's pocket when they crouched down to dig the shifting sand.

'What have you got, Liz?'

'Nothing, probably,' she mutters. 'It looks like part of a necklace.'

'Let me see.'

When I peer through the goggles again, the object is a tiny bird, with wings outstretched against a background of flames. Its minute feathers have been carved into the green stone with delicacy. The charm found in the dead girl's shroud could have been fashioned by the same maker, and bought from the same shop as the ones on Sinead Harcourt's bedside table.

'I need a photo, before you bag it.'

'Get on with it then,' Gannick snaps. 'Don't just stand there like a village idiot.'

'Stop cursing me, Liz. I'm running this investigation, remember?'

'How nice for you.' Her tone is pure venom. 'Did Madron finally cut you loose?'

My phone rings before I can answer. I don't bother to pick up, until it happens again a minute later. Isla has left a voice message, asking me to return to St Mary's fast. An emergency has come up that she can't fix. The line breaks down when I call her to find out what's wrong, leaving me frustrated. She's the calmest member of my team and never cries wolf, so it must be urgent. Isla hasn't put a foot wrong in the past three years.

'Something's kicked off on St Mary's, Liz. I have to go. I'll send Eddie over soon, to help you.'

'You're leaving just as the real work starts?'

'I'd rather stay, believe me.'

'Let someone else fix the bloody drama then.'

'I can't. The buck stops with me, as SIO.'

Gannick doesn't bother to criticise my leadership skills again, but unspoken words hang in the air when I step back onto the launch. The contempt in her eyes follows me across the smooth water of Deadman's Pool like a curse.

14

Isla's not answering my calls when I moor the police boat in Hugh Town harbour. Neither is Eddie, so I leave a voicemail, asking him to cadge a lift from a local fisherman and sail over to St Helen's immediately to help Gannick. The quay is deserted as I jog into town. I can see just two pensioners huddled on a bench, cradling takeaway coffees, watching a band of clouds roll in from the west.

I'm nearing the station when a text arrives from Isla, asking me to come to Porthloo beach. It's lucky that nowhere is far away in Hugh Town; the islands' biggest community is scattered across a landmass just five miles long. I take the police van, for the sake of speed, on the short journey. It sounds like it needs a service, the engine's chugging much too loud. The twisting road leads north from Hugh Town, through open farmland, where goats peer out from behind dry-stone walls. Isla is waiting for me by the turning down to the beach from the coast road.

'The boss is injured, sir.' She's usually serene, but her voice is crackling with anxiety. 'Phillip Warleggan called the station earlier.'

'It's okay, Isla. Just tell me what happened.'

'Phillip found him on the ground by his boat, unconscious. I think he fell from the deck.'

'Did you ring the hospital?'

'He won't go, that's the trouble. The DCI's adamant, but he'll listen to you. Phillip's trying to persuade him now.'

We follow the lane down to the beach. It's a sandy, horseshoe-shaped bay, where half a dozen small craft are raised on stages, to protect them from storm damage. Their decks stand fifteen feet above ground, so a tumble from there would cause anyone serious damage. Phillip Warleggan approaches as I park the van. The former bank manager looks business-like, as usual, dressed in a smart blue coat.

'It's lucky I was out walking; poor Alan's in a bad way. He's really not himself. He kept talking about smugglers and lost children. It didn't make sense.' The man's face is solemn. 'He climbed back onto his boat and now he won't leave.'

'Thanks for calling us, Phillip. You did the right thing,' I say. 'We'll handle it from here. Go home, please, and stay warm. I'll call you later with an update.'

Warleggan marches away, clearly glad to escape. DCI Madron's boat lies directly ahead. It's a beautiful four-berth wooden cabin cruiser, with a big fishing deck on the bow. It's a typical example of Ray's design and craftmanship, with every boat unique. Madron has kept the paintwork immaculate, brass portholes gleaming in the winter light. A ladder is propped against the side of the boat, for access. I head straight for it, still curious to know why he sailed out to St Helen's yesterday morning, just before I found the body, and why he's returned to his boat as our murder investigation gets under way. Isla comes to a standstill, and her usual calmness is missing. I've never seen her so anxious.

'Let me talk to him, Isla. Wait in the van, if you prefer.'

She backs away fast. I'd prefer to let Madron deal with his situation too, but that's not an option if he's injured. When I call out a greeting there's no reply. He's not on deck when I climb onto his boat. I step into the galley, where the light is murky. The DCI is frozen in place, hunched on a bench, gazing at the floor. I can see he's wounded, even in the half-light. There's a bruise by his hairline, and a patch on his forehead glowing an angry red. A few tools lie scattered at his feet – a hammer, chisel and a can of engine oil.

'Is everything okay, sir?' I ask.

Silence lingers on the air. 'I was checking my boat. I need it in good order. Maintenance is essential in winter. I was covering it with a tarpaulin.'

'And you had a fall? I can see you're injured.'

'It's nothing. Leave me alone, for God's sake. You've got work to do at the station.'

'Let's get that head wound sorted first, at the hospital.'

'I'm not wasting their time with a few scratches.'

My thoughts are slow to adjust. Madron has been a thorn in my side ever since I became his deputy five years ago. He's criticised everything I do, from taking Shadow out on patrol, to the brevity of my case reports. But none of that matters when I see his hands shaking uncontrollably. Madron doesn't protest when I pick up a blanket from the bench and wrap it round his shoulders.

'What's this about, sir? I saw your boat near St Helen's yesterday morning, just before I found that girl's body. What were you doing out there?'

He looks away. 'Hunting for smugglers, if you must know.'

'On your own, in storm season?'

'I've been patrolling the water at night.' He's unwilling to meet my eye. 'Those vermin are polluting these islands. I can't retire until it's under control.'

'That's a big ask, sir. Smuggling's gone on for centuries. It'll outlive us all.'

'Defeatism won't fix the problem. It's children's lives they're trading.' His voice rises to a shout. 'Can't you see, those bastards are ruining lives? I don't want that for my legacy. There's been enough misery in my lifetime.'

'How do you mean?'

'My wife pined for years. Our son never came back, even though we bought him a house.' Pain echoes through his words, his voice uncertain. 'Tall, good-looking, bright, like his mother. Dead in his twenties on that stupid motorbike. How come he never achieved anything?'

'You're rambling, sir. I think it's concussion. Come with me, please.'

'Stop interfering, Kitto, that's an order.'

'You're getting in that van, even if I have to drag you. Do you hear me?'

My boss is slumped in his seat. He no longer smells of

Brylcreem, soap and boot polish, just the bitter scent of fear. His face is slick with sweat, and there's a mud smear across his chest. But it's the distant look in his eyes that worries me, like he's watching events unfold miles away. Madron's an institution in Scilly. He's always seemed invincible, but his fall has reduced him to a frail old man in moments. His comments don't make sense. I don't understand his night-time vigils, or why he'd drive here to check on his boat, just as our investigation goes public.

When I look through the nearest porthole, Isla is clutching the steering wheel in the van, clearly shaken by Madron's fall. Our boss is easily the most annoying man I know, and maybe she feels the same, but he cares deeply about protecting the community. It's like we've been sheltering inside a building that appeared rock solid, and the roof's suddenly collapsed, without warning.

I work hard to coax Madron down the ladder, his movements unsteady. He flatly refuses to go to hospital, but he allows Isla to drop him at home instead. We make the short journey to his bungalow in silence. I follow him down the path to make sure he's safe, but he sends me away. He insists that he'll be at the station tomorrow, as usual, to check on our progress, then his front door clicks shut in my face.

Isla gives me more details as we walk back down the road. Apparently Madron's wife is in New Zealand, visiting their daughter. She's not due home for weeks. Isla's concern echoes in her voice. Our boss has won our loyalty by stealth, despite acting like a tyrant. I ask Isla to walk back to the station, then I drive uphill to the hospital to find her mother. If Madron won't seek medical help, I'll have to request it for him.

The abandoned baby enters my mind as I enter reception. I catch sight of him through a glass panel as I head down the corridor towards Ginny Tremayne's consulting room. She's caring for him, but he's bawling at top volume. It's hard to believe that such a small child could make so much noise. I stand still, trying to gather my thoughts. My brain keeps on trying to make links between the murder on St Helen's and the baby's abandonment, but I can't make a connection without valid proof. I'll have to enlist help from the medical team to search for evidence, before a link can be ruled out.

When Ginny beckons me inside, I see anxiety in the way she's holding the baby like he's made of glass. 'He should be on a neonatal ward, in an incubator,' she says. 'He's refusing to feed and so underweight his life's in danger. This boy needs comfort, like all newborns. The nurse dashes in here when she's got a minute, but she's busy on the ward.'

'Maybe a volunteer could help?'

'Everyone works, Ben. Do you know anybody who could put their life on hold at the drop of a hat?'

'I'll ask around.' I watch the infant's minute hands grasping at thin air. 'Would you mind if Gareth Keillor examines him? I need any pathology that could link him to the murder victim.'

She looks surprised. 'But he can't be the murder victim's baby. He's just a few weeks old, and she died months ago, didn't she?'

'His DNA could still help us.'

'Go ahead. Gareth won't hurt him. This baby's got bigger problems than another doctor examining him.'

There's sadness on Ginny's face when she lowers him back into his cot. Then she listens carefully when I describe Madron's fall and his refusal to get treatment. She promises to visit him at home soon, then hurries away. The baby is screaming louder now he's been put down. Instinct tells me to pick him up, but there's no time. It feels like another abandonment when I leave, then stand in the corridor texting Keillor to request his help.

I call at Phillip Warleggan's house on my way back to the station. He invites me inside, for the first time ever. The man's home is much more colourful than his appearance. The hallway is painted terracotta, and when I glance inside his living room the warm atmosphere continues, with handwoven rugs on the floor. His kitchen is full of old wooden furniture, the air scented by fresh coffee. There's a pin board covered in photographs that reveal a different side of Warleggan's personality. They show him with a group of younger friends on holiday, in blazing sunlight, his smile relaxed. He's always struck me as formal and austere, but it looks like he's got more than one identity. He seems relieved when I explain that Dr Tremayne will call on Madron soon, despite his refusal to seek help.

'Alan's been such a good friend to me over the years. It was awful, hearing him ramble like that.'

'Can you remember what he said?'

'He seemed ashamed of something, which seems odd. He's always been so public-spirited.'

'Would you mind keeping an eye on him, Phillip, in case he's concussed?' He nods his agreement, and I glance at his photos again. 'It looks like you've had some great holidays.'

Warleggan smiles. 'I help a charity that delivers free books overseas. Kids are always hungry for knowledge, when money's short. They know getting a professional job could liberate their families. They work incredibly hard at school.'

'That's impressive. I spent most of my education longing for the bell to ring.'

'Yet you've become a senior police officer. You must have a good work ethic these days.' His voice softens. 'Did you get time to see Sinead Harcourt?'

'I tried, but she's hard to pin down.'

'Between you and I, her father's struggling.' He looks down at his hands. 'Pete took on a big mortgage to buy their house. He needs to downsize before debts overwhelm him, but he hates to disrupt Sinead's routine.'

'He's lucky to have your advice.'

'The poor man's under too much pressure. It concerns me, to be honest.'

When I glance outside, I spot a low-roofed building at the end of the garden. The dwelling has shuttered windows, and it's surrounded by overgrown shrubs. 'I didn't know you had an annexe, Phillip.'

'There's a reason why it's neglected.' He follows my gaze. 'It was one of the main attractions when I bought this place. That building's an old smugglers' den, from the seventeenth century. The history fascinates me. I want to preserve it, but Historic England won't let me touch a single brick without their permission. They've never even sent a surveyor over to assess it, so my hands are tied. Would you like a tour?'

'Another time, thanks. I should get back to work.'

Warleggan smiles, but I can tell he's disappointed. Our meeting has exposed a different side to him. His remote manner disguises a warmth people rarely get to see, like the vibrant colours on his walls and his desire to protect the islands' heritage. It sounds like he's found the ideal way to avoid loneliness, by doing charity missions abroad.

Nina's suggestion that we try out life on the mainland returns to me as I head back to the van, questioning my own work-life balance. It took me years to readjust to the starkness of island life after my long spell in London. We're often cut off from the mainland in storm season, the Atlantic too rough for ferries to run. Warleggan has found his own way of dealing with island winters, when it can seem like madness to stay stranded on a handful of rocks, battered by vicious tides. Living here carries plenty of benefits too. The beauty of the place in summer is so uplifting, I'd hate to leave.

I stand motionless on the street, letting the view dilute the ugliness I've witnessed recently. The off-islands are changing from charcoal to pewter, and the sky's wide canvas is smudged with cloud. The case still feels like a gathering storm. First the girl on St Helen's, with no one to mourn her death, and now a baby no one will claim. My boss is too wounded to accept help, and his recovery may take days, leaving me in charge. I've wanted more responsibility for years, but the weight of it feels unnatural as I drive back to town.

15

I leave the van at the station then walk to Hugh Street in the centre of town, where the Tideline Giftshop is still open, even though it's almost 5.00 pm. I need to find out more about the jade charms left at the crime scene, but there's no sign of Emma Angarrack inside, even though her black Lexus is parked outside her shop. It always surprises me when people spend a fortune on transport when the island is only five miles long, but it's part of Emma's persona to advertise her success. I remember she was the same at school. Her parents had little money, like mine, but she was the first kid to get a Saturday job so she could buy clothes and makeup. She must have a trusting disposition these days. The door to her shop is unlocked, because stealing is rare in Scilly. Shopkeepers often nip out, leaving their doors open, so customers can still pick up what they need then leave cash by the till.

Emma's shop is packed with hand-painted cards, pottery, handmade bags and jewellery, produced by the islands' thriving community of artists. Ray calls the trinkets on display 'dust catchers', but their appeal is obvious, especially for children. Everything is shiny and bright, wrapped in ornate packaging, the air smelling of lemon and patchouli from soaps and scented candles.

The charms are displayed on the counter, with cards explaining each symbol. I pick up a turtle that's just a few inches long, matching the one inside the girl's shroud. The card explains that the creature's domed shell represents heaven and its square underside the earth. Maybe the killer hoped to guarantee the girl safe passage to the afterlife, but it takes a leap of faith to believe that a murderer might consider themselves spiritual, unless they're mentally ill.

I'm still rummaging through the charms when Emma's voice reaches me through the door to her stockroom. I can't make out individual words, but her tone is flat with anger. It sounds like a marital row, which takes me by surprise. The Angarracks are the islands' power couple – the headmaster of Five Islands Academy and the islands' mayor. I've never seen my old classmate show a negative emotion. Emma's tone is softening now, like she's on the verge of tears. Maybe she's exhausted by all the public good she does in her spare time, but I didn't come here to analyse her state of mind.

I focus again on my search, finding a copy of the second charm at the bottom of the pile. The phoenix, rising from the ashes, is described as a symbol of rebirth and renewal. Emma's strained conversation continues in the distance. I'm still considering why two symbols of eternal life were left at a murder scene, alongside a Vietnamese prayer shawl. It could be pure coincidence that one of the charms Sinead Harcourt collects ended up inside the shroud, but no one has admitted to owning them.

When Emma finally appears, she looks immaculate as always, not a hair out of place, but her face is flushed, and her eyes are glossy with tears. It's the first time I've witnessed her vulnerable side.

'Sorry, Ben. I thought the shop was empty.'

'I heard you on the phone, so I waited. Everything okay?'

'No, to be honest.' She hesitates. 'One of my suppliers missed the deadline for my order.'

'It sounded pretty heated for a business conversation.'

'They've let me down, in a big way. I'm already dealing with sky-high rent and energy bills.'

'Sorry to hear it. I just wanted to ask you about these charms, if that's okay. How long have you sold them?'

She appears glad to change topic. 'Two years or so. Kids love them.'

'Do you remember any adults buying them in the past year?'

'Steve and I gave some to Lisa, for her birthday. Pete Harcourt bought a few, and that older guy, from St Martin's, with the big speedboat. I've forgotten his name. He's lived there years, but only comes over to pick up shopping.'

'What does he look like?'

'Medium height, grey-haired.' She runs a fingertip along her jaw. 'A few scars on his face, like he was in an accident years ago.'

'Mark Lanner, the composer?'

'That's him. Quiet, isn't he? No one really knows him.'

'Maybe he needs peace, for his job.'

'We could all use more of that.' Her smile finally revives. 'Got time for a coffee, Ben?'

'Another time, thanks for your help, Emma.'

She manages a cheery wave goodbye. I get the sense that she's struggling to keep her public and private roles balanced, but concealing it with bravado. It interests me that a man like Mark Lanner collects good-luck charms. I've only met him a couple of times, but he struck me as a guy with his feet on the ground, not inclined to believe in spiritual forces. I'll have to pay him a visit soon.

Lawrie Deane is holding the fort when I return to the station. He's sitting in reception with his phone pressed to his ear and Radio 2 playing old-school pop in the background. He says it makes the station welcoming, but he can only have music while Madron's absent, because the boss hates informality. Scraps of paper are littered across Deane's desk. It looks like calls have been coming in thick and fast, but that's not unusual. We get obscure requests for help every day. Pensioners call in to report their cat missing, or that a kid has lobbed a brick through someone's window and needs a stern warning from a uniformed officer.

When I reach my desk, I look up Mark Lanner's phone number, to ask him about the charms he purchased, but he doesn't answer. There's bad news from the Coastguard Agency too. Their data system's down; they can't access photos from their patrol boats. The officer promises to contact me once the system's live again. I take the chance to ask about smuggling activity and human trafficking. His voice flattens when he explains that they're fighting an unstoppable tide. The traffickers are making serious money from transporting children and adults to the UK, by any means possible. They can afford bigger craft, equipped with sophisticated GPS, allowing them to evade patrol boats, and they're increasingly brazen. Their illegal passengers often get sick during their long voyages. A few boats have been seen dumping victims' bodies at sea, in broad daylight. I can't help remembering the victims cast into Deadman's Pool hundreds of years ago, but it doesn't explain the presence of a young girl's body on St Helen's, carefully wrapped and buried. It sounds like the traffickers are far less considerate, treating their victims as goods to be bought and sold, without any emotional value.

I wait until Deane has rung off then inform him of Madron's fall. Disbelief crosses his face when he hears our boss is refusing treatment. Deane has worked in the islands' force for two decades and remains loyal, even though Madron's controlling style sometimes irritates him too. I tell him that the boss is in shock, or concussed, yet he's still planning to report for work tomorrow.

'That's crazy. He needs an X-ray, at least. Want me to have a word?'

'If you can, Lawrie, it might help. Contact his wife in New Zealand too, please. Maybe she can talk some sense into him over the phone.'

'Will do, sir. They've planned that trip for months, to see their new grandchild, but Madron bailed at the last minute.'

'Do you know why?'

'No idea, sorry. He's not the confiding type, is he?'

'That's for sure. I saw his boat near St Helen's the morning I found the body. He said he'd been hunting for smugglers.'

'It's obsessed him for years. He often talks about them plaguing the islands.'

'He's been doing night patrols, alone.'

'That's a good way to get himself killed. But the DCI sees this place as his empire, doesn't he? He wants to retire with a clean sheet.'

'No one should intercept a smuggler's boat without help from the coastguard. They're terrified of jail and plenty are armed.'

Deane throws up his hands. 'God knows what drives him, or his wife. They've always been private. I water their plants if they go away, but the pair of them keep their distance from most people. They can be kind though. When they renovated their place, they gave me a load of furniture and bits and bobs, after my divorce. I get the odd Sunday lunch invite too.' He gazes down at the counter. 'You know, I could tell something was wrong last time I visited.'

'How do you mean?'

'The atmosphere between them was weird. The DCI never mentions his feelings, even though he's a good listener. He helped me a lot when Sally buggered off to the mainland with her fancy man. I was going round the bend, but he let me talk it out of my system.'

'You hardly mention your divorce these days.'

'We buried the hatchet years ago, thank God. There's no point in hanging on to bad feeling, is there? I couldn't let it upset my boys.' He glances down at the messages he's written.

'Isla's pretty upset about Madron getting injured. Can you check she's okay?'

'No worries, boss, if you deal with these messages.' He dumps a pile of notes on my desk.

'What happened with Sinead Harcourt, Lawrie?'

'She was in a right old state, going on about dark forces everywhere she looks. I suppose that baby could be hers, but she's too bright to get herself in trouble, and Pete's always protective. The mother could be any woman of child-bearing age, couldn't she?'

'We still need to find out about Sinead's trips to St Helen's, and the charms she collects. Can you set up an interview with her?'

'It's on my list.'

'Any more sightings of people sailing over to St Helen's?'

'Not so far.' He nods at the window. 'You've got a visitor. Shadow caught the ferry over from Bryher, by all accounts. How does he know where to find you?'

'Too much canine intuition.' Shadow often goes down to the quay to wait for me, if I'm late home. He's smart enough to realise that if my boat's missing, the ferry will deliver him to Hugh Town, so he can hunt me down.

Shadow's standing in the yard behind the station. When I open the window, he leaps straight through, his paws hitting my chest in his usual boisterous greeting, overjoyed to find me at last. He soon settles under Madron's desk, while I sift through Deane's messages, hoping to glean new information about anyone seen on St Helen's.

Two journalists have rung the station already. They've heard about the crisis unfolding, and it's lucky the weather's too poor for them to send drones over to take photos. They'd do anything for a big story, particularly about a murdered teenage girl. I've avoided them until now. Madron has always dealt with the press, because my blunt communication style alienates reporters, and the feeling's mutual. Most are like blood-sucking leeches. I made the mistake of trusting one early in my career, believing he wanted justice, but his motives were just like the rest. They just want a strapline and a photo to help them sell their story to the highest bidder.

I spend the next hour sifting through information on my laptop. The coastguard and port-authority reports for the past six months have arrived, but there are no photos. It's just a list of cargo boats, with names, destinations and shipping licences, that goes on for pages, but it's the tip of the iceberg. Many small and medium-sized boats make night-time landings in Scilly, and on the Cornish coast. I still believe the girl under the sand is more likely to have died here than on a boat, yet how could she remain invisible? It seems too coincidental that a baby was left for us to find, the morning after her body came to light, yet the events may not even be linked.

Deane's voice echoes through the station's thin walls, offering Isla tea and sympathy. Her voice is still flat with shock, after trying to help Madron. When I look outside, darkness has already fallen. I check the maritime weather forecast on my computer then grab my phone.

'Are you still on St Helen's, Eddie?'

'We've been here hours. Gannick's using battery lights, and she's got me scouring the island with my torch.'

'Make her pack up, then sail back here, fast.' I can hear waves hitting the shore, like bursts of ill-timed applause. 'A new storm's coming over. Stay at Tregarthen's tonight, you won't have time to reach Tresco.'

There's a rush of static, before our connection fails. I hope he ferries Gannick back to St Mary's before sea conditions worsen. I check my watch: it's 8.00 pm. Isla appears calmer when I enter the team office, while Deane fields yet another phone call. I hear him advising one of the islanders to take shelter with a neighbour if they're worried about their roof surviving the incoming storm. Reassurance is our biggest role in a community like this, where policing often feels more like social work.

'A woman just called from St Martin's,' he says, putting down the phone. 'A single mum, afraid her kid's in danger since that girl was found.'

'What did you say?'

'That it's an isolated incident, but she's still panicky. My son's worried about his boys too. I think all the young families feel the same. What if the killer attacks another child?' Deane's gaze shifts to the window, scanning for threats.

'Keep on telling people that the body may have been left by a passing boat, Lawrie. That's enough for today. Go home now and rest, both of you.'

Isla rises to her feet. 'We're going to the boss's place first, to check he's okay.'

'He may not welcome you.'

'I know, sir, but we'll get food for him, from the Co-op. It feels wrong, leaving him by himself,' Isla says.

'We can always leave it on his doorstep if he sends us away.' Deane joins her, putting on his coat.

'It's a kind gesture,' I say. 'Let's hope he appreciates it.'

My colleagues disappear into the dark outside, and their goodwill makes me feel guilty. They've both formed a decent relationship with Madron, despite his critical nature, while my own has never developed. Shadow can always read my body language. He picks up on my low mood, whining in sympathy, but regret's pointless. I need a ride home to Bryher before the storm hits, or I'll be staying at Tregarthen's too.

I can't see any familiar vessels on the quay, until I spot Ray's boat straining its mooring rope, like it's longing for a new voyage, but there's no sign of him. My dog guesses where he's hiding immediately, running back down the quay to The Ship pub. It's Ray's favourite watering hole on St Mary's, with sailing memorabilia on the walls, from the days when mariners relied on celestial navigation. I glance at the sextants, compasses and maps before I see Ray, alone at the bar. He's reading *The Cornishman*, always happiest when no one engages him in small talk. He rises to his feet when Shadow races over. Ray's an older version of me, tall with a hefty frame, stern-faced, with thick white hair.

'I'm your ferry, Ben. Let's go, before it gets worse.'

'Who told you I needed a ride?'

'Nina called me, after the storm warning.'

The conversation's terse, even for my uncle, who loves monosyllables. The sea is pitch-black when we reach his boat. Clouds race east at breakneck speed, obscuring the stars, as whitecaps surge through the harbour's mouth. Ray doesn't bother to check whether I'm prepared for a bumpy crossing. There's a glint of excitement in his eyes as we set off. He abandoned his naval career to return to Scilly and run his father's boatyard, but I know he misses the adventures.

Ray appears to be in his element as we leave the harbour's protection, the boat shunted sideways by rising waves. We're motoring at top speed, when conditions worsen. The sea starts to churn, making me wish I'd never seen *A Perfect Storm*. The boat labours up each wave's incline, like a climber reaching for the summit. Ray faces his boat into the swell to avoid being knocked broadside. It's like being trapped on a rollercoaster, long after it stops being fun. I'm relieved to reach Church Quay at last and moor outside his boatyard. The ground continues rocking when I step onto the jetty.

'Thank God you were steering, Ray. My bowrider wouldn't have made it.'

'Mine's seen plenty worse.' Shadow chases after him like he's found a new hero. 'Coming in for a drink?'

'Definitely, after that ride. Let me ring the hospital first.'

Ray climbs the steps to his flat with Shadow in hot pursuit, while I make my call. Ginny Tremayne tells me that Madron only let her carry out a basic health check at his home, refusing to get a head X-ray. He's still insisting it was only a bump. She's told him to take time off work until he's fully recovered. The man's stubbornness doesn't surprise me, but it adds to my list of concerns.

'How's the baby doing?' I ask.

'Not well, I'm afraid. Gareth Keillor examined him earlier, but I don't think he found anything for your case.' There's a moment's silence. 'He'll have to feed better by tomorrow, or he'll need a gastric tube.'

I hate the idea of a plastic line being forced down such a tiny child's throat, even to save his life. And it bothers me that Keillor found nothing to connect the two crimes, even though I was clutching at straws. My spirits only lift again when I enter Ray's flat over the boatyard. I spent so much time here as a boy, I learned from his example that a solitary life doesn't have to be lonely. Women are drawn to him, even now, but he's only had a few relationships in the past twenty years. They all end for the same reason. His real passions are his work and the sea. I know that's unlikely to change.

I'd like to pick his brains about anyone that's been sailing to St Helen's, but he hates being questioned while he's completing a task. I watch him pour out measures of Scotch then load plates with crackers and cheese. He dumps the tray in front of me without a word. I'm not much of a drinker, but I knock back half the whisky in a gulp, to thaw the sea air from my lungs.

'Who do you think buried that girl on St Helen's, Ray?'

'Why ask me? Everyone's got their pet theory.'

'I'd still like to hear yours.'

He considers in silence, his glass hovering in the air. 'Some sick bastard showed her no respect, but it's the mother of that baby I pity. Some poor girl's lost on these islands now, alone and terrified.'

Sinead Harcourt comes to mind. Why would a young girl run from me if she's got nothing to hide? She could easily have fallen pregnant and been too afraid to seek help. Whoever left the baby outside the station feared their own life would fracture under the weight of public judgement. I'll have to be systematic about checking every female of child-bearing age on the islands as the potential mother, starting with Five Islands Academy.

When I look at Ray again, his eyes are fixed on the black glass sea outside, while the storm gathers pace.

16

Mai wakes up hours later, her mouth dry with fear. The man is pacing outside the door. She knows what to expect. It always happens in the middle of the night, but familiarity only increases her terror.

When the door creaks open, her body is rigid. She prays to see Lao again, but the man's hands are empty apart from a lit candle. Something has changed. It could just be the flickering light, but she sees a new type of violence in his face, like he's got nothing to lose. He steps towards her with fists raised.

'No,' she screams. 'Don't touch me.'

The man never listens, yet instinct makes her fight him every time. She tries to kick out, but he's so much stronger, she can never win. He yanks back the duvet, then pins her to the mattress. She bites her tongue when his hot breath sears her cheek. The violation sends pain burning through her body like wildfire. Tears ooze down Mai's cheeks while he makes his vile grunting noise, and nausea rises in her throat. She wants to claw at his face, inflicting pain on him too, but she keeps her arms rigid, to avoid more punishments. It feels like an eternity until he rolls onto his back, leaving her spirit in tatters.

Mai avoids looking at him in the candle's guttering light. She'd rather pretend he doesn't exist.

'You should be loving,' he says. 'Is it so hard to show me tenderness when I've sheltered you all these years?'

'Give me my son. He's all I want.'

'Why him, not me? I've told you, we can live abroad, once I get you a passport, but that takes time. There are countries where people accept couples like us. We can get married. You want that too, don't you?'

The man's speech is hard to follow, but his tone is familiar. He sounds like a child begging for comfort. Mai wants to grab the nail she found and slash his eyes, blinding him, so he can never look at her again, but fear smothers her. Mai forces herself to caress his shoulder, like she enjoys the intimacy.

The man smiles. 'That's better, Mai. Some kindness, for once. Is there anything you need?'

'To walk with you, outside.'

His frown returns. 'Not after last time. How about something from the shops?'

'New radio, or book of English words.'

'You want longer chats, do you?' The man laughs. 'I prefer peace and quiet. I get enough people hassling me all day, making impossible demands.'

He takes his candle and leaves, locking the door behind him, while Mai's pain burns. She should have tried harder, pretending to care for him, but hatred always rises in her throat. Sometimes it feels like it's the only thing keeping her alive. He will kill her if she tries to attack him, yet the temptation is growing. She takes the nail from under her pillow and rubs it across the floor again. Mai repeats the gesture, over and over, until the spike is sharp enough to make him bleed.

17

Wednesday, 10th January

I wake early with a thumping heart. Last night's sleep was troubled by nightmares about giant children taking the islands by siege, trampling on buildings and littering broken dolls across the fields. Nina is still fast asleep beside me. She can relax at the drop of a hat, and that skill has deepened since our son was born. I often find her napping on the chair in Noah's room, while he sleeps in his cot, perfectly in sync. Her dark eyelashes are splayed across her cheek, her oval face beautiful. I'd love to stay in bed with her all morning, but there's no chance of it today.

When I check my phone I see that Isla texted last night, saying that Madron didn't answer his doorbell. She and Lawrie left the food in his porch. My alarm increases when I check the weather outside; the sea is one shade lighter than black, boiling with waves. The sky is solid grey, tarnished and dull, like rusted steel. Sailing is off limits for now, so there's no chance of calling on my boss to check he's okay.

'Shit fucking timing,' I mutter.

Wind screams down the chimney in the living room as my frustration builds. The storm has brought my investigation to a standstill. Inter-island ferries won't run, flights from the mainland will remain cancelled, and it could be days before Gannick can continue her work on St Helen's.

Shadow is scratching the front door, forcing me to act before he removes even more paint. The wind shoves me backwards when I open it, like a drunk spoiling for a fight, but Shadow's thrilled. He races away, hunting the eye of the storm.

Lights are on at Hell Bay hotel on the far side of the beach, meaning that Zoe is up already. Instinct makes me get dressed fast, then pull on a waterproof coat to brave the elements. I envy

Shadow his low centre of gravity when the wind pummels my face, but the ten-minute walk will be worth it to make sure Zoe's okay. The sea keeps hurling itself at the shore, leaving ribbons of pale foam in its wake. I've always loved how Bryher changes in a squall. The sea's roar is loud enough to wake the dead this morning, with tons of shingle being hauled inland, rattling like thunder. Drizzle coats my face, leaving a rime of salt on my lips.

I'm glad to reach the hotel's shelter, then run up the steps to the terrace, where Zoe is fussing over Shadow. She's dressed for DIY in paint-spattered dungarees and trainers full of holes. Zoe looks beautiful but vulnerable without makeup, like she did as a teenager.

'You're still gorgeous enough to stop traffic,' I tell her.

'That's a lie, big man, but I'll take it.' Her grin flashes on for an instant, bright enough to illuminate any room. 'Hoping for breakfast, are you?'

'You know me, babe. Food is always welcome.'

Shadow runs ahead of us, upstairs to the flat Zoe uses whenever she's home. It brings back memories of all the great times we had when her parents were running the bar and restaurant on the ground floor, while we watched TV and drank their booze. The place is lacklustre now, in need of new carpet and a kitchen refit, but it's still my second home.

Zoe produces a bag of croissants. 'How many?'

'Four, please.'

She gazes at me open-mouthed. 'No one eats more than two.'

'Except me. It takes fuel to run a big machine, and one's for the dog.'

I watch her put the tray in the oven. She's a tall, strong-looking woman who seems perfectly at ease, until I study her closely. There are blue circles under her eyes, her movements jittery. She passes me some orange juice, then dumps plates, butter and pots of jam on the table.

'If you're upset about me running off the other night, it wasn't your fault. Children are my Achilles heel, that's all.'

'I should have thought before blurting it out.'

She turns to face me, her expression neutral. 'You went through a blunt stage at school too, remember?'

'Christ, yeah. My communication style left a lot to be desired.'

'Especially with girls.' Zoe giggles. 'You tried asking Jane Elmore out but ended up mentioning the size of her feet instead. Where the hell did that come from?'

'Panic, I think. I suddenly noticed they were huge.'

'You'd fancied her for weeks.'

I shrug. 'It was a truth waiting to be spoken.'

'The poor girl must have been traumatised. I bet she never wears stilettoes to this day.'

'Jane was too smart for me anyway. She's probably a neurosurgeon by now.'

'Or a saddo, with a foot fetish.'

Zoe's banter continues when the food arrives. We could pass the whole morning like this, but I lean closer, forcing her to meet my eye.

'I've never seen you run away from anything, or anyone, till you split up with Dev.'

'Things have changed.' Her voice trembles. 'I can't have kids. I should have guessed it before my first IVF.'

'How, exactly?'

'It was stupid not to try earlier.' Her gaze drifts out of focus. 'Some evil bastard killed that child on purpose. That's what hurts.'

'I know, sweetheart, I'm sorry.' When I put my arm round her shoulder, she shifts closer, accepting the comfort. 'Where's Dev in all this?'

'Out of the picture, months ago.'

There's too much bravery in her voice. She's divorcing a man she loves because she can't have children, which strikes me as a mad self-punishment. Zoe wants to free him to start a family with someone else, but he's fighting her every step of the way.

'Dev loves you. He won't give you a divorce.'

'It's not his decision.' Her smile slowly revives. 'Eat your breakfast, big man. I'll tell you my plans for the next six months.'

'Not yet. There's another story you should hear, about a child that needs help. Want me to tell you now, before someone else does?'

'If you must.'

I take a long breath. 'I found a baby outside the station yesterday, in a cardboard box. He's at the hospital now, struggling.'

She stares up at me, unblinking, when I explain that he's tiny and frail. His chances are poor while he refuses to feed. What he needs most is comfort and round-the-clock care, until his mother's found.

'Are you serious? You came here to pressure me into looking after a baby, full-time, after I've had four miscarriages?'

'No, it's just for information. I'd never ask you to do something that hard.'

'Liar.'

'You'd have heard, sooner or later, Zoe. It was best coming from me.'

She bats the subject away, but I have no regrets. She'll have to face a world full of children one day, even if it hurts. I listen to her talk while I plough through croissants. I only quit eating when she announces that she's booked a round-the-world air ticket and her first destination is Japan. Her flight leaves next week.

'You promised to stay till Easter, to spend time with us and Noah. He's your godson, remember?'

'I'll come back, I promise, but a long-haul trip will clear my head. I want to see Vietnam, Laos and Cambodia. Then it'll be Australia and New Zealand. I'll find work when I run out of cash.' Her hands tremble as she picks up her coffee.

'Running away won't fix it.'

'I need a new adventure, that's all.'

'What about your life in India?'

'Give me a break, can you? Don't guilt-trip me for wrecking

Dev's life too.' She grabs my hand. 'Be happy for me, big man. The journey will sort me out, I promise.'

'You know I'll support any decision you make. But I'm allowed to miss you, aren't I?'

'I need you happy, big man. You're my rock, remember?' She touches my arm. 'I don't want this to be all about me. I'm glad Nina's so happy. She's great with Noah, isn't she?'

I nod in reply. 'She thinks he'd have a better life on the mainland.'

'Maybe that's true, but this place is in your bone marrow, isn't it? He can discover the world later, like we did.'

'Leaving would a wrench, that's for sure. I feel at home here, even on a shitty day like this.'

'It's worth considering. I'll always visit, wherever you go.'

Shadow gives a pitiful whine, like he's just realised one of his favourite humans is flying off on yet another trip. His complaints only stop when I chuck him the last croissant. He catches it neatly between his jaws, then swallows it in two gulps.

'Greedy bastard,' I mutter.

My dog fixes me with his ice-cool stare, immune to criticism.

The gale is still blowing when I give Zoe a hug then go back outside. Horizontal rain hits my face like a scattergun. My friend's claim about needing a new adventure doesn't ring true. Maybe hearing about the murdered girl on St Helen's was the final straw. She's in pain, and the islands no longer comfort her, but I can't change that. Once her mind's made up, she races ahead like a tornado.

I'm freezing when I get home. Rain has penetrated my coat, despite the waterproof guarantee on its label. I stand in the kitchen, dripping, while Nina feeds Noah oatmeal. He keeps trying to grab the spoon, for the simple pleasure of throwing it on the floor, but she evades him, shovelling dollops of food into his mouth. They're still at it when I emerge from the bedroom in dry clothes.

There's no chance of getting to work for the next few hours, so I disappear into the small office Nina uses for online counselling sessions. The rain-lashed sea lies three hundred metres outside the window, with no boats in sight. You'd have to be crazy to sail in weather like this, although the surging waves make a great spectacle. When I turn on my computer I could howl like Shadow. The internet's down, and my phone's stopped connecting. My world has shrunk to the size of Bryher, two miles long and half a mile wide, populated by fewer than a hundred souls.

I stare at the blank screen then draft some emails. They'll send once we're back online, but that could take hours, so I scribble a task list for when communication is working again. I need to contact local fishermen for any information about foreign boats seen sailing around Scilly in the past six months. It's a longshot, I know. Thousands skim past us before crossing the Atlantic, and no suspicious marine activity has been reported so far.

It must be possible to find out whose baby was left at the station. I send a quick reply to Denise Laramie, the counsellor at Five Islands Academy, requesting a meeting. She's been unable to identify any girls as potential mothers, likely to conceal their pregnancy. I should also call on Steve Angarrack, the headteacher, to see if he has any ideas. I can't believe a mature woman would hide the birth of a child, unless she were unstable, or trapped in a violent relationship. It still feels right to start with the islands' youngest women first.

There's no access to the census while I'm offline, forcing me to run through a mental checklist of islanders. Then an email arrives in my inbox, proving my connection's back in business.

The subject line reads: 'THE DEAD GIRL'. The anonymous message is just three words long: 'LISA ANGARRACK KNOWS.'

It seems odd that the message has named the headmaster's daughter, just as I'm processing information about the school. I'm afraid the sender's tapped into my emails, but that's impossible, when the system's encrypted. I search my inbox, but the signal fails again. I've got little chance of identifying the sender from such a crude message. Anyone on St Mary's could have used the library or one of the cafés to fire out the email then deleted the account.

Lisa Angarrack is the teenage daughter of Five Island Academy's headmaster and the islands' mayor. The girl fades into the background at public events, unlike her high-profile parents. I haven't seen her since her mother's inauguration at the town hall three months ago. Someone's gone to the trouble of sending an anonymous email, telling me to focus on Five Islands, but why would they have information about the buried girl? I'll have to question Lisa anyway when I speak to her father about vulnerable female pupils.

I look up from the screen and see the weather changing. There are glints of light between clouds, and the waves are flattening at last. It's a relief when my phone rings. I assume it's Gannick trying to contact me now the line's back on, but the caller is male, his voice low.

'Can you speak up, please?'

Mark Lanner tells me he's returning my call. His tone is polite when he agrees to a face-to-face meeting at his home today on St Martin's. I promise to sail over once the storm lifts. When I shove my phone back into my pocket, I do a quick search online, and discover that he's well-known as a composer of film scores. One of them won a prize at the Cannes Film Festival. It feels like a thin lead, but I have to chase down anyone who's bought those good-luck charms. The email interests me more. Someone has learned how to avoid leaving a signature, making sure it would remain anonymous.

Nina still has her hands full when I prepare to leave, with our boy in fight mode, hurling Lego at the wall.

'He's got cabin fever. I'll take him outside when the rain stops,' Nina says, her smile returning. 'Or we could swap him for a quieter version?'

'Shadow wouldn't let us.'

The truth is, neither would she. When she used to breast feed him in the early days, her eyes locked on to his, like nothing could ever pull them apart. Their connection is so complete, it sometimes feels like I'm a spare part, hovering in the background. I want to breathe her in when she rises to her feet to hug me goodbye.

Rain is still hitting the roof so hard it sounds like lead pellets dropping from the sky. I feel bad about leaving while Noah's in a strop, but it's how our lives work. We cover each other's absences with help from my godmother, Maggie, but never get enough time together as a family. I want that to change, but nothing will shift until this case is solved. My sense of urgency increases when I step outside into the pounding rain.

18

It's mid-morning by the time I reach St Martin's. When I moor my bowrider on Lowertown Quay, the sea is calm, as if it's pretending the storm never happened, as innocent as a blank sheet of glass. The Karma Hotel still has a sign outside, promising luxury spa breaks, even though the place is closed until tourist season starts at Easter. The island's focus has shifted to the winter flower-picking campaign, with daffodils and narcissi turning the fields gold. The land shimmers as I approach Mark Lanner's home on Top Rock Hill. I've never visited his place before, my curiosity rising as I climb. The man's home is typical of the local architecture, a grey stone cottage with two storeys, and I can tell he's spent a fortune on modernising it. The windows, solar panels and loft extension appear brand new. There's a smaller house next door, which looks neglected. It's empty, the shutters in need of paint, a few tiles slipping from the roof.

No one answers when I knock, but the door's ajar, so I walk inside, calling Lanner's name. Piano music drifts downstairs, the tune slow and haunting, each note more melancholy than the last. There's no reply when I call again, so I climb to the landing. A grand piano lies behind a half-open doorway, where a grey-haired man is playing with total concentration. Exotic objects fill every corner of the room. The colourful tapestry on the wall looks Indian, and an ebony statuette on his mantelpiece could be from Africa.

The melody suddenly falls silent when Lanner stops to scribble notes on his sheet music, then cross out a stave. He looks startled when I emerge from the shadows. It takes him a moment to rise to his feet, with hand outstretched. He must be retirement age, medium height, wearing expensive clothes. But it's his face that interests me. The man's features have the battered look of a professional boxer, not a classical pianist, yet his movements are delicate.

'Sorry, I didn't hear you arrive,' he says.

'I enjoyed listening to you play. Is that a Steinway?'

Lanner smiles. 'Class D, made in 1933, with a good pedigree. Gershwin composed on it once, so they say.'

'My wife would love to see it. She trained as a violinist.'

'She's welcome here, anytime.' He returns to the piano, stroking a finger across the keys. 'I'm guessing you play too; from the way you're admiring her. Want to play a few bars?'

'Your piano's way above my level, Mr Lanner.'

'Mark, please. I promise, you won't cause any damage.'

'Not today, thanks. I play now and then, just for myself. I never had lessons.'

He looks intrigued. 'You must have plenty of self-discipline.'

'It was just a hobby, in winter. My parents never bought a TV.'

'I watched far too many programmes as a boy. *Doctor Who* was my big obsession.' The curiosity on his face sharpens. 'It's not every day the police pay me a visit. I'm interested to know why.'

'It's about the grave we found on St Helen's.'

Lanner's face blanks. 'Take a seat, please. I'll make some coffee.'

The composer's reactions are difficult to read. His manner is genteel, but this could just be a veneer. His reason for buying this place hits me when I sit by the window. The view extends west for miles, from the green curve of Tean to the smooth waters of Deadman's Pool. His property lies closer to St Helen's than any other, as the crow flies, with a direct view. There's a high-grade telescope by the seating area, and I can't resist using it. When I adjust the viewfinder, the island's landscape comes into focus. I can count the boulders ranged across the beaches and see the stone-built walls of the ruined church and Pest House, plus dozens of seagulls wheeling in low circles. Lanner has an unobstructed view of the child's grave.

He takes the seat opposite. 'I look at the view whenever the tunes dry up. I stargaze sometimes, or watch passing boats. It always intrigues me when someone visits St Helen's at night.'

'Does it happen often?'

'Teenagers often sail over in summer for beach parties. Some still go, even in winter.'

'That's unusual.' Zoe and I used to sail over to Samson on a hot day, to swim and drink cider, but St Helen's never appealed. The religious history of the place and its legacy of illness put us off, but life is tricky for teenagers in small communities. If you want to misbehave, you need places to hide. 'We've been watching this stretch of water for smuggling activity.'

'I wondered why the coastguard have been patrolling,' Lanner replies.

'What about unfamiliar boats recently?'

He hesitates for a moment. 'I woke early on Sunday and saw a cabin cruiser sail past Tean, then on to St Helen's. It was around dawn. A young guy was steering, with a girl onboard. He landed on the quay, then another young woman walked down to meet them, carrying a rucksack. I didn't see her face clearly.'

'So she could have spent the night there. What happened then?'

'They headed towards St Mary's on his boat. It was raining, so the girls' hoods were up. I can't describe them, but the one he collected from St Helen's kept turning back, like she wanted to stay there.'

Lanner's story interests me. Why would anyone sail out to St Helen's, then spend the night in the freezing cold? It could be her that left the campfire and beer cans. I think of Sinead Harcourt and her belief that the island is full of spirits. Maybe she went there to feel closer to her mother, but she struck me as too timid to face the island's haunted atmosphere alone.

'Did you recognise any of them?'

'Not the young women, my life's too busy for much socialising. I'm lucky to be offered so much work, but it can feel relentless. Production companies call me morning, noon and night.' It interests me that he's talking about pressure, yet his calm manner never falters.

'What about the young man?'

'I've seen him before, working at the Co-op, always smiling. He's on the football team, I think.'

'That's Thomas Ford, he's got a job there till he goes to uni. I'll pay him a visit,' I reply. 'I hear you visited Tideline Giftshop recently and bought some jade charms. Were they for yourself or someone else?'

Lanner looks unsettled by the change of topic. 'My sister collects jade. I bought a couple for her birthday last year. She loved them, so I got some more.'

'Does she live nearby?'

'My family are all in London. I wanted something easy to post.'

I tap a note into my phone then glance outside again. 'Do you spend a lot of time, watching the sea?'

'Too much, probably. The ocean's my biggest inspiration right now. I'm writing a score for a film set in a lighthouse. The keepers get stranded, and their supplies run out. All they can do is wait, but the danger escalates. One of them goes mad.'

'No wonder your tune sounds ominous.'

'I want viewers to realise the characters are on a knife-edge.' Lanner appears preoccupied, like notes are still resonating in his mind.

'Have you seen anything else on St Helen's recently, Mark?'

'Not that I remember. The youngsters stuck in my head. I couldn't guess why anyone would stay there without shelter. It was like watching a movie unfold.'

'Did you see me finding the grave on Monday?'

'No.' He gives an odd smile. 'I do work occasionally, believe it or not.'

'If you see anything else, call me, please.'

He hesitates. 'I can keep a look out, if you like. I see most of what happens on St Helen's from up here.'

'That's a kind offer, but we'll be doing our own patrols. Just contact me if you spot something unusual. By the way, is the property next door yours too?'

'Yes, I'm turning it into a studio, with production decks and soundproofing, so musicians can use it for recording. The renovation's been a nightmare.'

'You'll have plenty of takers. Every family in Scilly has at least one musician.'

I catch a glimpse of Lanner's bedroom when he shows me out: a large bed faces another spectacular view, and there's a row of elegant landscapes on the wall. It's a different story downstairs, where all the doors are closed. I can see his garden through the glazed back door, neglected and full of brambles. He must spend all his time composing and peering through his telescope instead of tending his lawn.

I'm about to leave when a noise echoes through the floorboards beneath my feet, like knuckles rapping on wood.

'Is someone downstairs?'

'That's just my boiler. The pipework plays a symphony every time the temperature changes.'

'Doesn't it annoy you?'

'Not anymore, it's become part of my soundscape.' He smiles again, like we're sharing a joke.

'Do you live here alone, Mark?'

'That's how I like it, most days.' He hesitates for a moment. 'My girlfriend plays cello in the Berlin Philharmonic. We meet at her place in London when she's in the UK.'

'Okay, thanks for your help.'

The man's situation puzzles me as I walk away. Lanner's designer home feels too pristine, unlike Phillip Warleggan's, with its cheerful lack of order. And Lanner seemed a little too keen to get involved, but at least he's provided useful information about a girl who may have spent the night on St Helen's then been ferried home by two friends. I knew the boy's identity immediately from Lanner's description, and will pay him a visit. Scilly's different from the mainland, everyone's connected here, leaving few places to hide. Thomas Ford is the youngest member of the lifeboat crew, well liked by everyone. I'm certain he'll tell the truth about his trip to St Helen's and whether he saw anything there.

I thought that few people sailed out there in storm season, but guesswork is often wrong. I also assumed that Lanner's intense manner came from lack of conversation, yet it turns out he has a girlfriend. His situation strikes me as odd. Why have a relationship if you're going to be constantly apart? The thing I enjoy most about sharing my home with Nina is learning how she ticks. I hope to understand her completely one day, but that could take a lifetime.

When I get back to my boat I see that Liz Gannick has sent a text. She's on St Helen's with Lawrie Deane. The sea is still flat calm as I head northwest to join them, the wind falling to a whisper. Tean's empty fields are a vivid green as I pass its shores. The island teems with bees and butterflies in summer, but now there are only gulls hovering above its slopes, gathering energy for their next fishing expedition.

The police launch is moored by the quay on St Helen's. The island's odd atmosphere hits me again when I disembark, even though I'm not superstitious. The air is too still, my chest tightening as I walk inland. Deane is using a spade to dig the ground twenty metres inland, kitted out in white overalls. Gannick is standing by the cordon, making notes on her phone.

I can tell the forensics chief's in pain today. Her face is pinched white, the shadows under her eyes more black than blue. She told me once that her discomfort comes from a botched operation on her back, and even the strongest medication has stopped working, making a good night's sleep impossible. I expect her to snap at me, but she offers a grudging smile instead.

'Your sergeant's a grafter, isn't he?' she says. 'He puts you to shame.'

Deane is digging at a steady pace, too immersed to look up.

'Lawrie always goes the extra mile if a case bothers him. Have you found anything, Liz?'

'Just questions, for now, about the technical side of the killer's MO. The victim's body was wrapped in cloth then plastic sheeting, with a good luck charm inside.' Her stare is too intense, like she's drunk three espressos. 'An organised killer like that doesn't bury a corpse in shifting sand.'

'What are you saying?'

She frowns at me. 'I think they dumped her there because they panicked. Maybe they had a better place in mind nearby, where her body would never be found. But the ground took too long to dig.'

'And Deane's hunting for it?'

'I've told him to look for another burial site. I want to see if the killer tried digging inland, but had to quit when they hit a layer of rock.'

'Have you checked the items from the scene?'

Gannick's tone hardens. 'Give me a chance, for Christ's sake. I'll look at them tonight. Satisfied?'

She inhales a deep breath, preparing to harangue me, until Deane waves his spade above his head, signalling for our attention. He's standing near the prayer oratory. Gannick reaches him first, swinging over the sand on her crutches. Deane has uncovered some stones pressed into the earth, forming a granite cross about a foot wide. It was hidden under foliage. He saw that the stones were laid there on purpose, so he started to excavate. Now he's hit something hard, buried a few inches underground.

'You look tired. Let me dig now, Lawrie.'

'Take care, for God's sake,' Gannick snaps. 'You'll destroy evidence if it's a new victim.'

Deane's face is flushed with effort when I take over, clearing soil until a plank is exposed. Gannick yells at me to step back, only accepting help to prise up the old floorboard when she fails to do it alone.

I drop onto my knees and shine my torch into the opening. Someone has used a pickaxe to form a narrow hole in the rocky ground. The excavation would have been back-breaking work over many hours. I'm guessing they must have worked at night, to avoid being seen by passing boats and people like Mark Lanner. The narrow opening is about four feet deep and five feet long. I'm certain this grave was designed for a child's body, not an adult's.

'Tidy work,' Gannick mutters. 'Just like the shroud. And deep enough for more than one corpse.'

My head's pulsing with theories. If the killer feared being seen digging a permanent grave for the girl, they may have left her body in the sand, marking the spot with an object only they would recognise. They intended to return later, when it was safe.

Deane appears confused by the discovery too, and the weather's not helping. The clouds overhead are blacker than before, the encroaching tide icy and unforgiving. It's possible that the killer had a completely different purpose in mind. Maybe he was planning to bury more than one victim here. It's possible that a second child victim's life could be hanging in the balance, and the killer cares more about the next one. He, or she, deserves a proper headstone, and a permanent grave. But where are they being kept? When I rise to my feet, fresh rain pours down on me like a punishment for failing to understand. Even the landscape is against us, the slopes of St Martin's turning charcoal grey.

PART 2

19

We sail back across St Mary's Strait in separate boats. Lawrie Deane takes Gannick in the police launch, while I follow in my bowrider. They'll be keeping warm in the wheelhouse, while I'm exposed to the elements in my open-topped boat. It's perfect for fresh summer days, but now the rain feels as brutal as the case.

Deane looks relieved when I send him back to the police station after we moor, to inform Eddie and Isla about the empty grave. The man is a creature of habit. I bet he stops at the Island Deli to pick up his lunch first, but my own appetite has vanished.

'Gareth Keillor called earlier. He wants us at the hospital,' I tell Gannick. 'Wait for me in the shelter, Liz. I'll get the van.'

'I can walk, you know.' She narrows her eyes. 'I'm not a cripple.'

'That's not a word I use.'

'Paralysed then. Is that polite enough for you?'

'Stop it, for fuck's sake. We're on the same side, remember? It's pissing down, so let's drive.'

'I prefer to use my feet, thanks.'

'Go ahead, but don't moan about getting drenched.'

'Do I look even remotely dry to you?' she says, giving me a full-force glare.

She sets off without another word, leaving me to call the Angarracks' home. I still need to see Lisa, to follow up on the anonymous email claiming she has information about the grave on St Helen's. No one answers, so I leave a message, requesting an urgent call back.

Gannick is fifty metres ahead as I hurry down the quay. Her behaviour's changed since last time we met; she seems to be on a collision course with all humanity now, her hair-trigger temper even quicker to ignite, so I keep my distance. By the time we reach the hospital, I'm just a few paces behind, and rainwater is dripping from her hair. We're both so wet it looks like we've been for a winter swim, thanks to her need for absolute control.

Gareth Keillor is waiting for us in his office. It's the size of a broom cupboard, with his personality filling every corner. A pinboard is covered in family photos of his grandkids on summer holidays; his golf clubs lean against the wall. There's nothing in his in-tray except a single computer printout. The glint in Keillor's eye normally means that he's discovered something useful. He's too preoccupied to notice the brine dripping from our coats, forming puddles on the lino.

'I've got some results from the lab,' he says. 'Your murder victim had a miserable time, I'm afraid. She had a low iron count, vitamin deficiencies and anaemia. That suggests she was kept in the dark for months, or even years. The girl needed urgent medical attention, and no wonder her growth was stunted. Anyone's bones, skin and eyes would suffer, long-term, under those conditions.'

'Did you find any sexual abuse?'

'No evidence to confirm it, sorry. DNA degrades fast in wet, dark conditions.'

'What about her environment?' Gannick asks.

'She was kept somewhere with little ventilation, no direct sunlight, and had poor nutrition. Children don't suffer like this in the UK anymore. Illnesses like scurvy died out last century, but this girl had all the symptoms. It explains why she was losing teeth.' Keillor looks up from his report. 'That's where it gets interesting. I examined the baby you found yesterday. I took a nasal swab, then took a photo with my microscope and sent it to the lab. The baby has the same variant of *Stachybotrys* in his mucus as the murder victim.'

'That's black mould, isn't it?' Gannick interrupts. 'The type that grows in damp conditions.'

'Correct. It's a strong pathogen – the spores remained in the girl's airways underground.'

I stare at Keillor again. 'You think the victim and the baby were held in the same place?'

'The lab are ninety percent certain they were. The mould has a signature, apparently, based on dust and paint particles from the wall where it grows. All the major indicators match on the two images I sent. They need a physical sample to be sure, but I'm sure they were together, based on the evidence.'

The truth registers at last. Someone on these islands held our murder victim and the abandoned baby prisoner in terrible conditions, like the sailors that died in the Pest House on St Helen's after long sea voyages. It doesn't make sense. If a human trafficker wanted to profit from selling young girls into domestic slavery or the sex trade, they'd act fast to escape detection. Maybe another woman is still being held, after giving birth to the baby we found. I try to imagine her trapped in a dark cell, but the image won't take shape.

'There's one other thing,' Keillor says. 'I took photos of the baby's face and ran an ethnicity check, based on his face shape and features. It's ninety percent likely he's got Vietnamese heritage, mixed with European.'

'That's useful,' I say, meeting his eye. 'Could he have been kept in the hold of a boat?'

Keillor shakes his head. 'Most are fibreglass these days, which is mould resistant. The stuff in their airways is common in old houses and places with poor ventilation. You see it mostly in cellars and bathrooms.'

'Sum up, Gareth, please. We haven't got all day,' Gannick snaps.

'The girl was trapped somewhere damp, probably for years. The baby may have been born in exactly the same room, to a different mother.'

I turn the idea over in my head. There's poverty in Scilly, like anywhere, but we're a close-knit community with little domestic abuse. No one gets held prisoner by a sadistic monster in a place like this. That happens in horror movies, not small islands, where every drama plays out in public. It disgusts me that someone may have targeted the islands precisely because they seem clean and innocent.

'We still don't know if the female victim was British or Vietnamese, do we?' I ask.

'Her face is too damaged for AI to identify ethnicity, but the genealogy test should tell us,' Keillor replies. 'I'll ring them now and rattle their cage. I've already sent them a blood sample from the baby to see if he's related to the victim.'

'Can you ask for comparisons with every islander on the DNA database too, please?' I ask.

'I'll need a Home Office passcode for a large-scale survey, Ben.'

'You'll get it today.'

Gannick seizes the report as Keillor makes his phone call, her gaze devouring each line. Finding the killer seems to matter to her personally this time, making her temper even more caustic. I slip out of the room unnoticed, knowing that she will spend ages discussing technical details with Keillor.

I can't just stand still, knowing that someone on these islands is hiding a monstrous secret, so I go in search of the abandoned baby instead. I need to understand why a half-Vietnamese child was kept in the same environment as the murdered girl. I have to inform the whole team that we're looking for someone with a warped mindset, passing as normal in our small community, yet capable of torturing multiple victims.

I hear a woman's voice drifting down the corridor. She's crooning a soft ballad that's instantly familiar. The sound is so mellow, the case's ugliness fades from my mind. I follow it to a door that stands ajar. Zoe is sitting in an armchair with the abandoned baby in her arms, feeding him from a bottle. She's singing him a tune she wrote at music school, too preoccupied to spot me watching. Her voice is still beautiful. I knew she'd come here, sooner or later. She's always quick to help anyone in need, especially children. It proves she's stronger than she knows. But what will happen if we find the boy's mother alive? Sooner or later this child will be taken from Zoe too, and the hurt could knock her sideways.

Pete Harcourt is nowhere to be seen as I walk through the hospital. It's likely he's off duty, but his daughter isn't my top priority right now. Madron enters my mind again when I leave. Under normal circumstances he'd be tracking my work via constant texts and emails, and I could use a senior officer to offload the new information I'm carrying. It bothers me that he's not answering his phone, and that he kept Lawrie and Isla locked out last night when they called by. He could be out cold on his bathroom floor, thanks to his sense of pride. I don't want that on my conscience, so I head downhill to Pilot's Retreat.

The brass letterbox glitters when I reach Madron's bungalow, his door shiny with fresh paint. I stand in his porch with my thumb on the doorbell, but nothing happens, and my concern for him increases. I stoop down to peer through his letterbox, but see only his empty hallway, so I circle the building. Some windows have frosted glass, and the rest are obscured by net curtains. It's a house designed for a couple who value their privacy above all else. Instinct makes me run my fingers under the seal around his back door and try to lever it open. When I ring him again, his phone sounds in a distant room.

I'm about to shoulder down the back door when I notice that his bathroom window is ajar. I jemmy it open then try to squeeze through. My body's not designed for small spaces, but I force my shoulders inside with effort, then land on his bathroom floor.

Madron's home feels cold, like the heating's been switched off for days. I rush from room to room, looking for him, but finding only the precision he imposes on everything he touches. Even the cookery books in his kitchen are arranged in alphabetical order. There's no sign of him. I should be glad that he's not slumped in a corner, yet his absence feels worse. Madron's car is still on the drive. He could have wandered off anywhere, suffering from a concussion he refuses to acknowledge. I'll have to add finding him to my list of duties.

I spot a door that must lead down to his cellar from the hallway, but Madron can't be down there because it's padlocked on this side. It strikes me as odd that anyone would have an internal lock in their home in Scilly. Burglaries happen once in a decade, yet it seems fitting. My boss hates any type of risk.

His phone is lying on the hall table. Most days it's glued to his hand, from dawn till dusk, but now there's no way to contact him. There's an old-fashioned answering machine beside it, blinking with messages. When I play them back, three are from his wife. Each one sounds more anxious than the last, reminding him that he promised to Skype her in New Zealand. The final one is from Ginny Tremayne, her voice gentle when she urges him to visit her clinic for a head X-ray, to check there's no damage from his fall.

I let myself out of the front door, uncertain how to assist someone who refuses help, because I see life differently – if the worst happened to me, I'd expect my whole community to pitch in and lend a hand. I have to remind myself that Madron's absence is the least of my worries. Something's broken in our community if at least one young girl and a baby have been imprisoned in a filthy room for years. I'll have to work out every detail for the sake of the victim's wasted life. I want to know why the killer wrapped her body with so much care. He could be intending to kill another child to fill that second grave, but my first job is to find out which young islander carried out a night-time vigil on St Helen's, according to Mark Lanner. The girl must be brave, if she really spent the night there, accompanied only by ghosts.

20

Mai's body aches all over when she finally rises from her bed at 3.00 pm. Only her longing for freedom keeps her alive, and her anger at being trapped for so long. She can't give up. She drags the table over to the window. When she stands on it, her eyes are level with the glass. The opening is almost covered by weeds, obstructing her view of a grassy lawn and the edge of a flower bed.

She examines the window frame with care. The wood is dry, with paint flaking as she rubs its surface. The man hasn't noticed that it's falling apart. Mai removes the sharpened nail from her pocket, using it to loosen the surround. A piece of wood drops into her hand, leaving a narrow gap, cold air funnelling inside. Her heart lifts as she feels rain on the grate. Maybe she could work the whole frame loose, then pull it from the wall? She's stared at the window thousands of times, but never believed she could escape through it. Now it feels like there's nothing to lose. Getting out could be her only chance of seeing Lao again. It would take strength to haul herself up onto that ledge, and her attempt might fail, but she pushes her doubts aside.

Mai goes on loosening the frame, then presses the fragments back into place, so her work will go unnoticed. Most of the plaster around the frame feels solid; it will take days to break it apart with just a single nail.

She's still standing on the table when a noise sounds outside. Suddenly a girl's voice babbles, the sound high and urgent. Mai feels certain someone knows she's trapped, and elation floods her veins. She screams for help in Vietnamese, her knuckles rapping the windowpane. But when she stops to listen again, there's no reply.

21

Rain is still tipping down when I jog into town from Madron's place, leaving Gannick and Keillor exchanging information. Hunger nags at me as I call Eddie to bring him up to speed. There's a shocked silence at the end of the line when he hears that the victim and the abandoned baby were held in the same place.

'The killer may be planning to kill a second victim,' I tell him. 'The grave's deep enough for more than one body, and they meant business. It's pretty much hacked out of rock.'

'They used a pickaxe?'

'It looks that way, but it doesn't give us much. They probably chucked the tools into deep water so they wouldn't be found.'

I'm light-headed when the call ends. I'll have to eat soon to keep going, but need to check Mark Lanner's story first. The beauty of living in a small community is knowing almost everyone by sight. Only one lad working at the Co-op on Hugh Town High Street wears a ready smile and plays football for St Mary's. Thomas Ford is well known locally, thanks to his sporting record. Fordie's one of those kids that pick up every sport without effort, and he's won a place to do sports studies next year. I've always liked him, not least because he volunteered for the lifeboat crew the minute he turned eighteen, so our paths cross regularly at training and on shouts.

The shop is empty when I dash inside, out of the rain. I grab a packet of doughnuts, but there are no sandwiches, so I collect a ready meal instead, to microwave at the station. There are wide gaps on the shelves, which often happens in winter. The Co-op is the islands' only decent-sized supermarket, and it does a heroic job of feeding everyone on St Mary's, but it can't perform miracles. There's virtually no fresh produce when storms disrupt supplies from the mainland. Everyone stockpiles daily staples, or borrows from friends if they run out. I'm lucky that my godmother Maggie runs The Rock pub on Bryher, where food is always plentiful, thanks to half a dozen industrial freezers she keeps stocked all year.

Fordie appears when I approach the till, giving me an open-faced grin.

'Looking for bargains are you, boss? We were talking about you at football this week. At your height, you'd make a decent goalie for us.'

'No co-ordination, that's the problem. That's why I played rugby. All I had to do was knock people over.'

He laughs at the idea of me flattening grown men on the rugby field, but his expression alters when I admit that I've got a few questions to ask. I can see him tensing up, so I cut to the chase.

'You're not in trouble, Fordie, I just need info about your trip to St Helen's on Sunday. I hear you sailed there, bright and early.'

Fordie shrugs. 'It was nothing, we just wanted to see the birds.'

'I didn't have you down as a twitcher. And why go at dawn, with a female passenger?'

He blinks back at me, panicked. 'It's the best time to see the gulls and kittiwakes…' His voice tails away.

'You know a girl's body was found there, don't you? I need to hear what you saw there, and both girls' names, please. One of you may have a spotted a detail that could help us.'

'It's not us you should ask, Ben.' He pauses to stuff my shopping into a bag, his voice low. 'It's the people in power doing all the damage. They're making big profits.'

'I keep hearing about this conspiracy stuff, but where did it start? I need your help, Fordie.'

When his smile returns, it's running at half strength. 'I can't talk here, sorry. Anyone could be listening. Can we meet somewhere else?' He glances around, like the Co-op's aisles are heaving with spies.

'What time do you finish work tonight?'

'Six.'

'Come to the station then. We can talk it through.'

Fordie nods rapidly, then hurries back to his task, shelving tins of food. I can see why he'd be reluctant to share information in public, if he knows something relevant. But it surprises me that an upbeat character like him has accepted that dark forces are at work in such a peaceful place. I trust his judgement, though, because he's always hard-working, committed to the lifeboat team, and one hell of a footballer. It takes drive to develop that much skill; I'm certain he'll be able to unlock the conspiracy idea for me, provided he feels safe.

I shelter under the awning outside the Post Office, then eat two doughnuts in rapid gulps, thankful that Nina can't see me. She hates junk food, but sometimes it's necessary, to provide a quick burst of energy.

There's an hour to kill before my conversation with Fordie, so I take the short walk back to the station for the police motorbike. St Mary's is just large enough to make transport essential to our jobs. We patrol the other four inhabited islands on foot or push bike – it's the best way to stay connected to a community. People stop and talk to us, making it easier to nip problems in the bud, but there's no time to dawdle today. I still want to find out why Sinead Harcourt ran away after seeing me on the lane by her home.

The rain's lighter when I ride north from Hugh Town. There are few straight roads in Scilly, so I stay within the speed limit, framing questions in my head as the landscape winds past. Telegraph Hill only contains a handful of houses, scattered along the road. Lawrie Deane's house still looks bright and cheerful, unlike the Harcourts' place, with its high fences, keeping the world at bay.

Pete Harcourt opens the door soon after I ring the bell, dressed in a faded T-shirt and jeans. His mood seems lighter than when he's on duty. Classical music is playing on his radio, and this time I recognise the composer. It's Erik Satie, the melody pure and distinctive. Harcourt's relaxed air vanishes when I ask to see Sinead.

'Don't upset her, please.' He stands with fingertips pressed together in front of his chest. 'Sinead would never hurt anyone. If something bad happened last night, it'll be down to someone else.'

'Last night? Why do you say that, Pete?'

He hesitates. 'I caught Sinead trying to leave about 2.00 am. I sleep like a log normally, but her footsteps woke me. She wouldn't say where she was going.' He closes his eyes. 'Her looks make her a target for every lad on the island, don't they?'

'I'm not suggesting she's the mother of the abandoned child, but she might have witnessed what happened on St Helen's. She was so upset about the murdered girl, and the pair of you often visit the island.'

'It can't be Sinead.' Harcourt gazes down at his hands. 'We're close, you see. She'd never hide it from me if she got pregnant.'

'Has she had counselling since her mum died?'

'She refused to go. When Sinead digs her heels in, that's it.'

'Look, Pete, I need to speak to her today. Is that okay?'

'She won't know anything.'

'I have to check if she's got any details about the murder. It could explain why she's so caught up in conspiracy theories, couldn't it?'

'Most kids here believe that stuff. Sinead was happy, before Gail died.' Harcourt's voice falls to a whisper. 'All that conspiracy crap is just her way of grieving. She'd never get involved in something that dark.'

'I won't grill her about it, I promise.'

Harcourt looks too exhausted to argue. I glance around his kitchen again, while he goes upstairs to fetch his daughter. The remains of a Sunday roast sit by the oven, covered in tinfoil. I can tell he's trying to give Sinead the best life possible, since losing her mum, including home cooking. But I notice another padlocked door opposite me, like in Madron's home, even though burglaries here happen once in a blue moon.

When Sinead Harcourt finally appears, I understand her father's worries. Her face is delicate, and smooth dark hair spills over her shoulders. She looks like a Renaissance artist's model. Her eyes are the lightest blue I've seen, her movements quick and bird-like. Noah watches me with the same intensity whenever he's learning a new skill.

She's calm, unlike on our previous meeting. It feels like she's staring straight through me when she perches on a stool nearby.

'Thanks for coming down, Sinead. I've wanted to check you're okay since you ran off yesterday. Did I scare you?'

'I was just upset about that girl you found.' Her voice is a dry whisper.

'Because her grave was on St Helen's?'

She gives me the smallest of nods.

'Now, I need to know if you saw anything suspicious there.'

'The island's spirits used to protect it.' The girl's head drops suddenly. 'But bad things are happening there. The network treats it like their headquarters.'

'How do you mean?'

'They sail over, at night ... I don't trust anyone in the public eye.'

I leave a pause, in case she wants to give more details, but she's silent.

'Why do you call them the network?' I ask, keeping my voice low.

'Because they're everywhere, connected to each other. St Helen's is holy ground, but they do deals there, with dirty money. They smuggle drugs and human lives. Everyone knows it at school but they're frightened to say. Do you know what scares me most?' Now she's finally talking her speech is rushed and crackling with anxiety. 'The powerful ones are running it all: the mayor, Phillip Warleggan, the chief of police. Your boss started it. Their souls are evil, even though they go to church. You can see it in their faces.' Her eyes burn with conviction.

'Be careful, Sinead. Claims like that need evidence.'

'Adults never believe me.' Her words are shrill with conviction. 'You have to do something to stop them. I've told Dad and Lawrie, but they won't listen.'

I can tell she's sincere, but her story sounds like a fantasy spun by any grieving teenager. She's suffering so much mentally, even her environment feels unsafe.

'Let's focus on my questions, for now, please, Sinead. Tell me if you've heard anything about people getting hurt on St Helen's.'

She looks away. 'It was Mum's favourite place, but now people are dying there.'

'I think you sail over sometimes, with mates, at night. What have you seen?'

'Nothing.' She twists a strand of hair round her fingers, her gaze intense. 'The island's ghosts don't scare me. It's the living that commit evil, not the dead.'

I decide to change the topic, before we disappear down another conspiracy rabbit hole. 'How well do you know Lisa Angarrack? I got a message saying she knows something. She's about your age, isn't she?'

The girl's shoulders tense. 'We're not close anymore. Lisa and me don't see each other outside school.'

'Give Ben the full story, love.' Pete Harcourt's voice is gentle. 'She was your best mate for years, wasn't she?'

'Her parents sent me away months ago. They're part of the network.'

'Stop it,' her dad hisses. 'You're obsessed by all that nonsense.'

I agree with him but stay quiet. Sinead's suspicions don't seem to bring her much comfort; her pale eyes are glassy with tears.

'How about Fordie? He's just a couple of years older than you, isn't he?'

Her cheeks flush. 'We chat sometimes, that's all. He's friendly with everyone.'

'Do you ever go out in his boat?'

She shakes her head vehemently. 'Dad takes me to St Helen's, no one else. I told you that already.'

'Okay, that's enough questions for today, Sinead. But call me, please, if you remember anything suspicious happening on St Helen's.'

'It's the islands' children that need your protection.' Sinead's watching me intently, like a magpie observing something shiny glinting in the sun. 'Do you need many exams to join the police?' she asks.

'Level-three passes, plus GCSE English and maths. Are you thinking of joining us?'

'One day, maybe, after uni. But I'd never work for Alan Madron.'

I give a slow nod. 'Your dad says you enjoy investigating stuff. Is that right?'

'I like learning the truth about things and helping people.'

'Me too. But let us solve this, Sinead. Don't take risks. Your dad said you tried leaving the house alone last night. It's important you stay indoors after dark, until we catch the killer.'

'I needed fresh air; this place smothers me.' She blinks rapidly, then suddenly leans forwards to touch my wrist. 'What type of watch is that?'

'Tissot. My wife bought it for my fortieth, last year.'

'Was it expensive?'

'She won't say, so probably, yes.'

When I take it off and pass it to her, she weighs it in her hands, then examines every detail. She's either genuinely interested, or it's a smoke screen to throw me off course. The girl's avid expression makes me certain she's smart, despite her odd ideas about spirits and people doing bad deeds.

'How does the battery work?' she asks.

'It's solar-powered, each charge lasts six months.'

'Can you wear it underwater?'

'Down to thirty metres – pressure changes don't affect it.'

Sinead runs her fingertip over the back. Perhaps she's easily distracted by random details that catch her eye, and that's why she imagines crimes where none exist. I think she's concealing secrets about St Helen's too, but it would take time to win her trust. I'd stand a better chance of learning exactly what she knows without her dad monitoring every word.

'Thanks for helping me today, Sinead.'

The girl's beauty comes into focus again when she smiles. 'I can tell you're not in the network, but you're in danger too, with them in charge. They won't let you get in their way.'

'Let's talk about that another day.'

'That man on St Martin's is part of it. He's watching, every time me and Dad go to St Helen's. He pretends to write music, but he spies for the network. I bet he reports back to them every day.'

'I'll keep that in mind. Here's my number, if you remember anything about that grave on St Helen's, or the baby we found.'

The girl places my card in her pocket, then returns my watch, her gaze solemn. Pete plants a kiss on the top of her head as she leaves the room, but she barely responds before returning to her own world. Our conversation makes me certain that she sits upstairs, imagining dangers, while her father plays classical music in the kitchen. I'd like to know if there's a grain of truth in her conspiracy theories, but local kids would see me as part of the problem if I started interviewing them.

Pete Harcourt looks exhausted by the conversation, even though no voices were raised. He explains that Sinead has always loved make-believe. Her passion for fairies and Santa Claus morphed into an obsession with ghosts and conspiracies, since her mother died. Now she exists in a hinterland, lost between the real world and her imagination.

I bring the subject back down to earth by asking him about the padlocked door. Apparently he found Sinead rummaging through his power tools down in the basement years ago, when she was small. He's kept the door secured ever since.

'Can I take a look, Pete? We need to check basements in every property.'

'Go ahead, but there's not much there. It's just DIY stuff.'

Harcourt fumbles some keys from his pocket then undoes the padlock. The space is brightly lit when I flick the switch, but the air smells damp. It's a typical man cave, with tools arranged along one wall, plus a workbench with a circular saw. I'm not sure why the place leaves me disturbed. Maybe it's a fraction too neat, with no mess anywhere, or sawdust on the floor. It bothers me that the ceiling is stippled with black smudges of mould, yet the basement's only occupants appear to be spiders guarding their webs. Surely Sinead would know if her father was involved in abducting victims and keeping them imprisoned, but loyalty or fear might be preventing her from telling anyone? I swallow a deep breath; there's no proof that one of Scilly's most trusted residents is involved, yet Harcourt still looks anxious when I go back upstairs.

'Thanks, Pete. You've got a bit of rising damp, haven't you?'

'It needs treating, but my finances are screwed without Gail's wage. Phillip Warleggan's lent me money, but he'll need paying back one day.'

I turn to face him, surprised that the old man has given him a personal loan. 'You always have music playing, Pete. Does it ease the stress?'

'Not if Sinead's involved in something bad.' He hurries on before I can reply. 'She wants her independence, that's the trouble. Sinead's clever, but she's not ready for the adult world.'

'She seems pretty grownup to me.'

I bet many parents of teenagers feel the same when their child goes astray, but Sinead's attitude is too dark for her years. She seems to think that evil exists at every turn. It bothers me that she collects jade charms and could be making regular trips to St Helen's on Thomas Ford's boat. I'd love to be certain that she and her father have no connection to the dead girl, or the baby left on our doorstep, but it's too soon to judge. If Sinead's done anything wrong, she's found a neat way to deflect attention, by spouting conspiracy theories about the islands' powerholders. The certainty in her eyes disturbed me when she named those she believes are exploiting the islands for their own gain. She seemed afraid of Mark Lanner, on St Martin's, but described Madron as the worst of all. The conviction in her voice nags at me, even though there's no evidence that the islands' elders have done anything wrong.

22

I'm with Isla and Eddie at the station at 6.00 pm, holding an update meeting. Lawrie Deane has already been briefed, and I've sent him to check people's basements, using the council's property list. We need to search any that contain the black mould Keillor identified as priority. Most houses here are built on solid granite, so only a minority have cellars, due to the cost of excavation, but I want to chase down every scrap of information. We still know little about the girl left under the sand, except that she was kept somewhere cold and dank. It's possible our killer wanted to move her body to a permanent grave, but I'm still afraid that he's keeping more victims. It's even possible that the mother of the abandoned child is still alive, trapped in a dark room.

'Every few years some monster gets caught, torturing girls,' I say. 'Remember Marc Dutroux, in Belgium? His wife knew about the victims he kept underground and even took them food. She was a primary-school teacher at the time.'

'You think a couple could be keeping prisoners, sir?' Isla asks.

'We can't rule that out. It bothers me that local kids and teenagers seem obsessed by the idea that dark forces are at work. Maybe one of them knows something, but they're too scared to talk.'

She looks upset. 'Maybe the killer's got them all running scared. Someone violent might be drawn to a sleepy place like this, where no one's on guard. But if the baby's his, maybe he couldn't bring himself to kill it?'

'The good-luck charms back that up. Why would a murderer leave symbols of purity in a victim's shroud unless they have regrets?'

'The bastard must have spent days planning it all.' Eddie's voice is sharp with frustration. 'Passenger transcripts from the airport and the ferry don't help. I can't find any young girls arriving then never leaving again. They're all accounted for.'

'It could be a trafficker. They might be moving the victims around by boat. That's how they took the girl's body to St Helen's, after all.'

'Most families have one, sir,' Eddie says.

'That's why we need to focus on locating mould in properties first. Lawrie's already out there checking basements and cellars, but we need to check every property for signs of it in any of the rooms.'

The killer may have left the islands already, but few people are crazy enough to try sailing to the mainland on a small craft, over twenty-eight miles of Atlantic swell, during storm season. We lost two islanders doing that voyage last year, on a day the forecasters predicted would be clear. A freak gale boiled up out of nowhere. The rescue helicopter found their boat upturned, with no sign of life onboard.

Isla interrupts my train of thought. 'When can we search St Helen's properly, sir?'

'After Liz gives us the all-clear. She can't have evidence disturbed.'

I wish we could speed up the protocol, but we're in Gannick's hands with forensics. I use Madron's landline when 6.30 pm comes round, to find out why Thomas Ford is running late. He doesn't pick up, so I leave him a voice message, reminding him to report to the station immediately. I should have brought him straight here, but I know he's always well intentioned. I assumed he'd be the first person to volunteer information. Maybe he's too afraid to share what he knows, but it won't be hard tracking him down, with so few places to hide.

Eddie tells me the reason for Madron's absence from home when I return to the team room. Phillip Warleggan checked on him last night, as I requested, then persuaded him to stay at his place overnight. Warleggan rang the station and reported that he's concerned about Madron's health; he seemed stronger after a sound night's sleep, but still not himself. I feel daft for breaking into Madron's bungalow, convinced he was in trouble, when he may just have been visiting another friend. He appears to have accepted Ginny Tremayne's advice, to take time off work, liberating me to lead the investigation without him blocking me at every turn.

I'm about to dismiss Eddie and Isla for the evening when Steve Angarrack finally rings me back. The headmaster's tone is confident when he explains that work's been so busy it slipped his mind. He invites me to their home straight away. As I make my way out of the station, I send Eddie and Isla home, but they're not thrilled to leave. I get the sense that they'd prefer to stay and work on the case round the clock. We've all switched up a gear, aware that there may be limited time to find a second victim alive.

The Angarracks' home is in one of the best parts of Hugh Town. It's a steep climb uphill, directly above the harbour. They only bought it recently, and I can see why. The place has stunning views across St Mary's Sound. But it looks like the sprawling detached property needs work, after standing empty for years. The exterior will take money and effort to get it looking smart, unlike the brand-new car on the driveway. It strikes me as odd that the couple run two expensive vehicles in a place where most tasks can be completed on foot, but it proves they must be rolling in money.

I'm still interested to know why Emma had such a heated phone conversation at her shop. It sounded like a marital row, even though the couple always seem united. But they're both burdened with work responsibilities, and doing a place up can put a strain on family life too.

The wind is blowing harder as I wait in their porch, but Steve gives me a warm welcome. It's been months since we did our last lifeboat training session together, followed by a night in the pub. He's played a smaller role in the crew since becoming headmaster at Five Islands Academy last year, but he's still a fit-looking guy, medium height, with cropped grey hair smoothed back from his face. I've never seen him panic, even though we've been on shouts together, facing force-nine gales. He's responsible for the education of every child in Scilly, but his manner is upbeat when he leads me inside. He's wearing an expensive tracksuit, like it's his duty to look smart, even in his downtime. It's only when I look closer that tension shows in the tight set of his shoulders.

'Sorry to miss your call, Ben. Things have been hectic, for both of us.' He gives me a look of mock despair. 'We need more hours in the day, don't we?'

Emma is peering at her laptop in their brand-new kitchen, which looks so spotless it's hard to believe anyone ever prepares food there. She gives me a radiant smile, like she's keen to erase our last meeting from my mind.

'This place looks great,' I tell her. 'You're transforming it.'

'Don't be fooled, Ben. It's literally the only room we've finished.' She shuts the lid of her computer. 'Steve's always at school, and the Island Council love arguing about parking spaces, when we've got much more important stuff to fix.'

'You'll soon knock them into shape.'

'I bloody hope so. Meals on wheels is struggling, and the youth club's a disgrace.' She offers me a seat at the table. 'Sorry I was fed up the other day. I hate suppliers letting me down. That sort of thing has to be nipped in the bud, doesn't it?'

Steve busies himself making hot drinks while we talk. They may be one of the islands' power couples, but they still seem down to earth. The pair have risen to leadership positions in a community where having airs and graces makes you a laughingstock, yet something about their unassailable confidence strikes me as fake. They sit down opposite me, like I'm being interviewed for a job.

'What's happening with your case?' Steve asks.

'We're making progress, but I need more information. A witness on St Martin's has seen boats landing on St Helen's at night. Youngsters had beach parties there in the summer, so maybe a few teenagers have kept on going over. It's possible they witnessed the girl's burial.'

Emma looks appalled. 'If that's true, they must be terrified. Are you sure the girl you found on St Helen's was held captive?'

'The pathologist is certain, and we think the abandoned baby was held in the same place. I've seen the Home Office stats about child migrants and kidnap victims from abroad. Ten thousand kids were trafficked to the UK last year. We've even found asylum seekers stranded in a dinghy here.'

'The islands have always been a smuggling route for illegal goods, but not children, surely?' Steve looks shocked. 'Where would you hide them in a place this small?'

'This killer's smart enough to find an ideal hiding place, and one of your pupils may be able to help. I had an anonymous email, telling me to ask at Five Islands about the murdered girl, and a school flyer was left in the box.'

'I don't believe one of my pupils is the mother of that child, if that's what you're saying.' Steve's expression darkens. 'A concealed pregnancy's unlikely. We've improved sex education out of sight since I started teaching there, nineteen years ago. One of our girls got into trouble back then. No one saw it coming, until she gave birth on the bathroom floor at home.'

'That sounds harrowing. What happened to the baby?'

'She did a good job; raised him here alone. But it wasn't easy.' He shifts awkwardly in his seat. 'Our kids know they can talk to our school counsellor, Denise Laramie, about their problems. My teachers are trained to spot problems before they escalate...' His voice tails into silence.

'This isn't an inspection, Steve. Everyone knows you're performing miracles at Five Islands. I don't think any of your students are directly connected to the murder, or the abandoned child. I just need to find out if one of them witnessed anything, to explain what happened on St Helen's.'

He looks relieved. 'Denise can identify any students that seem unsettled.'

'I've interviewed Sinead Harcourt already. She was very upset about the murder, and the abandoned child.'

'And full of crackpot theories no doubt.' His voice sounds

irritable. 'Sinead's convinced plenty of other kids that the entire adult population is riddled with evil.'

'It sounds like it's the powerholders she fears the most. I can see why young people feel let down. Plenty of them will have to leave, to make a living.'

'Ask any questions you like at school. Just remember that they're kids with vulnerabilities.' The look in his eye is protective. I can tell he's back in headteacher mode, ready to defend his school to the hilt.

'My first step will be a chat with Denise tomorrow.' I put down my coffee. 'There's one more thing, I got an anonymous email, claiming your daughter has information about the murder.'

'Lisa?' Emma's face blanks. 'Why would she be involved?'

'It implied she knows something about the victim.'

'That's rubbish. It'll be some coward spreading rumours behind our backs.'

'I still need to ask her, I'm afraid.'

'Lisa's a hundred percent focussed on her schoolwork right now.'

'But it's possible she's heard something about the murder and kept it to herself. Some kids may know why that girl died, but they're too scared to talk.'

'Lisa never keeps secrets from us,' Emma snaps. It's the same hot tone I heard her using on the phone.

'Don't get upset, Em. Ben's just doing his job.' Angarrack's voice is measured.

Emma's lips clamp shut. I can't tell whether the look in her eye is anger or fear when I ask my next question.

'Does your daughter see much of Sinead Harcourt? I hear they used to be close.'

'Lisa has other friends now,' Steve says, not missing a beat.

The picture suddenly falls into place. 'You separated them?'

'We just asked her to choose more appropriate friends. Lisa's bright, with her feet on the ground, while Sinead's a troubled soul.'

Steve Angarrack's hand settles on his wife's wrist, like he's restraining her. 'Kids often outgrow each other at that age. It's our duty to protect her.'

'Can I see Lisa for a minute, please? Then I'll leave you in peace.'

'She's at drama club till nine,' Emma says.

'No problem. I'll catch up with her tomorrow at school.'

'One of us should be there, if you interview her. She's only sixteen.'

Steve turns to face me. 'Lisa won't mind answering your questions. But even so, I'd still like to be present, if that's okay?'

'Of course.'

Emma stares at me. 'Why aren't you holding regular public meetings if you really think some monster's locking victims away? The community expects me to keep them safe, in my role as mayor.'

'That's our job, Emma. Protecting the islanders is our responsibility, while you run the council.'

'But it's a thin line, isn't it? Alan Madron involves me in his decision-making.'

'He's ill. I'm running the investigation, and the police team, for now.'

She releases a sigh, but keeps her thoughts to herself.

Steve breaks the silence: 'I'll bring Lisa to the counselling room tomorrow. Denise will call me when you arrive.'

His wife's face is flushed with an anger that I don't understand. But his manner remains calm when we say goodnight.

'Sorry about that, Ben. Emma always wants things fixed straight away.'

'That's a good quality in a mayor. We need someone to fight our corner.'

'Let's just hope she doesn't burn herself out.'

Steve's face blanks, as if the ugliness of the case has finally registered. His front door clicks shut behind me fast. I can see why kids like Sinead would feel excluded from their affluent world, where some of their daughter's friends are judged unworthy. I'd love to be a fly on the wall in their designer kitchen. I feel sure he's marching back down the hallway now, to face another row with his wife, about issues they prefer to keep private.

23

I make it home just before the next storm hits, with rain still spitting in my face. Nina sent a text, saying she's at The Rock with Noah, even though it's 10.00 pm. I hurry north across the beach to my godmother's pub. It lies half a mile away, over the next headland. The wind feels biting. Whitecaps are cresting on New Grimsby Sound, and Tresco's coastline is picked out by moonlight, its curved form floating on the sea, like a sleeping giant. It's a relief to step inside and take off my dripping oilskin, even though the case is still rattling around my head.

The Rock hasn't changed much since I was a boy, with a fire burning in the inglenook hearth and most of the island's eighty-strong population filling the tables. I assume the hot topics are the murder case and the abandoned baby, because conversation falls to a buzz when the crowd spots me. I keep my head down, keen to avoid direct questions. It would be wrong to encourage speculation without solid facts to share.

Nina is in the corner, talking to Ray. My uncle can appear taciturn, a lifelong bachelor with little tolerance for fools, but he always relaxes in her company. The expression on his face could almost be a smile. It vanishes when I reach their table, as if he'd prefer to keep my wife to himself, but she reaches up to kiss my cheek.

'Noah's been grizzly, so I came here for some adult company.'

Our son appears to be in his element too. He's charming people at a neighbouring table, red-cheeked from teething, being passed from lap to lap. That's how childcare works on Bryher. The pub is great for free babysitting. It makes the islanders seem more like relatives than friends, complete with enmities and fierce loyalties. I've seen fights break out here, and tempers run high, but tonight's atmosphere is peaceful.

My godmother is behind the bar, running the show. Maggie

Nancarrow is small but mighty, a force of nature, with a cloud of grey ringlets framing her face. When my father died my mother retreated into herself as her MS took hold. She died in her fifties, and ever since Maggie's loyalty to me has never faltered. I feel lucky that she's filled a grandmother role for Noah from the day he was born.

She peers up at me through her red-framed glasses, scouring my face for information. 'You look hungry, Ben. How about a brandy, then I'll get you some grub?'

'The drink sounds good, but no food, thanks. I just came to collect Nina and Noah.'

'He's staying with us tonight, to give you two a break. I've got everything he needs till morning.'

'You're a lifesaver, Maggie. How come you always calm him down? He was screaming blue murder this morning.'

'I'm a baby whisperer. Can't you tell?'

'Write a book, you'll make a fortune.'

'It's not rocket science. Your boy loves fresh air, so me and Nina put him in his stroller and took him out for an evening walk. He'll sleep like a log tonight.' She studies me more closely. 'Did you hear Zoe's looking after that baby you found, up at the hospital?'

'She's still there?'

'Stuck to him like glue, apparently, and the kid's rallying. It's her I worry about.'

'You can't look after everyone, Maggie, but it's great you try.' I reach over the bar to plant a kiss on her cheek. 'If I was single, I'd marry you tomorrow.'

She beams at me. 'You're too tall.'

'Heartbreaker.'

'What's the news from St Helen's?' Her eyes glitter with interest. Maggie's capable of discretion, but it's too soon to tell even trusted family members that I'm afraid of finding another victim, and that the powerholders in Scilly appear to be keeping secrets.

'We're making progress; that's all I can say.'

'Tight-lipped, as ever. Get yourselves home before Steve hears we're babysitting.'

Maggie's elderly boyfriend remains in the kitchen most nights. He's a gifted chef, ruling his empire with a rod of iron. The man looks like a veteran Hell's Angel. I can't imagine him enjoying a boisterous one-year-old's company after a long shift, so I follow Maggie's advice before he changes her mind.

The storm has released its grip on Bryher by the time we get outside, with Shadow chasing our heels. Stars glitter in the gaps between clouds, and the only evidence of the latest deluge is puddles on the ground, the wind falling to a breeze. Nina pulls me to a halt by the shore. We stand side by side, looking out over New Grimsby Sound to the lights of Tresco, a few hundred yards away.

'I've been thinking about the future, Ben. Want to hear my suggestion?' Nina asks.

'Can't we just be here now, looking at the stars?'

'We can do that too.'

I look down at her. 'Go on then, hit me with it.'

'It's simple, really. You want to stay here, and I want us to have another child. Maybe we could do a trade? We could compromise and carry on living here for good, with another baby?'

'You'd give up the mainland for a bigger family?'

'Provided we make more trips to see my parents. A week or two at Christmas, Easter and summer.'

I take a breath, letting my thoughts settle. 'That's a decent plan.'

'You agree?'

'Okay, yeah. If we both get what we need.'

Nina beams up at me, then leans in for a hug. I know that I've been played. This is the outcome she planned all along, but who cares? The solution was waiting right in front of us. She barely speaks on our walk home to Hell Bay now the subject's agreed, her arm linked through mine. Her capacity for silence intrigued me from the start. My wife never speaks unless she's got something useful to say, which suits me fine. She reaches up to kiss me in the porch, with a sudden burst of heat.

'We're alone for once, Ben. Let's enjoy it.'

'Fancy a bath?'

'Or just getting naked on the living-room floor?' She's already peeling off her jumper. 'Babies need making, you know.'

'Happy to volunteer,' I say, grabbing her waist. 'No more condoms, thank God.'

'What about Shadow? He's still outside.'

'Let him find his own woman.'

I lean down, fingers racing to take off my boots. It seems like months since we had time for tenderness, or the good old-fashioned lust I feel for her every day. My body's out of practice when she tugs my shirt over my head, then flicks out the light, even though there are no close neighbours to peer inside. Nina looks beautiful by moonlight. Tall and slim, with a dancer's lithe body, unlike mine. I catch sight of my reflection in the window's black glass. We're beauty and the beast. My hulking shoulders are ugly by anyone's standards, but the chemistry between us never seems to fade. Nina gets her wish sooner than expected, on the sofa, instead of the floor. Even a barbarian like me has standards.

She falls asleep immediately, with her head on my shoulder, legs still wrapped around my waist. Nina doesn't even wake up fully when I carry her to the bedroom, but the long overdue sex hasn't lulled me to sleep. My eyes stare at the ceiling while starlight drifts through the window. My head's fizzing with information, yet it's Alan Madron who surfaces, vulnerable and alone, after a lifetime in control. Why would a young girl like Sinead Harcourt claim he's the most evil man in Scilly, and why would a decent lad like Fordie run and hide?

Old certainties are vanishing, even though it's a relief that we're staying put. I know that more changes lie ahead. Madron can't do his job forever, no matter how tightly he clings on to his power. If he retires, another officer will be recruited to take his place, or I'll have to step up. Ideas about the case chase round my mind, like a greyhound on a track, unable to stop.

The house feels unnaturally empty, with the baby monitor silent for the first time. Someone must be grieving for the young girl we found under the sand, and for the abandoned child, yet the truth's still out of my reach.

24

It's the middle of the night. Mai is freezing cold as she stands on the table, scratching plaster from the window with her sharpened nail. She keeps her courage up by picturing the outside world as she works. Mai remembers her village by the Red River delta, with its pagoda and banyan trees; her family's cabin was built on a raised platform, to protect it from floods. She used to play with Tuyet and their cousin Kim on the muddy ground below, drawing pictures in the dirt. Even though she's been away so long, the longing for home still tugs at her, making her eyes well with tears.

Mai has never seen the UK, except the woodland where the man took her to walk. The sea must be nearby, because, with her ear pressed to the glass, she can hear waves pounding the shore in winter. Will she have enough courage to escape if the chance comes? The world outside tempts and terrifies her at the same time.

She screws her eyes shut and pictures Lao. He felt so small in her arms, and fragile, like he was made of air. She must find him, there's no other choice. She runs her nail down the side of the window to loosen the frame, until something catches her eye. There's a thin beam of light outside. Its radiance cuts through the weeds shadowing the glass. Mai presses her hand to her mouth to stop herself calling out. It could be the man, but why would he poke around in his own garden in the middle of the night? Someone is passing the window now – their feet are level with her eyes, in green rubber boots like the ones her mother wore each winter.

Mai hits the glass with the palm of her hand until the frame rattles. The torch beam suddenly zigzags away. She can no longer see through the tangled leaves, yet her hopes are growing. Maybe someone is searching for her at last? The dream stays in her mind long after the light fades from view.

25

Thursday, 11th January

I'm on auto-pilot when I wake at 6.00 am, expecting to hear Noah chuntering to himself about the new day, until I remember that his cot's empty. It's an odd quirk of human nature that I've been longing for time alone with Nina, only to find myself hating his absence. She's in the shower already, singing at top volume, while I make breakfast.

My wife looks rested when she appears in the kitchen, her expression content as she pours honey over her porridge. It's a fact of life that once a decision's made, Nina rarely has regrets.

'Missing him, aren't you?' she says.

'Not the shrieking, or the nappies. It feels quiet, that's all.'

'Enjoy it; we'll soon have two to think about. A proper sleep was bliss.' She takes a gulp of coffee. 'Can I get a lift with you this morning? Maggie's keeping Noah today.'

'We owe her and Steve big time for all this babysitting.'

Nina laughs. 'Noah prefers them. Maggie carries him round in a sling.'

'She'll have him running the pub next. You'd better get a move on, if you're coming with me.'

'Ten minutes, that's all I need.' Nina puts down her coffee, leaning closer to observe me. 'I wish you didn't have to work this weekend. The case is getting to you, isn't it?'

I tell her about the investigation's slow pace, without revealing the awful conditions our victim endured, and that the baby was held there too. But I do let slip that the killer could be keeping another victim locked away. Nina looks shocked. The baby we found came from another mother, not the victim under the sand.

'So it's possible a second girl's trapped somewhere dark?' she asks.

'We found a grave the killer's been digging on St Helen's, hacked from stony ground,' I say. 'It's deep enough to hold several victims.'

'It takes commitment to do all that work. Maybe he wants to leave them somewhere pure. I might feel the same, in his shoes.'

'Burying her near a shrine doesn't erase the violence.'

'Perhaps it does, in their eyes.'

'I still don't get the Vietnam link. The girl was wrapped in a Buddhist prayer shawl, the jade charms are from there, and the baby's got Vietnamese heritage.'

'Has anyone travelled there recently?' Nina asks.

'No one's admitted to it, except Phillip Warleggan. His place has already been searched.' I dump our cereal bowls and mugs in the sink. 'I may not get back till late tonight. It feels wrong to stop working while someone could be locked in a dungeon somewhere.'

'You won't find them by running yourself into the ground.'

'I'll take breaks, don't worry.'

She shakes her head. 'Come home for dinner. It's my turn to cook.'

I nod in reply, relieved that the atmosphere between us is back to normal. Simple details keep me sane when an investigation's slow to unfold. Our conversation is disturbed by a high-pitched bark from the hall. Shadow is poised outside the nursery. His pale eyes lock on to mine, full of questions. He puts back his head and gives an ear-splitting howl.

'Calm down,' I tell him. 'Noah's with Maggie.'

My dog hovers in the hallway, unable to decide whether to guard his territory or follow us outside. He squeezes out of the door at the last moment, then sticks to our heels like glue. Shadow's psychology often baffles me, but today it makes sense: he's always a hundred percent focussed on Noah, staying close, especially at night. He appears happier when we reach the quay. Shadow shares my love of the ocean, his tail wagging as the bowrider's engine starts first time, and our journey gets under way.

I watch the sky as we sail. A cyclorama of clouds races overhead, which suits me fine. It's the ones that hang around that cause most grief, but the air still feels charged. I'm certain more storms are coming, but Nina appears relaxed. She sits with Shadow in the prow, dressed smartly for her day of counselling. I'm glad she loves her job, but it gives me a twinge of envy. I'm responsible for finding a killer who enjoys imprisoning children, and I realise now that Madron does more than rearrange paperclips in his office. My phone is buzzing with messages that I'd rather ignore. Journalists keep calling me, now that he's absent.

Nina kisses my cheek when we reach St Mary's, then hurries along the quay, leaving me to secure the mooring rope. Shadow is still behaving oddly. He normally races across the shore, looking for adventures, but he remains close by, as I head for Tregarthen's. My first appointment is with Liz Gannick. The place is her favourite in Scilly, with an unparalleled sea view from the end of the quay. The receptionist smiles when I walk inside. She emerges from her desk to stroke Shadow, even though dogs are forbidden. He's charmed most of the islanders over the years, giving him access to plenty of homes, and constant free food.

I walk up to Gannick's rooms on the second floor, braced for verbal abuse. It's only 8.30 am, but she's already at work. Her kit is spread across the table in her suite, including a professional-grade microscope, slides and specimen jars.

'Keep the bloody dog out,' she hisses.

I squeeze through the door fast, leaving Shadow behind. His barks of protest echo through the wall, but Gannick has already forgotten my existence. She's balancing on her crutches, peering down her microscope with total concentration. The table is cluttered with vials of liquid and sheets of litmus paper.

'How are you doing, Liz?'

'I'm having a ball, can't you tell?' She carries on with her work. 'I've dealt with the prayer shawl. It's mixed silk and cotton; the weave's thin, from heavy use. It's clean, apart from one patch of bodily fluids, most likely from the corpse.'

'But you found something else?'

'Several things, actually. Grains of pollen, from agapanthus flowers.'

'Island lilies? They grow everywhere here.'

'Someone could have washed the shawl then hung it out to dry when pollen was on the air. It's more proof that the killer's local, and someone may have seen it.'

I remember Lawrie Deane's certainty that he'd seen the lotus symbol somewhere before, so maybe it was flapping on a washing line. It's not much to follow, but I keep my mouth shut. If I question Gannick's findings she'll catch the next plane home.

'The biggest news is another link between the baby and your victim, like the mould in their airways. Come and see.'

Gannick lets me peer through her microscope. The slide contains two scarlet threads, which appear identical, lying side by side. They're so enlarged I can see every twist and fray.

'Are they from clothing?'

'Let me explain, for God's sake,' she snaps. 'One of them was in the girl's shroud, the other was on the baby's blanket.'

I straighten up fast. 'What type of fibre?'

'Carpet. The pigment's faded, so it must have been down several years. I can't give you an exact scenario, but the killer probably laid the shawl on a carpeted floor to wrap the girl's body, because there are more of the same fibres on the plastic sheeting. It looks like they dressed the baby in the same room.'

'That's a breakthrough, Liz.' My brain's already making lists. We'll need to search the island again, for properties with red carpet, as well as damp.

'I'll spend more time on the charms. No fingerprints on those, but there's a chance of DNA.'

'When can we go back to St Helen's for a full search?'

'Not yet. I want to check the area by the second gravesite, once the weather clears.' She lifts her gaze. 'You think they'll kill again, don't you?'

'It's the baby's mother I'm worried about. It's possible she's alive and still being held; there may be other victims too. Someone's treating the island like their own personal graveyard.'

'Go and catch them then,' Gannick snaps. 'Don't let anyone touch the crime scene without my permission. Now bugger off and let me work.'

I pause by the door. 'You don't fool me, you know.'

'Why are you even still here?'

'There's a decent human trapped inside you, longing to be let out. I'll come back tonight for a catch-up. I may even bring food and alcohol.'

She scowls at me. 'I'm not here to socialise.'

'Life's different in Scilly, Liz. I need your information, and we believe in welcoming people, even during a murder case.'

Gannick tells me to clear off again at the top of her voice. Shadow looks smug when I return to the corridor, clearly happy that she bawled me out, after being banished during our brief conversation.

I feel better as I jog back downstairs. Information has been thin on the ground, but now everything suggests that the killer is an islander, taking captives, from an unknown source. The pollen on the shawl is too common to help us, but the carpet fibre is a new direction. It might be traceable, and a shred of evidence is better than none.

26

The police station is empty when I arrive. I put my head round Madron's door, but there's only the familiar scent of air freshener in his office. He's made no attempt to contact me since his fall. I expect he's being cared for by his friend Warleggan, while he recovers, but it still feels unsettling. Until now he's been hard to avoid. Maybe it's his old-school formality and the layer of mystery he cultivates that makes him seem dangerous to a fragile teenager like Sinead Harcourt.

Back in the team room I pause to look at the paperwork on Lawrie Deane's desk. He loves charts and spider diagrams, and this case is no exception. I can tell it's obsessing him too, from his lists and scribbled notes. I should follow his example, instead of holding most of the information in my head.

Eddie and Isla both appear tense when they arrive, like the case is getting to them. My deputy looks his age for once, his blond hair dishevelled. His face only brightens when I share Gannick's discovery. We now have even more proof that the girl's killer kept the baby in the same place as the victim, thanks to the matching carpet fibres. My two junior officers pay attention to all Gannick's findings, including the pollen from native lilies. The killer may have been in their own property when they prepared the body for burial, so we need to know which homes on St Mary's contain red carpet.

'The house could be on any of the islands, couldn't it?' Isla says.

'Let's start here with the biggest population and collect carpet samples in labelled evidence bags. If Gannick finds a match, we've got a direct link. I want every property on St Mary's searched, new or old. Use volunteer stewards to help us, please. We'll cover the off-islands next. And can one of you organise volunteers to help comb the area around the church ruins on St Helen's tomorrow, after Gannick's finished? I want to do a wider search in daylight for anything the killer could have dropped.'

'That's tricky, boss. I spoke to the Science Council yesterday,' Eddie says. 'They won't overrule the law on disturbing sites of special scientific interest without agreement from Scotland Yard. We're already in violation, according to them.'

'What part of "it's a fresh murder scene" do they not understand? Call the Yard, please. Get authorisation today.' I look at them each in turn. 'Any other news?'

'Thomas Ford's done a runner. He hasn't turned up for work at the Co-op,' Isla says. 'It's really weird. Fordie's never caused anyone trouble, or hidden stuff. He's brilliant on the lifeboat too.'

'Maybe he's scared, if he knows something big. Put out feelers, can you? I need the names of the girls he's been ferrying over to St Helen's.' I glance round the office. 'Where's Lawrie?'

'Checking the boss is okay. He sounded weird on the phone, apparently. Lawrie's been going flat out. He did a trawl of houses with cellars last night, but none contain black mould.'

Before I can reply, my phone buzzes in my pocket. Gareth Keillor sounds excited, his voice racing the moment I pick up.

'I've got news about the dead girl's DNA at last, Ben. There's a twenty-five-percent match with a pupil at Five Islands Academy.'

'That's brilliant, Gareth. Give me the details.'

'Her name's Kim Durgan. Her DNA result's listed on Ancestry.com. It proves that the victim on St Helen's was one of her first cousins.'

The news is a great step forwards, but it leaves me baffled. The Durgan family are well known in the community as foster parents. I can't see how a kid they've adopted could be related to a young girl that was held captive here for years when no one's been reported missing. Eddie and Isla also look surprised by the news.

'Kim hasn't got any living relatives, to my knowledge, boss,' Isla says. 'My family knows hers pretty well. She was eight when the Durgans adopted her. Fifteen now, I think. She's sweet, but incredibly shy.'

'I'll talk to her parents now.'

My junior officers get back to work with new energy, last night's exhaustion dropping away. They're both placing calls to recruit searchers. I'd like to help, but Kim Durgan may have vital information, and I can't question her without informing the parents first, because she's a minor.

Layla Durgan sounds nonplussed when I call to ask her to meet me at the school counsellor's office, to discuss Kim's situation, urgently. There's a shocked silence on the line when I explain why, but she agrees to the meeting, insisting that her husband will be present too.

Lawrie Deane is rounding the corner as I leave. He looks burdened by his visit to Madron, keeping his head down. He's clutching the shopping bag he always brings to work, no doubt full of cakes. Deane may not be the quickest officer alive, but his predictability is comforting. He'll be a steadying influence on Eddie and Isla while they organise the island-wide search.

Five Islands Academy lies ten minutes west of Hugh Town on foot, close to Old Town Bay. My own time at the school was mixed. I'm used to being conspicuous these days, always the biggest man in the room. It often works to my advantage now, but it was a challenge back then, until I took up rugby and boxing to let off steam. I developed a passion for books, thanks to a great English teacher, but got detentions in other lessons for constant daydreaming. The place looks freshly whitewashed, but it smells just the same – of floor polish, angst and overcooked food.

Shadow appears as I head inside. I've had permission to bring him onto the premises since I gave a talk here about the police's canine search-and-rescue unit. It gave the pupils time to question me about my job too. Shadow stole the show, as usual, weaving through the packed hall, collecting strokes from every kid in the building.

The counsellor's office lay in the same place during my time here, at the end of a quiet corridor. I got sent here twice, to see a strict-looking man who sat behind his desk, firing out questions about my father's death. My teachers hoped that talking about it would improve my concentration in class, but it had the opposite effect. I sat there in silence both times, wishing the ground would swallow me up.

Denise Laramie gives me a warm welcome, then gazes up at me through gold-framed glasses. She's a pretty woman with auburn hair caught in a ponytail, a down-to-earth manner and a genuine smile. If she's surprised to see Shadow, it doesn't show. I can tell how gentle she is from the way she pets him, and my dog settles at her feet when we sit down, gazing at her adoringly. I know little about her, except that she lives alone and is popular in the community. She'd just left Five Islands when my time here started. The walls of her counselling room are a tranquil green, with a few pot plants and easy chairs grouped in the corner. The ugly formality it held twenty-five years ago has gone, thank God. Denise only looks concerned when I share my new information.

'We've had a DNA result linking a pupil here to the murder victim. The test shows that the teenage girl on St Helen's was Kim Durgan's cousin.'

Her mouth drops open. 'I thought she'd lost all her biological relatives. Kim hates talking about her birth family. It's a huge trigger for her anxiety, you see.'

'I've invited her parents here. I think they're in shock too.'

'Let me give you some background,' Denise hurries on. 'The Durgans fostered Kim, then went on to adopt her. She's one of the lucky ones, but it's still a huge trauma. I referred her to the hospital recently to help her panic attacks. Kim's been seeing Nina since the start of term.'

'It's affected her badly?'

'I can't share her personal details, but it's common knowledge she was trafficked into the UK. Her journey from Vietnam was harrowing.' Denise looks uncomfortable. 'Life hasn't been easy for her here either. Five Islands' culture can be hard for vulnerable kids.'

'There's bullying, you mean?'

'The pressure's top down, with everyone working flat out. High performance is expected from pupils and staff here, round the clock, but Kim might feel overloaded. At fifteen she's faced more stress than most adults ever see.'

'So she might be suffering because of the regime here? I don't quite understand what you mean by the pressure coming from the top?'

She hesitates. 'The management team want OFSTED to grade us outstanding: that obsession affects everything. Institutional stress is pervasive, you see. It's worse if a child's already afraid.'

'It sounds pressurised. Maybe that's why conspiracy theories are going around?'

'You've heard about that, have you? I thought it was just whispers among the kids, but maybe there's more to it.'

'I've asked to see Lisa Angarrack, in case she knows anything. Steve will be present too during that interview.'

Laramie looks anxious. 'Please don't mention what I said. He's an amazing headteacher, I respect him more than anyone. His targets are challenging, that's all.'

A rap on the door ends our conversation. Layla and Joe Durgan look like old-school hippies, with tattoos, piercings and colourful clothes. Layla's hair is styled in thick dreadlocks, and Joe's ragged curls prove their love of deep-water surfing, even in winter. The couple have been foster parents for twenty years, as well as running a landscape-gardening business together. Their relaxed outlook is well known across the islands, yet there's no sign of it today. Joe is a foot shorter than me, but his hands keep bunching into fists, like he's aching to throw a punch. Words babble from his mouth before he's even sat down.

'This is wrong, Ben. It must be. We put Kim's DNA on Ancestry.com years ago, but no matches came back.'

'Not a single one,' Layla echoes. 'She hasn't mentioned her cousins for years. All three girls were kidnapped in Vietnam, then trafficked here. We think the other two died in transit.'

'I didn't know there were any Vietnamese nationals on the islands.'

'There aren't,' Joe says, shaking his head. 'Kim's our daughter now, with full British citizenship. She's got the same rights as you or me.'

'I still need her story, to find out anything she knows. One of her cousins may still be alive.'

Joe looks less angry, leaving just concern on his face. 'She cried her eyes out every night for months, at the start. Losing her birth family broke her heart. That's why we adopted her; a traumatised kid like her should never end up in care.'

'Sorry, but it's my job to find out why Kim's cousin died here. She was murdered less than six months ago.'

'We can't just drag her out of lessons to tell her something this upsetting. We need to tell her gently tonight at home, before anyone goes digging up the past.' Layla Durgan rises to her feet.

'I'll be guided by you, but I'm sorry, the latest we can wait is tomorrow morning.'

Layla gives a nod of acceptance, then exits the room with Joe trailing in her wake. They're among the most decent people on St Mary's, but I can tell they're defensive, afraid their adopted daughter could get harmed as the truth unfolds. Kim Durgan is lucky to have found adoptive parents who will fight on her behalf; the pair seem a hundred percent united in their cause.

Denise Laramie urges me to conduct tomorrow's meeting at the Durgans' home, where Kim feels safe, and to include Nina, because the girl will need psychological support from a trusted source. Once the subject's dealt with, she makes a call, inviting the head and his daughter to the counselling room.

Steve Angarrack appears in a well-cut suit. He looks more like a football manager than a school leader, confident his team will win every match. He seems different from the quiet man I remember from our shouts on the lifeboat. Steve's ultra-confident work persona strikes me as fake, yet Denise Laramie hangs on his every word. I've encountered men like him before, leading gangs in London, full of bravado. They mask all their fears and cultivate reputations as tough guys, with members afraid to question their decisions.

Lisa Angarrack seems much gentler. The head's daughter is wearing a pristine uniform, her dark hair tucked neatly behind her ears. Shadow is keeping his distance, waiting for his chance to approach, even though he normally loves young people. Lisa's glance flicks rapidly between Denise's face and mine, but Steve speaks first.

'I'm here to support Lisa and answer any questions. We're both keen to help.' His speech is forceful, like he's setting the agenda, not me.

'Thanks, Steve. I appreciate you making time for this.'

'Will it take long?' Lisa's tone is anxious. 'My teacher's not thrilled about me missing a chemistry test.'

'I'll be quick, don't worry. I just need to ask you about the grave we found on St Helen's.'

'Sorry, but I've only been there once, on a field trip, to see the birds.' Her answer sounds rehearsed.

'I got an email suggesting you might know something about the girl that died. It was anonymous. Can you think who sent it?'

'No one comes to mind.'

'You're not being accused of anything, Lisa. I just need to check every angle.' I push a little harder: 'Have you ever sailed out to St Helen's since, with a friend?'

'Like I said, just once, on a supervised trip.'

'Sinead Harcourt seemed upset about the murder victim and the abandoned baby. Wasn't she a friend of yours?'

'Ages ago.' The girl's shoulders rise in a tight line. Shadow seizes his moment to approach, placing his muzzle on her knee. Lisa remains silent while she strokes his fur, her hand settling on his back. 'Me and Sinead drifted apart, that's all. I'm concentrating on getting top grades, so I can't socialise much.'

'That sounds like a lot of pressure.'

Angarrack holds up his hands like he's stopping traffic. 'Five Islanders enjoy a challenge. We're all high achievers here, aren't we, Lisa?'

The girl blinks rapidly. 'I just want to achieve my full potential.'

It sounds like she's spouting her father's mantra, not her own. The quaver in her voice makes me believe she'd answer differently without her dad breathing down her neck.

'Thanks, Lisa, that's all for today. If you think of anything else, call me, please.'

When I pass her my card she leans down to stroke Shadow again, smiling properly for the first time. I can't help feeling sorry for her. I bet she has to work hard, every day, to meet her parents' standards.

Denise Laramie looks on edge when the room empties. Our conversation switches back to Kim Durgan's life since arriving in the UK, and losing contact with her biological family.

'You think her cousins were on that boat too, don't you? But why would someone take just two girls, and leave the third to drown?' Denise says.

'I'm hoping Kim can tell me.'

'Please don't upset her. She trusts Nina, so she could lead the questions.' Her smile wavers. 'If Kim pulls up the drawbridge, we've lost the battle.'

'Nina will support her, don't worry. But can you tell me more about the culture here, before I go? I need to understand why conspiracy theories are flying around, but none of the kids have come forward with information.'

She hesitates. 'I hate seeing them too frightened to say what's wrong. No child should experience trauma alone. Lots of them seem gripped by the idea that evil exists at the highest level in Scilly. One child told me it's about smugglers exchanging huge amounts of money.'

'For goods or services?'

'They claim it's to do with child trafficking.'

Panic rises in my chest. What if they're right? I can't prove anything without evidence, but stories like Kim Durgan's must be adding fuel to the fire.

'Children have vivid imaginations, and the strict regime here probably doesn't help,' Laramie says. 'Hearing about that girl being murdered on St Helen's has sent their panic spiralling. They need answers, soon, to help them move on.'

I can hear the conviction in her voice, and her desire to defend every pupil. If my counsellor had been the same, I might have trusted him enough to offload the nightmares that dogged me for years. It interests me that Denise made Steve Angarrack and the other senior managers sound so obsessed by their goal of success that the pupils might be damaged by it. He used to be a laidback geography teacher, but now he appears to be striving for perfection, and his daughter is paying the price. Teenage life is complex enough, without sky-high parental expectations. His wife has a strong personality too, with her own set of demands.

Shadow seems reluctant to leave when I say goodbye.

'He'd make a great therapy dog,' Denise says.

'Don't tempt him. He'd switch career right now for a few biscuits, but be warned – he's ninety-nine percent wolf.'

Shadow growls as I lead him away, telling me he'd rather spend his days doing a cushy indoor job than roaming the islands with me. My frustration's building too. I've learned plenty about childhood vulnerability and the headteacher's passion for success, but little more about the victim on St Helen's, or the abandoned baby.

27

It's midday when Mai hears a vehicle arrive, with tyres spinning on gravel. She shoves the table back into place and waits by the door. She's got blisters on her fingers from trying to loosen the window, so she buries her hands in the pockets of her thin dress when the door opens at last. The man stands on the threshold. He's dressed in his black coat, a woollen cap pulled low over his forehead, his gaze intense.

'You don't look well, Mai. I've brought you some fruit.'

He places a shopping bag on the table and a bottle of water. Mai knows she should run into his arms, make him believe she's grateful, but her feet remain glued to the floor. She wants to attack him, but her sharpened nail is concealed under her pillow, too far out of reach.

'I got you something else.' He produces a small radio, with a lead to plug into the wall. 'Music will cheer you up. It's the one thing that gives my life balance.'

'Thank you.' Mai hugs the box to her chest. 'Let me come with you, outside, please.'

'Not today, but at least you're grateful, for once.' His face turns serious. 'I fell for you the moment our eyes met on that boat. Your age didn't matter. It was two souls connecting. I know you felt it too. Tuyet got in our way. I should have thrown her back.'

She remains silent, biding her time.

'I love you more than anything, Mai. We'll be a couple forever. Do you understand?'

'We can look after Lao, like husband and wife.'

'No, it's just us now.' The man looks away. 'I can't bring him back.'

'Don't say that, please...'

Mai feels her strength fading. The man seizes Lao's basket, and even though she tries to grab it, she can't stop him. Fury fills her mind as he marches out. He's taken the one thing that still connects her to Lao. Mai drags in a long breath, and her need to escape bubbles to the surface again. It's her only way of finding the truth. If the man has murdered Lao, he won't go unpunished. If she ever gets free, she will return to kill him: a life for a life.

28

Eddie is alone at the station when I get back. Lawrie and Isla are out, rallying search teams for more house searches on St Mary's.

'Let's check the evidence again,' I say. 'Then you can update the incident log.'

'The chief wants it done fast,' Eddie says. 'He still sounds groggy on the phone, but he's insisting on coming back tomorrow.' Eddie rolls his eyes. Madron's refusal to follow medical advice is only to be expected. The DCI has ruled this place with a rod of iron, yet his absence hasn't slowed us down. I don't want him here unless he's fully recovered, but it's not my decision.

'Forget about him for now. That DNA result changes everything,' I say. 'We know Kim was trafficked into the country six years ago, and the school kids know about it. They've started a rumour that's still going on, and it's spun out of control. Kim is the only islander with Vietnamese heritage. We know one of her cousins died here, after being held captive somewhere. We can't know exactly what happened to the third girl, but maybe they were together, and she's been locked up all this time.'

'Why do you think that?'

'I can't be certain, but we see rare cases like it in the news. A torturer kidnaps girls, and some of them end up pregnant. Sometimes they have accomplices, or a whole network. Maybe sex is the biggest driver.'

'You seriously think some pervert could abduct two girls without raising any suspicions and enlist mates to help? You can't sneeze without someone knowing round here.'

'I know, and the whole conspiracy thing could just be Chinese whispers, but we have to take it seriously. Some of the islands' youngsters might know a man here's been trafficking kids, but kept two girls just for himself, then one fell pregnant. Maybe they're too terrified to speak.'

'Jesus, that's a sick idea.'

'It happens, Eddie, in places just like this. Dennis Nilsen must have seemed like Mr Average when he murdered his victims; he'd been in the army and spent time working in a job centre. Our abductor probably acts just like the rest of us. The only sure fact is that they're living among us, undetected. He could be a middle-aged loner, but some are married with kids, using their family as a smokescreen.'

'So it could be pretty much any able-bodied bloke, with access to a boat, mould in his basement and red carpet on the floor?'

'Checking every house should expose him.'

Eddie looks concerned. 'Scilly's full of old stone houses. Most of them probably have mould problems in winter. We get it round our bathroom window every year.'

'Let's focus on people who're acting suspiciously first.'

'Fordie's still hiding from us. Apparently he was seen taking mates out on his mum's boat a lot last summer, for picnics and to swim on the off-islands.' He meets my gaze. 'I don't get it. He's such a great character, larger than life, always making everyone laugh, but he's got a conscience too. How many lads sign up for the lifeboat that young?'

'Hardly any, and we've both been on shouts with him. He must have a good reason to hide. We need to interview him urgently. If he knows the killer's identity he may be scared of reprisals. He's friends with Sinead Harcourt too, our biggest collector of jade charms.'

'Isla put an announcement on local radio, asking people to call us, if they know of any property with red carpet. It'll be from an older person's home, won't it?'

'What makes you say that?'

'Loads of people prefer hard flooring these days. The DCI told me he took up a load of carpet a few years back, to replace it with laminate.'

I nod in reply; half the islanders will have done the same. When

I moved into my parents' cottage I ripped up acres of worn-out carpet, then sanded the floorboards. The only things covering them now are some handwoven rugs Nina brought from her flat in Bristol. I flick through the investigation's timeline on my laptop.

'What about men living near St Helen's, with access to a boat?'

'You've interviewed Mark Lanner on St Martin's. His place is closest, and he's got a big speedboat.'

I remember the odd atmosphere at the composer's home and his love of watching the sea. Sinead Harcourt described him as a spy. 'Lanner was a bit too keen to help,' I say. 'He even offered to keep watch over St Helen's for us. I was surprised to hear he's got a girlfriend. He seems like the solitary type to me.'

Eddie looks surprised too. 'I've never seen him with a woman.'

'She plays cello with the Berlin Philharmonic, apparently. Do a background check on him today, please.'

He taps a note into our case file. 'I can't believe Lanner would be involved in trafficking kids, though, the bloke's so mild-mannered.'

'It must be someone local, Eddie. They could have taken multiple victims over the years, for all we know. The killer must have a short fuse, to throw that girl against a wall.'

'Whoever did it's a fucking monster.'

'Anger won't help us.' I peer out of the window. 'We've blocked the press till now, but the longer this lasts, the harder they'll push. They'll send drones over for pictures if they sense a big story.'

Eddie studies me again. 'What else should we be looking for?'

'Changes in behaviour. Whoever put amulets in the girl's shroud seems to regret their crime. We'll see the signs if we keep our eyes open.' I glance at messages scrolling across my phone. 'Do you know any details about how Kim Durgan was trafficked into the UK?'

'I looked up the press report, just now. It happened when I was at uni. A boat was found adrift on Deadman's Pool, six years ago.'

'They were picked up here?'

He nods. 'There were no adults onboard, just ten kids, mainly girls, captured from different countries. Kim stayed with the Durgans that first night. Apparently, she was mute for the first six months. They tried to find her birth family in Vietnam, without any matches.'

Eddie's already tapping away on his computer, but the traffickers from six years ago could be in any country by now. Thousands of kids are brought into the UK illegally every year, via perilous journeys from countries like Albania, Romania and Vietnam. They're abducted, then sold for domestic slavery, drug running and sex work. The islands seem too quiet for such an ugly trade, but that could be their biggest draw for the traffickers.

'Kim may not remember anything,' Eddie mutters. 'I'd want to forget that journey, wouldn't you?'

'Lawrie will know the details if the police were involved.'

I set off alone to visit Thomas Ford's mother. I'm praying he hasn't been dragged into working for the traffickers, paying him to make boat trips, or run errands. The girl he picked up from St Helen's could be wrapped up in it as well. I try to leave Shadow in Eddie's care, but his skill as an escape artist is unbeatable. He squeezes out of the door behind me, determined not to be overlooked. Lawrie and Isla have taken the van, leaving me to use the police motorbike, and Shadow isn't impressed. He howls the minute I put on the helmet. The noise follows me down the road, high and keening, like a wolf protecting his territory. I never enjoy leaving him behind, but it can't be helped.

29

I head for Five Islands Academy to see the catering manager, who also happens to be Thomas Ford's mother. I've grown more cautious in my driving since Noah's arrival, following the lanes that thread across St Mary's at a steady pace, while dusk thickens. We've only had a few accidents here in recent years, but it pays to go slow. Occasionally, cars hurtle round blind corners like they're competing on the Isle of Mann. The island's quiet this afternoon, and so is the school. Kids are still trapped in their classrooms. I see them through the windows with heads bowed low over their tables. They look far more industrious than me at their age, but a few are glancing at the wall clocks, longing for the bell.

The fire exit is open when I reach the kitchen, where condensation streams down the windows. Annie Ford is hunched over a steel table, dicing carrots at terrifying speed. She's younger than me, a big woman, dressed in an apron that's so food-stained it will never again be sparkling white. Her cap must be intended to stop hair contaminating the food, but most of her short blonde curls have escaped. She was a skinny little girl when I escaped to London. By the time I returned she was a single mum, working as a kitchen hand to make ends meet. Annie is a larger-than-life character now, always the first to sing at karaoke nights in The Atlantic pub. I've heard her belt out 'It's Raining Men' and 'I Will Survive' at top volume. She pretends to be tough, but her son, Fordie, is her world. I saw her shed a few tears of pride the night he was formally welcomed into the lifeboat crew. Annie normally greets me with a smile, but today her expression's wary.

'If you want Fordie, you're in the wrong place. He takes care of himself these days.'

'Put the knife down, please, Annie. Killing me would get you twenty years.'

'I'm too busy to chat.' She lowers the blade slowly. 'What do you want, exactly?'

'Food, please, if you've got some. I've hardly eaten today.'

Her anger dissolves in an instant. She whirls around her kitchen, light on her feet for a woman carrying at least fifteen stone. Annie soon produces a bowl of soup, plus half a cottage loaf and a family-sized wedge of cheese.

'You're a lifesaver.' I glance around at boxes stacked with fruit and vegetables. 'This is way better than my school meals. It was mostly pizza and chips.'

'They're not getting any ultra-processed crap on my watch.' She settles on the stool opposite, her gaze razor-sharp. 'You didn't come here for dinner, Ben. If it's police business, spit it out. I haven't got all day.'

'Fordie was meant to call by for a chat at the station. He never turned up, and he's skipped work too.'

'He'll have his reasons. My lad never lets people down.'

'That's why I'm concerned. You know he's been using your boat to sail over to St Helen's, don't you?'

'Only in summer. He wouldn't hang out with mates there in the cold.'

'He was seen there at dawn last Wednesday, with a passenger. He picked up another girl, who may have camped on St Helen's overnight. I need their names.'

'How would I know? He's a good kid, everyone trusts him.' She lets out a heavy sigh. 'I've got no reason to worry.'

'Yet you do, Annie. I can see it. Why?'

She frowns at me. 'He makes me proud most days, filling shelves at the Co-op to save cash for uni next year. Most other kids would run up debts and to hell with it.' She drains her mug, then slams it down. 'It's a miracle he's turned out so well. Being a single mum wasn't easy; boys need strong male role models. Best you stay married to that beauty of yours.'

'That's my plan. Do you know many of Fordie's friends?'

'He's mates with everyone, you know that. But he's known Sinead Harcourt longest. They've always been close.'

'He's staying here till she finishes school so they can go to uni together – is that it?'

'Ask him yourself.' She hauls herself upright. 'Now let me work, Ben. The kids will need feeding tomorrow.'

'Thanks for the soup. It's the best I've had in years.'

She gives a grudging smile. 'My grandma's recipe.'

I try one last time. 'I think Fordie knows what happened on St Helen's, that's why he's hiding somewhere. He may even know why a girl gave birth here in secret, with no help from anyone.'

'So you came straight to me. You think I'm the expert on that subject, like everyone else?' she mutters, her voice bitter. 'No one lets me forget it.'

'You've lost me, Annie.'

She narrows her eyes. 'My boyfriend ditched me when I fell pregnant as a girl. He didn't care whether I kept the baby, so I panicked and tried to disguise it. I was fifteen and home was a nightmare.'

Steve Angarrack's words return to me, about a teenage pupil having a concealed pregnancy, years ago. 'That can't have been easy.'

'I didn't accept it myself, till Fordie arrived. I'm lucky Steve gave me work here. I owe him a lot.'

'You were brave, keeping your baby.'

She lifts her chin, eyes shining. 'Fordie knows I don't regret it. If you go bullying him, you'll have me on your back.'

'I won't,' I say, rising to my feet. 'Where do you keep your boat, Annie?'

'Waterman's Cove.'

The bay lies on St Mary's northeastern coast, with few houses close by, due to flood risk. Fordie and his passenger could easily have sailed away early in the morning, unseen.

'Contact me, please, when Fordie gets home.'

She shakes her head. 'I won't go ratting on my own son. Try the old youth club. He sometimes hangs out there with mates, but don't tell him I sent you.'

Annie is already back at work, chopping at frantic speed. It's a wonder her fingers are still attached to her hands. Maybe the pressure coming down from the school's management is affecting her too. I had no idea that Fordie came from a concealed pregnancy, but that doesn't prove much, except that he may be harbouring low self-esteem behind his ready smile. A killer could groom a boy like him, without a father's protection, from a young age. He may even have been paid to dig that grave in the rocky soil.

I ride straight to the old youth centre on Quay Road in Hugh Town, just five minutes away. The youth club has moved to Carn Gwaval, because the old site is too dilapidated to use. The two-storey building looks desolate now the winter dark has arrived. It has boarded-up windows, but still holds memories for me. I used to come here with mates after school, to play table tennis and ogle girls, but it's been neglected for years. Paint is flaking from the exterior walls. The only sign that anyone's entered recently is a loose plank nailed over one of the openings. I walk down the side access without making a sound. Fordie must have seen me arrive, though. I catch him scrambling out of a window, ready to sprint down to the beach below, until I grab his arm.

'Stop running, for God's sake. You promised me a chat, remember?'

'I can't talk about it.' He looks furious as he tries to wrench his arm free.

The lad mutters a stream of curses when I drag him inside. The place is freezing and pitch-dark, apart from streetlight filtering through the only open window. The youth club used to run music nights and talent shows, years ago. There's nothing here now except rat droppings in the corners. The only impressive thing is the graffiti on the walls. It pictures a nightmare version of the islands, complete with phantoms, thunder clouds, and red-mouthed vampires. I spot an old mattress in the corner. Fordie must be in deep trouble to hide somewhere this squalid, when the rest of his life has been about success and acceptance, until now.

He looks haunted when fresh shadows flicker across his face, still more boy than man.

'Tell me about St Helen's, Fordie. A girl's dead, remember?'

'That's not my fault.'

'Talk to me then. What's the real reason why you've been sailing there?'

'Kids pay me to ferry them over, that's all.'

'Not in winter they don't. You're running errands for smugglers, aren't you? Maybe you've even been digging graves.'

He stares back at me. 'If that was true, why would I be doing a shitty job at the Co-op? I'd have money to burn. But I've got a conscience, believe it or not.'

'I know you, remember? You don't have to prove it. But you collected a girl from St Helen's early on Sunday. Why?'

'A friend wanted to stay the night there, alone.'

'Tell me her name.'

He swallows a deep breath. 'Sinead Harcourt. She's convinced the network's using the island as a base.'

'The network being who, exactly?'

'You must have heard the rumours about the power holders. Children are being trafficked; the islands are a stop-off point for the smugglers.'

'Who told you this?'

'Every young person knows about it. Have you ever stopped to ask yourself why your boss, DCI Madron, takes his boat out every night?'

'He wants to stop drug smuggling, that's all.'

Fordie gives a slow laugh, like I've told a lame joke. 'It's not just him. Phillip Warleggan and others are involved too. Sinead wanted to catch them in the act. Take photos. But she wouldn't let me stay there with her.'

'And the other girl?'

'My ex-girlfriend. We were getting on fine till they separated us.' Misery shows on the boy's face. 'Her parents forced her to end it.'

'Tell me her name, Fordie.'

He chokes out the words. 'Lisa Angarrack.'

'The headmaster's daughter?'

'The three of us have been mates since nursery school,' he says, nodding. 'Lisa's taking a big risk, sneaking out to see me and Sinead. Her mum and dad don't approve. They say we're not high-fliers.'

'That's ridiculous. You're a role model for kids here: joining the lifeboat crew, and doing sport to a high level, making a life for yourself.'

'Her parents want her to go to Oxford and become a doctor, with a big flashy house.' I recognise the anger straining his voice, even though he's normally so good-natured. I felt the same teenage fury at his age, with little respect for adults' decisions.

'Why did Lisa want to go to St Helen's?'

'She's worried about Sinead. Her mental health's been shaky since her mum died. She was mad to risk chasing down the network on her own.'

'Did Sinead get photos of these people?'

'She wouldn't show us. She said that would put us in danger too.' Fordie stares down at his hands.

'I thought Lisa and Sinead didn't see each other anymore.'

'No one can separate us three.' He forces a smile. 'The minute I told them I was going to Leeds uni, they decided to apply there too. We'll always be mates, whatever happens.'

I'm beginning to understand the boy's situation. His two closest friends are suffering, for different reasons. He made that boat trip to help them. No wonder he's angry about being forced apart.

'Lisa will be in trouble if you tell her parents any of this.' There's sadness in his voice, as well as blame. 'Please don't. She's terrified of her dad.'

'Why?'

'He hides behind all that Mr Nice Guy bullshit. You should arrest him for mental cruelty.'

The flickering light is playing odd tricks with Fordie's face. He appears to have aged twenty years, his eyes set in deep hollows. I'm certain now that he's played no direct part in the murder, yet he still looks haunted by an idea neither of us fully understands.

My phone is pulsing with messages when I get outside. One is from Eddie, telling me that the Coastguard Agency's data storage is finally back online and they've sent photos of boats sighted near St Helen's, from recent night-time patrols. Eddie's forwarded some to me. The latest ones show lobstermen's skiffs collecting their creels before dawn. Most of the boats' names are familiar. I often follow the fishing fleet as they head back to harbour when I'm sailing to work.

The next picture pulls me up short. It shows Phillip Warleggan's lapstrake fishing boat, moored near the Pest House. I recognise it instantly because I helped Ray to build it, the summer before I left the island, twenty years ago. The picture was taken last Friday, just days before I discovered the body. I can't see anyone on board, but my thoughts are spinning. Phillip was at the meeting when I asked people who'd been to St Helen's recently to come forwards, yet he never said a word.

What if the email I received, telling me that Lisa Angarrack knows about the girl on St Helen's, was meant to throw me off course? Phillip Warleggan has placed himself in the public eye. That's wise for a man with secrets. It's easier to carry out offences in plain sight if you've built a reputation for public kindness. Who would ever doubt a former bank manager, renowned for his community work?

30

Mai is listening to English voices on the radio, trying to follow the conversation, when her strength deserts her suddenly. She's dizzy, her vision blurred. It takes effort to crawl into bed. The cold feels bitter, even with her duvet wrapped tight around her shoulders, her teeth chattering. What if she dies without seeing Lao again? She tries to sit up, remain strong for him, but soon collapses back onto the mattress.

She drifts between sleep and wakefulness. Her dreams feel more real than the nightmare of captivity. Mai pictures herself running down to the river with Tuyet. Women from their village are fishing there, casting their nets from the bank, but their mother is braver than the rest. She stands waist deep, facing the torrent, as water rushes past, smooth as quicksilver. Tuyet asks how many fish their mother will catch today.

'Four,' Mai says. 'One for each of us.'

Their mother throws her net again, and this time her skill pays off. She throws a fish into the basket. Mai watches it writhe, its sides flecked with gold. Then she smashes a stone on the fish's head, hard enough to kill it, while Tuyet hides her face. It's her duty to end their suffering because she's the oldest child.

Now the dream changes. The man is lying at her feet; his gaze is terrified when she lifts the stone and lets it fall. It's his turn to squirm in the mud, powerless, like the dying fish.

Mai wants to stay in her dream, free of the man at last, but a sound rouses her from sleep. It's a tapping noise, like rain falling on the tin roof of her parents' cabin. When her eyes open, a girl is gazing down at her through the window. Is she real or imaginary? Her face is beautiful but ghostly, framed by long dark hair. When Mai opens her eyes again the vision has gone, leaving only brambles pressing against the glass. Sleep claims her once more as the fever takes hold.

31

It's 6.00 pm when I leave the motorbike at the station and jog to Pilot's Retreat. Warleggan has chosen the ideal property to keep watch over the town. He can see people toiling up the lane, and fishermen emptying crates on the quayside, from his back patio. It's my duty to interview islanders who appear to be acting suspiciously, but I don't relish the idea of interrogating a man I've always respected. Warleggan's gravitas has seemed unquestionable until now, his quiet certainty that his moral code is always correct.

I'm heading up his pathway when the front door flies open, and Lisa Angarrack rushes out. Her face is stark white, and it's clear she's been crying. Warleggan's home seems an odd refuge for a distressed teenager. She barges past me before I can stop her. Phillip appears in the doorway a moment later, looking shaken.

'This is bad timing, I'm afraid, Ben. Can it wait until tomorrow?'

I stand my ground. 'Sorry, we need to talk. It's urgent.'

'Forgive me.' His politeness is slowly returning. 'Come in, please. It's freezing out here.'

Phillip leads me to his kitchen, leaving the rest of his house in darkness. His appearance is scruffy for once, his grey hair in need of a comb. The sink is full of dirty crockery, and laundry is heaped on a chair, waiting to be folded. There's discomfort in his body language too. Men like him hate being caught unprepared, with no time to hide their clutter, but I'm in no rush. Quiet works wonders when someone's on edge. Most people will crack under the pressure of absolute silence, but a minute passes before he opens up.

'Lisa came here for advice,' he says. 'Your interview today upset her. She thought you were linking her to that girl's death, on St Helen's.'

'That wasn't my intention. Are you close to the Angarracks, Phillip?'

'They're good friends. I've known Lisa all her life.'

'Why was she crying just now?'

'The girl feels trapped.' He folds his arms across his chest. 'She wants more freedom, but I can't intervene. Lisa's furious with me for not taking a stand for her.'

'It sounds like a tough situation.'

'Lisa will soon be able to make her own decisions, even if it means disobeying her parents.' Warleggan still looks upset, but I remember Sinead Harcourt claiming he was part of a network, running the islands for their own gain. It still seems far-fetched, but there could be some truth in it. Lisa might actually have come here to challenge him about something.

'Look, I'll cut to the chase, Phillip. Your boat was seen moored on St Helen's, late last Saturday night.'

His mouth flaps open. 'That's impossible. I haven't taken her out for weeks.'

'The Coastguard Agency sent a photo, with the time and date.' I show him it on my phone. 'No one was on board, and the island appeared empty too. Can you explain it for me?'

'I wasn't there. Someone must have taken it. Why on earth would I sail to a deserted island on a bitter night?'

'You tell me.'

The man's persona appears to change in the blink of an eye, from polite to defensive. I watch Warleggan scrutinise the picture, from the boat's make and model, to its name stencilled on the prow: *Winter Dream*. When he hands my phone back, his voice is strident.

'How can I prove my innocence when I live alone? No one can account for my movements.'

'That's convenient.' I keep my voice calm. 'I just need the truth, please, then I'll leave you in peace.'

'Anyone could have taken it. You don't need a key for the engine, it's push-button ignition.'

'You think another islander towed your boat down to the water, then sailed it to St Helen's, without asking permission?'

'I can only tell you the truth. I was here all evening.' His calm is slowly returning, but he still looks aggrieved. 'Maybe someone didn't want their own boat to be spotted. I'm sad you doubt my word, Ben. I've spent my life supporting this community. Doesn't my public standing mean anything to you?'

'Of course, but this is a murder case, Phillip. I have to explore the evidence, even if it's uncomfortable.' I glance around the room. 'Would you mind me taking a look around, while I'm here?'

'Lawrie Deane already did a search. Do you really have to rummage through my belongings all over again?'

Warleggan's tone is sour, but neighbourly relations matter less than finding the killer. He grumbles, then finally concedes.

I take my time over the search, and discover a patch of mould on the ceiling in one of his back bedrooms. There's no other sign that he could have kept the abducted girls hidden here. I look everywhere, but there's no red carpet either. The only possible link to the crime scene is the unexplained presence of his boat on St Helen's.

I peer through the back window of his dining room at his overgrown garden and the old smuggler's cottage he plans to renovate. He's tackled the weeds nearest the house, but the rest have run wild. I head outside, with drizzle spitting in my face. The old cottage appears empty when I peer through the windows. All I can see is the low-beamed ceiling and bare floorboards. It's a reminder of how humble lives were on the islands two centuries ago. The fireplace in the corner would have been the only means of heating the building. It's more likely that the baby's mother is hidden in a bunker, with a secret entrance. The tangled weeds could easily conceal one, and my actions may have damaged the girl's chances. If Warleggan's the killer, he may panic and kill her, as his escape routes shut down.

'Want to see inside?' The old man is standing so close I can feel outrage emanating from him in waves. 'Let me unlock it for you.'

'There's no need. I can tell it's empty from here.'

'Finish your search, please, then let this be an end to it.' He snaps out the words.

The overhead light fizzes when he unlocks the door, like the wiring's unstable. I can't see anything incriminating, but the place will need serious investment to preserve its structure. It's a single large room, with wattle-and-daub walls turning to dust and a fireplace blackened by centuries of use. I tap my heel on the floor and listen to the echo. Smugglers hid in half a dozen cottages on St Mary's, whenever customs-and-excise officers arrived from the mainland. Some of the cellars are too shallow to stand upright, but a few are deep enough to hide cargo, after shipwrecks.

'Where's the entrance to the cellar, Phillip? This is a false floor, isn't it?'

'It must be in the garden somewhere.'

'You've never found it?'

'Historic England told me not to go looking without their permission. The place may fall apart before I can preserve it, at this rate.'

Warleggan is playing the part of an abused citizen to the hilt. I run my fingertips over the floor and find a concealed trap door. I try to prise it open, but it was probably sealed a century ago, the grooves thick with dust. If he's been accessing the space below, it must be by another entrance.

It's pitch-dark when I leave the building. There's no point in searching for an entrance until daylight, so I inform Warleggan that another officer will return tomorrow to complete the search. I ask if he owns any more properties on the island, but his answer is a flat no. The man's politeness has vanished like Scotch mist. He looks even more annoyed when I ask for Lisa Angarrack's phone number. He gives it to me with a show of reluctance then says a curt goodbye.

My head's still packed with suspicions when I emerge onto the street. I'd like to know the true reason why Lisa fled from Warleggan's home in distress, but she doesn't pick up when I ring her number. My next call is to Eddie, to tell him about Warleggan's boat being sighted on St Helen's and his denial about sailing there. I hear disbelief in his voice, but I've seen a different side to the former bank manager tonight, colder and full of resentment.

When I look up again, at the quiet cul-de-sac lined with bungalows, my boss's home lies in darkness. It will be an irony if the killer turns out to live so near the chief of police.

I'm past worrying about his health, or where he's spending time, so it's a surprise to spot DCI Madron walking towards me when I reach the quay. There's confusion on his face when our eyes meet, yet his tone is as critical as ever.

'The station's empty. Why are none of you working?'

'Because it's late, sir. Our search will begin again tomorrow, at first light.'

'We can't let that monster get away with it. Do you hear?' His words are slurred, and he's unsteady on his feet. The man's pig-headedness about accepting medical care doesn't make sense. I can't drag him to the hospital, kicking and screaming, but I can limit the damage he might cause.

'If you won't accept medical help I'll have to tell headquarters, sir. It's obvious that head injury's affecting you.'

'Are you threatening me?' He sounds incredulous.

'I'm protecting the case and your best interests. You're in no state to work. I'll call HR tomorrow.'

'I'll report you for insubordination. They'll take my word over yours any day.'

'Go ahead. That's your choice, sir.'

Madron turns his back on me. He cuts a lonely figure as he stumbles down the path. The man no longer seems like a sergeant major, marching on parade. He looks battle-weary, as if the first strong wind could blow him away.

32

I feel tempted to stay on St Mary's, but darkness has ended our search. My hands are tied until daybreak. Frustration gnaws at me, as does my hard conversation with Madron, but at least we've made progress. Volunteer stewards have covered dozens of houses, searching for signs of girls being held captive and the red carpet Gannick's identified. Volunteers have begun searching the off-islands too. If the girl's still being held underground, we'll have more luck tomorrow. Now it's just a process of making sure no property is overlooked.

I reach Tregarthen's at 7.00 pm, with Shadow prowling at my feet. The receptionist looks unnerved when she hears that I plan to visit Gannick. I bet she's witnessed the forensics chief's temper firsthand; Liz will harangue anyone in her path if she's in a bad mood. When I tap on her door, she looks unimpressed.

'Go away, Ben,' she says. 'I'm not stopping for dinner; there's too much to do. If you really think another victim's being held prisoner, you should keep working too.'

'The killer must have found a perfect hiding place. I'll need daylight to find it, and we both need a break. You're coming home with me.'

'I'm your senior, remember? You can't force me to do anything.' Shadow approaches to lick her hand, but the air's fizzing with tension. 'Clear off and take your bloody dog with you.'

'Get your coat, Liz. I'm not leaving without you.'

Shadow finally nudges Gannick through the door, onto the dark street outside. She's still fuming, even though the stars are glittering above us, too beautiful to ignore. I ignore her protests as she trails after me along the quay.

I keep my gaze on the sea as we sail home. This is the time of night when smugglers' boats appear, then vanish again before dawn. The sea's immensity offers a perfect place to hide, with moonlight turning the water silver. Tresco's outline soon fills the horizon, with white pinpricks along its shoreline, like a chain of fairy lights.

Two fishing boats are churning out wash as they head for the Atlantic Strait, five miles to our west. My job felt like a battle today, but it's still preferable to being a trawlerman, like my father. I've seen the ocean in its worst moods since joining the lifeboat crew. Sailing into the teeth of a storm requires courage, yet hundreds on the islands risk it all year round. Most fishermen in Scilly do it out of necessity, to put food on the table, in a place where money is hard to earn.

We reach Bryher after a bumpy twenty-minute voyage. Gannick shows no interest when I pause outside Ray's boatyard. Hammer blows sound through the doors, proving he's still at work.

'My uncle's a master boatbuilder. He's a workaholic, like you.'

'That's not who I am.' Gannick spits out the words. 'I spent three weeks in the Seychelles last year, lazing in a hammock. I loved every minute.'

'Great, you can tell us about it over dinner.'

'I'm going straight back after the meal.'

The woman's brooding silence returns during our half-mile trek from Church Quay to Hell Bay. I take in the changing view as we drop down to the beach. The ocean's reach has turned pure black as the clouds thicken.

Music is blasting from the house when I kick my boots off in the porch, and time appears to have slipped backwards. Nina is playing seventies disco, with 'Boogie Nights' blaring through the windows. That's the beauty of living somewhere so isolated. You can play the Bee Gees' 'How Deep Is Your Love?' at full volume, and no one will question your taste. Noah is gripping Nina's hands while he jigs to the beat in front of the fire. His grin is so wide, he doesn't notice us until the track ends.

Nina swings him up into her arms. She only looks startled for a moment, before smiling at Gannick.

'You must be Liz,' she says. 'I've been wanting to meet you. Ben says you're the UK's top forensics mastermind.'

Gannick's frown lingers. 'He got something right, for once.'

Nina dumps our son in my arms. 'Come on through to the kitchen, Liz. I've just opened some wine, and I could use a hand. You're a decent cook, right?'

'How did you guess?'

'Scientists always are, in my experience. You understand the processes.'

I watch dumbstruck as my wife's charm wins the day, but Noah is whimpering, now the music's over, or maybe he's picked up that my body feels tense as a board, after a day of frustration. I carry him to the battered piano my parents inherited from the pub. He stops crying after a few notes, and playing unwinds me too. His gaze remains glued to my hands when I tap out some ragtime, then an old pop tune, his body swaying to the beat. Music always delights him. It could be thanks to Nina keeping the radio on constantly in the last months of her pregnancy, feeding him harmonies before he was born.

My playing's clumsy tonight, while my brain grapples with the case, but Noah doesn't seem to mind. I listen to the wind overhead and follow its tune until a new sound reaches me. Laughter echoes from the kitchen, loud and infectious. Wonders will never cease. My wife's ability to unlock even the hardest personality has triumphed again. I've rarely seen our forensics chief laugh in five years of acquaintance, yet it took Nina just twenty minutes, even though we've been chasing an ugly murder case all day. I shut the piano lid and spin Noah round to face me.

'Bedtime, pal, and we've got company, so no whinging tonight, okay?'

My son lets me carry him into the bedroom without complaint. He soon drifts into sleep once I've changed him then laid him in his cot. I plant a kiss on his forehead, inhaling his talcum-powder smell, then back out of the room with fingers crossed, leaving the door ajar.

Nina and Gannick have downed most of the wine by the time I reach the kitchen, the air heavy with the smell of browning cheese and oregano. The two women appear to be getting on famously. I'm not that hungry when Nina produces home-made pizza from the oven, after my meal at the school, but it's smothered in olives and anchovies, too good to miss.

'Leave room for pudding,' Nina says. 'My mother made pistachio ice cream last time she came over.'

Gannick looks relaxed, for once, her cheeks flushed with wine. I'm amazed when she speaks about her husband. She's guarded her privacy for years. The man likes exotic holidays, apparently, and finds her temper endearing. His one vice is cats. She lets him keep two Russian blues, as a reward for his tolerance.

Shadow rarely misses out on food, but there's no sign of him, until I check the nursery again. He's lying across the doorway, his muzzle resting on his paws.

'Why are you sulking?' I ask. 'Come and socialise.'

He releases a quiet whine. It sounds like exasperation, and I know he won't budge.

'Please yourself, mate. You're missing great pizza.'

When I get back to the kitchen the conversation has switched to the case. Gannick is passing on the news that the victim on St Helen's is related to Kim Durgan.

Nina looks shocked. 'Kim hasn't spoken about her family yet; losing them is still too raw.'

'DNA proves the victim was definitely her cousin,' I say.

'Kim thinks both her cousins died at sea when they were trafficked here.'

'She's wrong about that. And the second one might still be trapped on the islands. We've been hunting for her all day. I need to hear Kim's story tomorrow, with help from you.'

'She may clam up,' Nina says. 'Trauma can silence people, particularly adolescents.'

I'd like to know more, but it's the wrong time to question her about counselling Kim Durgan. I'm making coffee when a fresh band of rain batters the roof so hard, it sounds like nails are being hammered into the slate tiles overhead.

'Time I went back,' Gannick says. 'We need an early start tomorrow.'

Nina looks amused. 'Sorry, Liz. You're stuck here with us till it's safe to sail.'

'I didn't bring any night things.'

'Don't worry. We've got toothbrushes, a warm guest room, and food for breakfast.' I should have warned Nina not to enter personal territory with Gannick, but she rushes ahead. 'Ben says you suffer from back pain, Liz. Is that right?'

Gannick frowns. 'I keep that to myself, but some people are indiscreet.'

'It's a compliment,' Nina says. 'Ben never mentions anyone unless they interest him. When did it start?'

'Years ago, after a botched operation. I've tried booze, opioids, massage. Nothing works.'

'Who's your chiropractor?'

'I've been there, done that. None of it helps.'

Nina shakes her head. 'It will, believe me. I know the best person for you.'

My wife hurries away to find her phone, and Gannick turns in my direction. 'Nina's lovely, and I've enjoyed myself, but don't try humanising me, please. You'll only be disappointed.'

'You've been great company tonight, Liz.'

'That's just the wine. I'll be a bitch again by tomorrow.'

'Don't, please. I need you on side. Plus, I've always liked you, for some reason. The masochist in me enjoys a good kicking.'

'Happy to oblige.' She puts down her glass. 'What's getting to you about the case? I've never seen you this worried.'

'The second girl's in danger, now we're closing in – if she's even still alive. But there's bugger-all we can do in the middle of the night.'

'His DNA will be all over the hiding place. He won't get away with it.'

'I want her alive.'

'Me too, but this one's a psycho, isn't he? Anyone that blocks him is a target.'

'Including you.'

'I'll go down fighting,' she says, laughing. 'Nothing scares me these days.'

'Even a guy who loves seeing women suffer?'

'I'm a survivor, Ben. Worry about the second girl, not me. I can take care of myself.'

Gannick hurries off to bed. There's a gap between her self-perception as a warrior and her frail physique. And it's the first time she's shown me genuine support, instead of contempt. The outside world is comfortless, though. When I pull back the curtain, breakers are lashing the shore. Seabirds are returning to Bryher in flocks, scattered by the breeze. It feels like we're at the mercy of some savage force that's trying to tear these islands apart.

33

Mai is too weak to move when the man returns. She's lying motionless, with her face to the wall. Candlelight flickers across her face, and for once he's gentle when he checks her temperature. He babbles a few English words, but she doesn't bother to listen. Memories are more powerful. She wants to drift away on them and never return.

'Your fever's worse, Mai. Let's get you warm.'

The man hauls her into his arms then carries her upstairs. She can tell that lifting her has left him exhausted. His breathing is ragged, but she's too weak to escape. He covers her in blankets, then lifts her back into his arms. She can't tell how long the journey takes, but he puts her down in a room that's flooded with light. It's much too dazzling, after months in semi-darkness. He lays her on a sofa that's much softer than her bed. The air is warm, but she's shivering hard, and her teeth chatter.

'I'm sorry,' he mutters. 'It's my fault, for neglecting you.'

Mai is too ill to care about her new environment when he forces tablets into her mouth then holds a water bottle to her lips. It sounds like he's praying, the words whispered under his breath. She tunes out his voice. It's easier to picture her mother waving at her from the riverbank, but summer's floods could soon wash her away.

The man's tone changes to the whine of a frightened child. 'Don't die on me, Mai. I need you.' He's kneeling at her side, crying into his cupped hands.

'Where did you take Lao?'

'Listen to me. We're leaving, soon. I've planned it for years. We'll go to Spain, you and me, then India. We can get married one day.'

'If Lao's gone, let me die.'

The man's head is bowed when a fresh wave of fever surges through her body, plunging her back into darkness.

34

Friday, 12th January

The storm has played itself out when I wake at dawn. Nina is up already, the window revealing acres of grey sky and gulls surfing the breeze. The first thing I do is grab my phone and message Eddie and Isla to set up a public meeting on St Mary's – today at 1.00 pm. In a place this size, the public can be your eyes and ears, provided they know what they're looking for. I can hear Noah burbling to himself while he waits for breakfast. When I go into the kitchen, Gannick is at our table, wearing Nina's spare dressing gown, with my son on her lap, perfectly content. It proves that she's not stone-hearted after all. Her smile vanishes when she spots me, like I've caught her red-handed.

'I can't stand kids as a rule, but yours isn't too bad.'

'High praise, Liz. He seems keen on you too.'

'Let's not get sentimental.' Gannick passes him to me in a hurry. 'The weather's cleared, at least. Lawrie Deane's collecting me at eight.'

'What have you done to him? He always starts at nine.'

'I've scared him into submission,' she says, smirking. 'The poor man quakes in my presence.'

Gannick disappears down the hallway to our bathroom, with a towel draped over her shoulders, like she owns the place.

'Tough cookie, isn't she?' Nina whispers. 'Emma Angarrack was the same when she campaigned to be mayor. I admire people with that much focus.'

'How come you see the good in everyone?'

'By looking for it, I suppose.' She pulls her phone from her pocket. 'Layla Durgan's been texting me about Kim. Apparently, she cried all night. Are you sure this interview's necessary?'

'I need to know what she remembers about being trafficked here. It could explain why one of her cousins died.'

Noah is doing a workout while we speak. He's hanging onto a chair, then hauling himself upright, his cheeks pink with effort. I'd like to stay here and watch him preparing to walk, but it's not an option.

'Kim needs to feel safe,' Nina says. 'It'll be another violation if we say the wrong thing.'

'You can lead the questions. Okay?'

Nina looks more comfortable knowing that she will set the pace, because Kim trusts her already. We discuss the interview while our son continues doing pull-ups, his gait too wobbly to sustain him for long.

'Kim's only been able to describe her experiences since she arrived in the UK, not the past. She's still too traumatised to talk about being taken, or the terrible journey that followed. We shouldn't be rushing her.'

'Her other cousin's life may depend on it, Nina.'

She rises to her feet. 'Get Noah ready, can you? Then I'll ring Maggie. She's taking him again today.'

My wife's slow body language signals her reluctance to put a vulnerable teenager at risk, but I can't worry about that on top of everything else. There's so much to do. Each citizen on the islands must be treated as a potential witness, or suspect, including members of the police. My team's homes will have to be searched today, like the rest of the population, eating into the time left to find the girl alive.

Gannick says a courteous goodbye to Nina, before scowling at me then setting off to meet Deane's boat. I stand in the porch, watching her prowess on her crutches. She swings her bodyweight forwards, while her legs hang in a vertical line, which must take stamina. The woman's fierce nature often irritates me, but I can't fault her tenacity.

My next task feels like a betrayal. I send an email on my phone, informing police headquarters on the mainland that Madron is too ill to perform his duties. I set out his situation, including his refusal to accept medical help. Then I forward Ginny Tremayne's phone number, so they can get a medical opinion. It feels wrong, reporting him unfit for duty, but he's left me no other choice.

I'm still outside when Maggie arrives to pick up Noah. My godmother's grey hair is flying in wild curls in the breeze, and her smile's electric. I know from experience that she's capable of enjoying almost any situation life chucks at her.

'Where's my boy?' she asks. 'I've got big plans for today. I'll get him a tattoo, teach him bomb making, then get him drunk as a lord.'

'He likes tequila.'

'Sophisticated tastes for one so young.'

Maggie waves us out of the house, with Noah beaming up at her, knowing his day will be fun. He's used to a wide variety of people caring for him, which is a blessing. If you ask for a favour out here, it's rarely turned down, our lives are so intertwined. Shadow remains at the house, for once. He seems keen to watch over Noah instead of tagging along with me.

Nina shares a few more details about Kim Durgan as we cross Bryher, heading for the quay. The girl has terrible nightmares about her past. I'm surprised when Nina jumps onto our bowrider first. She normally prefers to let me steer, but today she starts the motor herself, her expression determined as we sail through New Grimsby Sound. It's 9.30 am and the sea is unsettled as we head for St Mary's. There's no sign of storm clouds yet, but the pressure weighing on the back of my neck announces that another weather system is coming our way, and the fishermen have sensed it too. A gaggle of trawlers drifts on the ebbtide in the harbour. They've returned to Hugh Town early, after racing home from their nightly hunt for mackerel and brown crab, in the depths of the Atlantic.

The Durgans' house lies near the quay on Church Street. The ramshackle property sits opposite St Mary's Hall Hotel. I've been here several times in recent years, to parties in their large garden, with Nina. The Durgan clan includes an assortment of foster kids, and grandparents, who live in a garden annexe. The family's parties always last until the small hours, with plenty of booze and dancing, but the place is unnaturally quiet this morning.

Layla and Joe soon appear in the porch. Their laidback style is still missing today. Now the facts have sunk in about Kim's cousin being killed recently, they both look even more worried.

'Please be gentle with Kim,' Layla says. 'She's hardly slept or eaten since she heard the news.'

'I promise we'll take it at her pace.' Nina keeps her voice low.

The couple's home is full of life, with vibrant kids' drawings lining their hallway. Joe stands in the kitchen opposite me, talking in a low Cornish drawl.

'Kim's made so much progress. We had to watch her like a hawk at first, in case of self-harm. All she remembers about being trafficked here is the fear,' Joe says. 'Do you know how many kids we've fostered over the years?'

'Dozens, I imagine.'

'Over a hundred, but Kim was the most damaged of all. Those bastards kept her locked in the back of a van for months. Then she was forced onto a boat, with a dozen other kids. The traffickers panicked and left them to drown. She'd have died if Alan Madron hadn't intercepted that dinghy, floating on Deadman's Pool.'

'Madron?' My thoughts grind to a sudden halt. 'I thought the coastguard rescued them.'

Layla takes over. 'Alan was there first. He got a call from St Martin's, then sailed straight over. He was a hero that night, bringing all those kids back to St Mary's, for shelter with anyone that had a spare room. Kim stayed with us. She had no papers, and hardly any English. The authorities tried tracing her parents, but Kim's birth family was never found. We couldn't risk such a fragile child getting lost in the care system, so we adopted her.'

This new fact could explain the conspiracy idea that kids like Sinead Harcourt believe. If they think Madron is involved in child trafficking, maybe they think he stole some of those children for himself. The idea's hard to fathom, but it's no wonder they see him as evil.

'Kim's lucky to have a second chance,' I say.

'She deserves it,' Joe insists. 'Kim's the bravest kid ever. I know you need answers, but even she's got limits. She might crumble if you force her to remember stuff that's too painful.'

'I promise to take it slow. If I see she's struggling, we'll stop the interview,' Nina says.

Layla appears relieved. 'It felt awful telling her that one of her cousins died here a few months ago, after being held prisoner. I think Kim feels guilty for not finding her years ago.'

The couple finally lead us upstairs. We skirt past abandoned toys, bits of Lego and muddy trainers on the landing. Layla and Joe hover behind us when Nina taps on Kim's door. It opens by only a few inches after she calls her name.

'Is it okay to talk with you for a minute?' Nina asks.

The girl's dark eyes are puffy with tears as she assesses us in turn. Her hands are shaking when she finally lets us enter, while her parents hover on the landing, yet she's holding on to her composure. Kim's room is tiny, with little furniture except a narrow bed. I drop onto a chair in the corner. The last thing she needs is me looming over her while she revisits the terrors of her past.

Nina perches on her bed. 'I like your room, Kim. The view's lovely.'

The window overlooks the garden outside St Mary's Hall, but a wall hanging catches my eye. It's a blue shawl with a yellow lotus in the centre, like the shroud at the murder scene, providing a direct link. I'd like to ask Kim about it, but she still looks tense, so I nod at Nina instead, to ask the question for me at some point in the interview. She already knows that an identical one was used as the victim's shroud.

'This won't take long, I promise,' Nina says. 'Ben just needs to understand about the girl they found on St Helen's. We know she was a cousin of yours, from her DNA.'

The girl doesn't react.

'We think she was living here, hidden away,' Nina says. 'What were your cousins like? It would help us to know. Take your time, then try and share a few details with us, if you can.' Nina waits a few moments before prompting her again. 'Were they smart, like you? Your last school report was great, wasn't it?'

Layla interrupts, calling through the open doorway. 'Take your time answering, love. Remember we're right here, if you need us.'

Kim's shoulders relax by a fraction, then she whispers her answer. 'They lived in the next village. They were older than me, braver too.'

'Can you tell us their names?' Nina asks.

'Tuyet and Mai. More like sisters than cousins.' Her eyes screw shut. 'The three of us walked to school together, every day. They were always kind to me. Mai was so clever, she won a prize for her English.' Her speech suddenly runs out.

'It sounds like you were really close. Remember, you're not to blame for any of this.' Nina glances at the wall. 'Can you tell us a little bit about your prayer shawl?'

'We took them to school with us, when we visited the temple.'

'And you carried yours all the way from Vietnam?'

She lowers her face. 'It's from my family. Everything else is lost.'

I lean forwards slowly, joining the conversation at last. 'Can I show you some items, Kim?' I take out my phone, find the photos and turn the screen towards her. 'It would help to know if these are your cousins'.'

The girl peers at the jade figurines and the shroud pictured on my phone. 'That looks like Tuyet's shawl, but I've never seen the charms.'

'How did you three girls get separated?' Nina asks.

Kim takes a breath, then words rush from her mouth like a dam's broken. 'Our kidnappers left us in a dinghy, on open water, and sailed away. It was so cold, Mai wrapped my shawl around me. I was terrified we'd all drown. When another boat came, a man grabbed Mai. Tuyet clung to her, so they were both taken. I kept screaming their names as his boat sailed away. A long time passed before the policeboat collected the rest of us.'

'Do you remember anything about the man who took your cousins?'

'I thought he was a rescuer, at first. It was too dark to see his face.' Kim's voice crackles with anxiety. If she knows anything, I can tell she's too afraid to reveal more, her eye contact dropping away.

'Is it someone from the islands, Mai?' I ask, but she doesn't reply. 'Maybe he threatened you, to keep quiet?'

She gazes down at her shoes. 'He yelled at us, but I couldn't understand. I was too afraid.'

Joe appears in the doorway. 'Maybe it's time for a break? I can see Kim's getting tired.'

'No, Dad, it's okay,' she whispers. 'If Mai or Tuyet is alive, I want to help, more than anything. They're my cousins.'

'You're doing great, Kim,' I say, as Joe slowly retreats. 'Try and remember what the man looked like, please. Any details could help.'

She shuts her eyes again. 'He must be old by now, from the way he moved.'

'How do you mean?'

'His movements were slow, but he was strong enough to lift Mai and Tuyet onto his boat. They didn't stand a chance. For years I wished he'd taken me as well. They're all I had.'

'I promise to look everywhere for your cousin, Kim. Thanks for helping us.'

I retreat onto the landing, aware that I may have done more harm than good. The lotus flower on the wall stays with me. The fabric is worn, like the one on St Helen's, yet it's the only decorative item in the room. It takes a big imaginative leap to picture Kim's cousin, just a few years older, giving birth alone, in a squalid room. I'd like to ask Madron about finding the children adrift on Deadman's Pool, but his hostility since his fall puts him out of reach.

Nina stays with the family once the interview ends. Outside, I call Isla. Her voice is breathless as she explains that her search of Phillip Warleggan's garden and the old cottage have yielded no direct link to the crime scene. The only connection is his boat moored by St Helen's, a few nights before the girl's body was found. The possibility of his guilt nags at me. It could just be that the man is too squeaky clean, or that Sinead Harcourt has planted seeds of doubt in my mind with her conspiracy theories. I can't question him again unless solid evidence leads me back to his door.

35

Mai is too weak to keep her eyes open for long. She can't tell whether it's morning or afternoon, with no light piercing the shuttered windows of her new prison. She's still lying on the sofa, so hot and feverish it's high summer in her dream. Mai pictures herself sitting outside her family's cabin, with her legs dangling from the wooden platform. She can see the river winding through rice fields, a blue ribbon shimmering in the heat haze.

A voice cuts through her stupor. It's coming from outside, a girl calling out in English, her voice loud and unfamiliar. Maybe it's best to let the fever drag her under for good and not keep trying to resurface. She shuts her eyes again, relaxing for the first time in years, until something cuts her ribcage. It's the nail she's sharpened, hidden inside her dress. The pain is a reminder to keep fighting.

Mai drags herself upright. She can see a kitchen through the doorway, with an oven and a fridge, and instinct drags her upright. Maybe she can find a better weapon to use against him? She takes a few tentative steps before falling. Her skin is slick with sweat, yet her fighting spirit is intact. Her vision swims as she crawls over the wooden floor, determined to protect herself from another attack.

36

I stand outside the Durgans' house, while Nina remains indoors, comforting the family. Relationships matter in such small communities, so I want to make sure Layla and Joe are okay before heading back to the station. When Layla emerges into the late-morning light to join me, she's clutching cigarette papers and tobacco. The collar of her padded shirt is turned up against the breeze.

'Sorry that was tough for Kim,' I say. 'I could see you're worried.'

'No need to apologise.' Her voice sounds shaky. 'You're only doing your job, and Kim's a survivor. She's an amazing girl. We love her, you see. The pair of us turn into rottweilers if anyone upsets our kids.'

'They're lucky to have you.'

Layla raises a smile. 'The thing is, Kim was so traumatised when she came to us, she couldn't even speak. She still has bad days, even now. Today's the only time she's called Mai and Tuyet by their names. I'd hate for her to suffer like that again.'

'There's a chance one of those girls is still alive, Layla.'

She presses her hands together, like she's offering a prayer. 'That would be wonderful for Kim. I hope you find her soon.'

'Me too. We're doing everything in our power.'

Layla perches beside me on a garden bench. I notice that soil is trapped under her nails, from her work as a gardener, her cheeks reddened by the winter cold. When she offers me a roll-up I shake my head but appreciate the gesture.

'Don't tempt me. Nina would kill me if I start again.'

'She's great at her job, you know. I hear Kim laughing with the other kids sometimes. It's like a burden's lifting from her shoulders. Maybe her nightmares will pass too, with more counselling.'

'Can you tell me anything about Kim's prayer shawl?' I meet Layla's eye again. 'Her cousin was wrapped in one just like hers. It interests me that she's managed to keep it safe all these years.'

'She was freezing cold that night. If Alan hadn't found her, hypothermia would have killed her. The kids on that dinghy had no possessions, or life jackets. Those traffickers deserve the death penalty.'

'Or a lifetime in jail.'

Layla's words remind me that I've been lucky. My parents left me the small house my grandfather built on Hell Bay, but the only thing tying Kim Durgan to her past is a threadbare piece of silk. The ones I'd like to punish are the traffickers themselves. Layla grinds her roll-up under the heel of her boot, then hurries back inside.

When I check my phone, Ginny Tremayne has left a message, summoning me to the hospital straight away. My spirits sink. If the baby has died overnight, Zoe will have to grieve all over again.

I tap out a quick message to Nina, then head off up the hill to Ginny. She is waiting for me in reception, white coat flapping as she leads me to her consulting room. Her face is grave when she shuts the door; she must want to keep our talk confidential.

'Alan Madron's ill, Ben. It's serious,' she says.

I nod rapidly. 'I had to report him unfit for duty today.'

'That was the right decision, but he's unbelievably stubborn. I found him wandering down the coast road on my drive to work. It took a lot of persuading to get him here. He needs assessment by the neurologist at Penzance Hospital, the minute we can fly him there. Our facilities here are too basic.'

'How's he doing?'

'His head injury's caused a stroke, which could have been prevented if he'd come sooner. It's affected his speech.' She holds my gaze. 'All I can do is give him blood thinners. Some patients recover quickly, but others suffer long-term effects.'

'Have you told his wife?'

'She's changing flights, but it could be a couple of days before she's home. I'm afraid Alan might try to leave when he comes round, if he's got the strength. He's obsessed with helping you find the murderer.'

'Can I see him, please?'

'Keep it gentle, if he wakes up. Don't get him agitated.'

My boss is asleep, when I enter his room, and dressed in blue NHS pyjamas. The sight of his vulnerability dispels any anger I've held over the years. I find myself babbling, for no reason. Madron's eyelids flutter when I talk about random subjects, like Noah learning to walk. Minutes pass before he wakes up, his gaze cloudy. My boss studies me in silence, like he's struggling to recall my name. When he finally speaks, his voice is a raw croak.

'Progress? Work? Tell, tell.'

'The case is going well, don't worry. How are you feeling?'

'Brain fog, headache.' He shields his eyes, then mutters another broken sentence full of jumbled words.

'Want me to draw the curtains?'

'No, no.' His voice is suddenly fierce. 'Details. All of it, give me.'

'Okay, just a quick outline. The girl we found on St Helen's is one of the Vietnamese kids you rescued from traffickers, six years ago. I need to know about you sailing over there to collect them, after you've rested.'

His face trembles. 'Bastards, no conscience.'

'That's for sure. Who rang you, about the boat?'

'Piano man, St Martin's.' He rubs his forehead again. 'Brain fog, headache. More update, now.'

'Gannick's found threads from a red carpet in the girl's shroud, and on the baby. They must have been held somewhere together.'

His eyes widen suddenly, his claw-like hand seizing my wrist. 'Carpet, living room. Red, dusty.'

'Where, sir?'

'My, my.' His eyes are wild, but he's not making sense. 'Mine!'

'You need to rest now, sir. We all have to accept help sometimes, now it's your turn.' I touch his arm. 'Stay here and rest. You've given me a breakthrough.'

Madron must be describing Mark Lanner as the piano man, with his vintage Steinway. It makes sense that the composer would have spotted the dinghy full of children adrift on the tide from his vantage point on St Martin's, yet why did he only call the police? The tiny boat could have entered the shipping lane and been smashed apart by a tanker ploughing across the Atlantic. Lanner could have used his powerful speedboat to reach them before making that call. But why would a successful man like him seize two young girls then hold them captive for years, unless he's a paedophile? It chimes with Sinead Harcourt's claim that he's not trustworthy. But such a bizarre act would make him insane.

I bump into Zoe on my way out. She looks exhausted but happy, holding a cup of coffee from the machine in the corridor, too focussed on the abandoned baby to leave him for long. Zoe flings her arms round me for a hug, then slips away. She appears in her element when I peer through the doorway. The boy has stopped screaming, now that he's receiving years of frustrated love. He calls out to her, eager to be held. I watch her lift the baby, then hug him close. There's no point in thinking about the emotional road crash that will happen if she's separated from him anytime soon.

Eddie calls me after I leave the hospital. He's already done the background check I requested on Mark Lanner. There are no female cellists in the Berlin Philharmonic Orchestra, so Lanner's girlfriend doesn't exist. What else has he deceived us about? I send Eddie to search his house on St Martin's immediately, then give the man a call.

'I'd like you to come to the police station as soon as possible, Mr Lanner,' I say.

'Is that really necessary?' His voice sounds hesitant. 'I'm in the middle of something. Could we talk on the phone?'

'I'm afraid not; and we'd like to search your property at the same time. May I have your permission?'

He hesitates for a moment. 'Of course, if it's important. I'll sail over this morning.'

'I need you here by midday at the latest, please.'

'I'll set off now.'

The composer sounds surprised to be summoned to the police station, but Madron's words make him a person of interest, and I want to speak with him before the public meeting. Sinead Harcourt's theory might even contain a grain of truth.

37

The police station is empty when I arrive. Lawrie Deane is over on Tresco, searching the last few properties for signs that the girls were kept there, and Isla is at Inn on the Quay, checking that everything's ready for our public meeting at 1.00 pm. It bothers me that time slides by without contact from Lanner. He said he'd sail straight here, but maybe he's making a desperate attempt to clean up his property, before it's searched. I keep busy doing paperwork for the case, but irritation has turned to anger by the time Mark Lanner finally arrives, at 12.30 pm.

'You're late, Mr Lanner. I told you it was urgent.'

'Apologies,' he says, with a slow nod. 'My boat wouldn't start. I tried to get the engine running, but no luck. I had to borrow a neighbour's.'

'Come with me, please. Let's not waste any more time.'

Mark Lanner is dressed too smartly for island life, in a tailored coat, new jeans and expensive boots. The wind has played havoc with his grey hair on his ride over, leaving it dishevelled. The overhead light exposes his damaged features in stark relief. It looks like his nose has been broken several times, and one of his cheekbones too. The composer's expression is blank when I offer him a seat in Madron's office then close the door.

'I need your help on the case. There's a personal matter to discuss too.'

'That's intriguing. I assume that's why you're searching my house?'

'Yes, we're scouring the islands for a young girl being held captive.' I examine his face as he nods, then decide to get straight to the point. 'Tell me what happened, please, the night you spotted that dinghy adrift, six years ago.'

'I can hardly remember the sequence of events, after all this time. But let's see ... I think I rang the police station first, and my call went through to Alan Madron.' Lanner blinks rapidly. 'He sailed over so fast, he reached the children before the coastguard.'

'Why didn't you rescue them yourself?'

'I had a smaller boat back then, too weak for those currents.'

'Were any of the kids brought to St Martin's?'

'No, I think they were taken to St Mary's, then social services took most of them to the mainland in the following days.'

'You saved their lives.'

'Alan Madron did that.' Lanner looks awkward. 'I just made a few phone calls. Anyone would do the same.'

'Did you spot the dinghy with your telescope?'

'I saw it with my bare eyes, just before nightfall.'

'Okay, that's useful, thanks.' I hold the pause for a moment, and he places his hands on the arms of his chair, about to get up. 'There's something else, Mark. You mentioned having a girlfriend, but that's not true, is it?'

He sinks back into his chair, his face flushing. 'I knew that would come back to haunt me.' He stares down at his hands. 'I said it out of embarrassment, I suppose.'

'There was no need. Being alone isn't a crime.'

'It is in my case. I wasted a good relationship through sheer carelessness.'

'Explain that for me, please.'

'I met a woman in Berlin, on a film set, years ago. She was a musician, like me. We lived together for a while, but I took her for granted. She left me, then moved to America, found someone else.'

'How long ago?'

'Almost a decade. She was beautiful and talented. I always hoped we'd get back together, but she found a new life. If I block out my mistakes, it's easy to believe we're still together.'

'What else have you lied about?'

'Nothing.' His intense gaze holds mine. 'She slipped through my fingers because I didn't show her enough respect. It's easier to retreat into music than accept she's gone.'

'That sounds painful.' I study him again. 'Do you mind telling me how you got your facial injuries?'

Lanner flinches. 'My stepfather took a dislike to me as a boy. He beat me black and blue several times.'

'How come no one reported him?'

'My mother was too scared. She sent me to boarding school, as protection, but the older boys were vicious too.' There's bitterness in his voice now, as well as loss. 'Sadness made me a composer. The piano gives back far more than it takes, but I've never had a lasting relationship, except the one I threw away.'

'You've travelled, at least. There's exotic artwork all over your house.'

'I miss those voyages. I don't need them anymore, thanks to the internet, but each country taught me something new.'

'Including Vietnam?'

'I went to the Red River delta, just once. The poverty back then was horrifying.'

'When was this?'

'Eight or nine years ago. I can't remember the exact date.'

Lanner has regained his composure, but his lie still seems strange. There's no stigma in being single, with millions of people living alone. I can see why Sinead Harcourt might fear a man like him, because he seems out of reach. He's experienced the kind of childhood that leaves people broken, never learning the difference between right and wrong. It's no excuse, but if he turns out to be guilty, that experience could explain why his moral boundaries became blurred.

I'd like to keep him at the station while Eddie searches his property, but no hard proof links him to the abductions, so I'm forced to let him walk away. Lanner tells me that he's planning to attend the public meeting, then hurries away.

When I arrive at Inn on the Quay, islanders are waiting in a noisy crowd. Isla has done the lion's share of preparation when I join her. She's laid out chairs in the restaurant and set up a microphone on the small stage. By 1.00 pm the room has flooded with people. I wait until everyone has filed inside, then a buzzing noise makes me glance through the window. A drone is hovering close by, flashing red as it takes photos for the press. I'd love to shoot it down, stopping them from stealing our images, but the only way to prevent the media reporting on the case will be to close it fast.

I explain that the girl we found buried on St Helen's may have been trafficked here from Vietnam, then could have been held captive for six years. The news is met by a stunned silence, until I continue. We think her sister could be the mother of the abandoned baby, and may still be alive. The whole community must be sick of the gossip about potential culprits, but everyone looks alert when I explain the story fully. Two sisters of nine and ten were seized from a trafficker's boat on Deadman's Pool six years ago, before the coastguard arrived. One died a few months ago, and we think the other may still be being held against her will.

There are grumbles of disbelief. I can hear people murmuring that such an ugly crime couldn't possibly be committed here, but I need to change their minds.

'This is ideal territory for traffickers, with free access to all the islands by boat,' I say. 'If anyone suspects that a neighbour, colleague or friend could be hiding a young girl in a damp room, with mould growing on the walls, you need to tell us straight away. We also need to know about any properties with red carpet on the floor.'

I'm halfway through my announcements when I notice that Mark Lanner is missing, despite his promise to attend. Maybe he sailed home for a solitary conversation with his piano, but it confirms him even more strongly as a person of interest. There's no sign of Steve Angarrack, Phillip Warleggan or Pete Harcourt in the audience either.

The atmosphere is downbeat when the meeting ends, just

before 2.00 pm. Lawrie Deane is manning the station, leaving Isla to deal with the people lingering behind. She greets each one with courtesy, which is how she's been trained. You're more likely to open someone up by being genuine and polite, instead of going through the motions.

I'm about to leave when Emma Angarrack tracks me down. She's well dressed, as usual, but her confidence is less convincing now I know that her daughter has been sneaking outside at night to meet friends. She looks fragile for the first time ever.

'Can we have a private word, please, Ben?' she asks, her voice falling to a whisper. 'Not here though, I don't want anyone else listening.'

'What about your shop?'

She nods rapidly. 'I'll wait for you there.'

Emma's face has drained of colour by the time she hurries away, but there's no time to reflect on her odd manner. Another member of the Island Council is waiting to speak to me. He's a retired builder, who made a fortune from property on the mainland. I've never seen the guy upset until now, his face beetroot red with anger.

'Your strategy doesn't make sense. Why are you bothering people who've never put a foot wrong? My home's been searched twice, turned over, like my family are grubby criminals.' He spits out the words. 'I'll phone Scotland Yard if you come back.'

'Sorry you feel that way, but we're looking for a murderer who may still be holding child victims. We have to search the entire island.'

'I bet no one's gone rummaging through your place, have they?'

'Every residential property will be searched, including mine.'

'That had better be true, Kitto. Believe me, I'll check.'

The man's glare is furious, then he marches away. I should have worked harder to placate him, but right now the islands' self-styled elite are the least of my worries. I have a quick word with Isla, letting her know that I'm going to speak with Emma Angarrack in her shop.

It only takes me five minutes to get there. The 'closed' sign is hanging on the door, but Emma rushes to open it, and my curiosity rises. She leads me to the back room, which is lined with cardboard boxes, a place where we won't be seen or heard. I notice her pallor again when we sit down on chairs in the corner.

'Take your time, Emma. I can see something's wrong.'

She looks down at her hands. 'It's about Steve.'

Instinct tells me to remain silent. If I push too fast, her bright façade will shatter.

'It's all such a mess.' She drags in a deep breath. 'We started out just like any other young couple. He was a trainee teacher and I was a shop girl, enjoying our lives, until ambition took over. Steve switched up a gear when Lisa was born, and I got dragged into it, to keep up. He wants perfection in everything we do. Poor Lisa's cracking under the strain.'

'That sounds tough on you both.'

'Like you wouldn't believe.' When her eyes blink shut, a tear rolls down her cheek. She doesn't bother to wipe it away. She just takes a deep breath. 'I think he's involved in your case, Ben. I can't cover for him anymore.'

I keep my voice level. 'How do you mean?'

'Steve's destroyed my trust. I've found out he's got a secret life.'

'Are you saying that Steve harmed that girl on St Helen's?'

When her head drops, my heartbeat accelerates, until it's hammering against my ribs. I can't believe that one half of the island's power couple is suggesting her husband could be the murderer.

'I'm sure there are others. He's not acting alone.'

'I need proof, Emma. Give me any details you know, please.'

She blots her eyes with a tissue. 'He leaves the house at night. When I challenge him about it, he just says he sleeps badly. That he takes long walks instead of disturbing me. Maybe he's so obsessed about improving that bloody school, it's broken him.'

'But there's no proof he's involved. Your property's been

searched, and so's the school. Where would he hide two young girls for all these years?'

'Last week I followed him to Church Cove. He dragged our speedboat down to the water at 2.00 am, then set off alone ... He was sailing towards St Helen's.'

'Is there anything else – anything that makes you think he's involved?'

'He's got two personas these days: calm and powerful at school, but he flies off the handle at home, for no reason.'

'I overheard you rowing the other day, didn't I?'

'It's been going on for months,' she says, nodding. 'The other night I thought he'd hit me. It doesn't feel safe being around him anymore. I'm moving Lisa out, before anything bad happens. We'll stay at my mum's.'

'I'm sorry, Emma.'

She blinks her eyes shut. 'Don't be nice to me, please. I'll cry my eyes out.'

I wait while she gathers herself, then ask: 'Where's Steve today?'

'At the school. He's got meetings all afternoon and into the evening. I won't tell him we're leaving until we're gone. There's no way he's hurting Lisa.' Her hand grips mine for a second. 'Please find out what he's done.'

Emma's eyes are still glistening when I say goodbye. The Angarracks are one of the most influential couples here, but she must be at her wits' end to accuse her husband of murder. If the islands' headmaster has really been keeping girls in a bunker, it puts him on a par with monsters like Jimmy Savile and Jeffrey Epstein. People in positions of power can commit terrible crimes with ease, influential enough to silence every critic. He's plausible, and he may even have persuaded his high-powered friends to cover for him.

38

I ride the motorbike straight to Five Islands Academy next, with Emma Angarrack's accusations filling my mind. No concrete proof connects her husband with the murder victim, but I still need him to explain his night-time boat trip. It's only 3.00 pm, but dusk is already gathering, and the kids will soon be going home. When I arrive at the head's office, his PA tells me that he's got staff appraisal meetings planned and he can't be disturbed. She looks furious when I march into his office anyway. When I spot the faded red carpet on the floor, my thoughts slow to a halt. He could have brought the girl's body here before burying it, to avoid leaving evidence at home. It's a stretch to imagine one of the island's most successful men could be involved, but his wife's comments can't be ignored.

Angarrack is on his computer, but jumps to his feet when I enter. Something's changed since last time we met. His appearance is no longer flawless. He's abandoned his jacket, and his tie hangs loose around his throat.

'Didn't my assistant tell you I'm busy today, Ben? I've got a load of meetings about to start.'

'There's a problem we need to discuss first. Some of the island's power holders have been lying to me.'

His face darkens. 'About what, exactly?'

'We found fibres in the dead girl's shroud, and matching ones in the baby's blanket, left at the station. They're from a red carpet like this one. I'm surprised you didn't modernise your office, like the rest of the building.'

'The science labs had to be refitted. The kids' needs matter far more than the state of my office.'

'That's very noble, but I still need answers. You've been taking your boat out at night, in storm season. Why, exactly?'

His mouth flaps open, but no sound emerges. A smart man like him knows that silence is his best defence.

'The killer wrapped his victim in a Vietnamese shawl, then plastic sheeting, in a room with carpet just like this. She was placed on a boat and taken to St Helen's at night. You need to explain your actions, Steve.'

'Time alone on the ocean keeps me sane.' He raises the palms of his hands, like he's testing the air for rain. 'Everyone sees me as this magician, working miracles for the children, but it takes its toll.'

'Why not resign, if the stress is too much?' I stare at him again. 'It could be you taking those girls prisoner.'

He stares at me. 'Is Emma behind this? She was upset this morning, but that's crazy. I took this job to protect kids, not harm them.'

'But it gives you access to young girls every day, doesn't it? That must be a big perk of your job, if you're involved.'

'That's a sick accusation.'

'Put me straight, then.'

'I'll sue you for reputational damage if this gets out.' His voice is strident. 'I want a lawyer present for the rest of this conversation.'

'Go ahead and appoint one, please. I'll search the building in the meantime. I need to take a sample from your carpet too.'

'Be my guest.'

Angarrack's face is rigid with anger. I pull on plastic gloves then pluck a few carpet fibres and bag them, for Gannick to compare, and leave his office without a word. The PA still looks angry when I ask for keys to search the school premises on my own.

The outbuildings in the grounds don't take long. All I find is an industrial mower, gardening equipment and the stink of creosote. My hopes only surface again once I enter the cavernous cellar under the main building. The air smells of mildew, and when the strip lights flicker into life, I see drops of water are running down the end wall. Rolls of old carpet are stacked in a pile, alongside crates full of documents. If I rummaged around for long enough, I'd probably find my own disastrous school reports, telling me to quit daydreaming and apply myself.

I stand in the middle of the space with my senses alert. The girls could have been kept here, with no natural light, growing dependent on their captor. But it's not private enough. I trace the walls slowly, running my fingertips over the surface, hoping to locate a concealed entrance. I check the concrete floor too. My search yields no fresh clues. Steve Angarrack wouldn't leave them in such a risky location for long. Maybe that's why he took his boat out at night, to transfer the second girl to another hiding place on the off-islands.

When I return to the ground floor the last bell of the day rings, and moments later the corridor ahead floods with smiling children, jubilant to be set free. I have to cut through the chattering crowd to return to Angarrack's office.

The headteacher has regained his calm during my absence. He refuses to speak when I ask again about his midnight boat trips. I'd like to detain him in a holding cell at the station until the island-wide search is over, but the only hints that he could be involved are too flimsy for an arrest. There's just his wife's claim that he's behaving suspiciously, taking his boat out at night, and the red carpet in his office. Angarrack looks triumphant when I ask him to report to the station first thing tomorrow, to explain his actions. He promises to be there by 8.30 am, with his lawyer.

The full horror of the kidnap victims' experience dawns on me as I leave the building. How long would my own sanity last if I was locked in a bunker? If one of the girls is still alive, she must have real courage, to endure it for so many years.

When I get back on the motorbike the winter sun has vanished. The only problem with living in an area with hardly any light pollution is that night-time darkness is absolute. The moment the sun sets, it's like a black-out curtain has been thrown over the islands, with only thin starlight to guide me. I can't do much to help me find the girl alive until morning; we're more likely to find the hideaway in daylight hours. But it gives me time to prioritise searching the team's homes too, or face public criticism. I call Deane, telling him that I'll go to his place first, then he can check Eddie's flat on Tresco. Deane has lived in Scilly most of his adult life, so he's a useful asset, knowing every inch of territory. Eddie can search my place on Bryher, and Isla's family home has already been visited.

Deane tells me to go ahead, his front door is never locked, like many properties in Scilly. Searching there feels pointless, when a terrified young girl may still be trapped in a dark room, but I have no choice. My breath crystallises on the air when I park outside Deane's bungalow. It looks like a typical bachelor pad inside. The hallway is painted white, with few decorations on display, except a framed photo of his older son's family. I can't resist looking in his fridge. It's well stocked with local delicacies, including smoked salmon and artisan cheese, proving the man's passion for food.

The bedrooms are tidy and simply furnished. There's no cellar, like most bungalows in Scilly. Developers stopped building them years ago, due to the cost of excavation. Deane's garden looks orderly even in the depths of winter, with dogwood bushes providing a splash of colour, their leafless branches a vivid red. He's built a summerhouse since my last visit, with buckets, spades and kites for his grandkids stacked in a corner. His place has given me some DIY inspiration, but my search has been a waste of police time.

I put through a call to Gareth Keillor, hoping he's got more information. His voice bubbles with excitement when he picks up. He's talking so rapidly, I have to ask him to repeat himself.

'The lab just confirmed it, Ben. The baby you found is related to Kim Durgan, just like the victim. Twenty-five percent of his DNA matches hers, so his mother must be one of Kim's cousins.'

I mutter my thanks, then shove my phone back in my pocket. The facts support the picture emerging from the evidence. Someone on these islands took both of Kim's cousins the night she arrived by boat. One of them died six years later, then the second girl gave birth to a son, only a few weeks ago. I'm praying she's still alive. All I have to do now is find her, before she meets the same fate as her sister.

39

I promised to return to Bryher to help finish the island-wide search hours ago, and my phone is pulsing with messages when I reach the quay. One is from Nina, but the signal's poor. The only fact I can glean is that Maggie still has Noah. She mentions bad sea conditions too, but St Mary's Sound is like a mill pond now, with barely a ripple. It's 6.00 pm, and the sky overhead is already pulsing with stars when I sail north for home. Things fall into perspective during my journey. All that matters now is finding the missing girl, even if it means offending a few high-profile islanders along the way.

I'm still tying the mooring rope when Maggie rushes down the jetty, calling my name.

'You never answer your bloody phone. I left three messages.'

'I've been working, Maggie. What's wrong?' When I put my arm round her shoulders, her body's hard with tension.

'Noah's missing.' Her panic registers with me for the first time.

'Nina will have collected him. They'll be at home by now.'

'Listen to me, for God's sake. Nina came to the pub earlier. She put Noah in his buggy then ran back indoors for her scarf. We chatted for a few minutes. By the time she went back outside, his buggy was empty.'

I stare at her as the penny drops. 'He'll be with someone.'

'We've called everywhere. Someone's taken him, Ben.'

Reality hits me suddenly, my energy draining away, into the sea. 'Where's Nina?'

'At home, waiting for you.'

I set off at a run, with fresh rain pelting the back of my neck. Why in God's name would the killer steal my child? I can hear Shadow howling a hundred metres away. The sound is so high and piercing, it sets my teeth on edge.

Nina looks ghostly when I get home. She's standing in the

living room, gabbling into her phone, her face chalk white. I can hear Eddie at the end of the line, giving reassurance. She doesn't protest when I take over the call.

'Get over here fast, Eddie. Noah's been taken. I think it's punishment for us getting too close.'

I hear Eddie's feet pounding as he races down the lane, heading for his boat in Tresco harbour, without bothering to ring off. Isla and Lawrie react fast too, when I call and tell them to declare a lockdown. There can be no sailing between the islands until Noah's found. My words are garbled, but they listen intently. I tell Isla to come over to help the search on Bryher, while Lawrie should man the station on St Mary's. It dawns on me that if Steve Angarrack took the girls, he must be working with an accomplice, because he's still over there. He couldn't have taken my son, but Mark Lanner could be anywhere by now.

Nina is speechless when I face her again, swaying on her feet. I've never seen her this afraid, even when she gave birth to Noah and kept passing out. Her eyes are glazed when I make her sit down. It's a relief when Maggie appears, panting for breath, in the doorway.

'People are checking the coast, down to Great Par,' she says. 'What else can I do?'

'Get Ray to run the search party, Maggie.'

I'm about to leave when Nina stops me. The fierce strength in her gaze is reviving when she forces me to look at her. 'I trust you, Ben. Don't come back here without Noah.'

'I won't.'

My wife releases my hands, and I'm in freefall. She's placed her faith in me, but I'm too wired to stand still. Shadow is panicking too. He claws at the door, desperate to get outside. My spirits lift by a fraction. He's stood guard over Noah obsessively, ever since we brought him home. There's a chance he can follow his scent trail if I act fast.

I grab one of Noah's sweaters, then let Shadow sniff it. My dog looks up at me, his pale eyes as clear as glass. His baying gets louder when he scratches the door again, his movements frantic. Maggie is on her phone, telling islanders to assemble at the pub, and to bring torches and flares. When I look at Nina for the last time, she's frozen in place, motionless by the fire as the flames dwindle to ashes.

Shadow speeds off like a bullet when I open the door. He's my best hope of finding Noah safe and sound, but he slows to a trot on Shipman Head Down, checking that I'm keeping up. Hope surges in my chest when he pauses outside the boatyard. Maybe it's just a misunderstanding? Ray sometimes collects Noah, then brings him home, if we're running late. My spirits plummet when I see my uncle dressed in waterproofs, holding flares for the search party.

'Has he been found?' Ray calls out.

'Not yet. Eddie's on his way, and Isla. Break windows if need be. Search outbuildings, and every bit of ground.'

My uncle's hand skims my shoulder then he marches away. I need reassurance, but Ray never gives false promises. Light spills from the open door of his boathouse and all I can hear is silence. My son would be safe now, if only I'd kept watch. Stealing him in plain sight was an act of desperation, or obscene confidence. My thoughts spin until the truth dawns on me. I'll have to stay rational, to find him alive.

Shadow is waiting on the quay. It looks like he's about to dive into the churning waves, until I grab his collar. His grey eyes glint back at me in the moonlight. I'm certain my dog understands that we must bring Noah home, because he's protected him since he was born.

When I release his collar Shadow leaps onto my boat. He stands on the prow, too busy sniffing the air to notice me starting the engine. When I glance back at my native island, every house is lit up like a beacon. Voices sound in the distance as the entire community heads north on foot. I trust my friends and neighbours to scour the island, but Shadow is my best witness. He may even have tried to tackle whoever stole Noah from his buggy an hour ago. His behaviour makes me fear that my son has already been taken to another island.

Rain pelts my face as we sail through open water, but Shadow's head is still raised, trying to catch Noah's scent, his body angled towards St Martin's. We'll start there, with Mark Lanner. His behaviour has bothered me from the start, and he failed to show up for the meeting, after giving himself time to wipe evidence away.

Shadow appears calmer, now Bryher is behind us. He remains on the prow as we sail. I stare ahead at the neighbouring island's dark outline, praying that my son is somewhere safe and warm. I'm gripping the wheel so tightly, as I navigate the oncoming waves, my fingers are numb.

PART 3

40

Mai feels stronger since she slept, and her fever has broken. The sharpened nail is still in her pocket. She's stolen a knife from a drawer too, with a five-inch blade. Her squeamishness has gone. If the man touches her again, she will defend herself. Mai places the weapon inside her dress, wrapped in kitchen towel. She gazes around the room, desperate for a way out. There are shutters over the windows, sealing out any hint of the world beyond, but at least she's warm, for the first time in weeks. Mai tenses again when footsteps sound on the gravel outside.

She's not prepared when the door suddenly opens and she hears a baby's cry, raw and pitiful. Mai's escape plan flies from her mind. The man is returning Lao, at last. She can forgive everything he's done, just to hold him again. When the man appears he's holding a package of food and a Moses basket tucked under his arm.

Mai drops to her knees, with arms outstretched. The man finally places Lao in her hands. He's lying in his Moses basket, under a blanket, but when she pulls it back, a different baby observes her through startled green eyes. Lao's eyes are brown. And this child is much bigger, his form curled tight inside the basket. She's horrified, yet the man continues smiling down at her.

'You'll be happy now, won't you, with a baby to look after? We can live as a family abroad.'

She cries out, *'Don của tôi ở đâu?'*

The man's tone is bitter. 'Speak English, for God's sake. I've spent long enough teaching you.'

'My baby. Where is he?'

'I told you, he's gone. You won't see him again.'

'No, please. I need my child.'

'This one can drown then. We're leaving tonight, by boat.'

Mai imagines the boy's mother weeping and terrified. She holds the baby tight in her arms, unwilling to let him be sacrificed. Her thoughts are racing as the man bundles her down a dark corridor, still cradling the child. Mai wants to lash out with the knife, but protecting the baby matters more. She knows the man can't be trusted. Maybe he plans to kill them both, then flee the country, with his crimes forgotten?

Soon the man forces her downstairs, back to her old room. She hoped never to return to this filthy dungeon, but she's got a new reason to live, even if Lao is gone.

'We'll sail tonight, I promise.' His gaze searches her face again. 'I'll leave the food here. You want the baby, don't you?'

'Of course. He's perfect.' She manages to smile.

The man crouches in front of her. 'People are coming after me. They won't accept what I've done, if I'm found. I'd rather die than go to jail. You understand me, don't you?'

'Always,' she whispers.

The man kisses her cheek. Mai forces herself to return his gesture, her lips touching his cheek, but all she feels is revulsion. He hurries away, leaving another woman's baby in her arms. When she peers down at him, the boy begins to cry, as if he's realised the danger he's facing.

41

Shadow barks again when I moor on St Martin's Quay. His call is loud and urgent as he races uphill from the harbour. I keep thinking of the facts I've gathered. Mark Lanner fits the typical profile for an offender who commits such terrible crimes: a lone male, failing to integrate. He's a fantasist too: a man with too much pride, embarrassed to be caught lying about his personal life. He may not even be attracted to women, only to young girls. Lanner phoned the police telling them to rescue the children adrift at sea, but could easily have taken two girls for himself before placing that call. Eddie has searched his home, but may have missed something vital. The composer is smart enough to conceal his crimes with ease.

Lanner's house stands in darkness while Shadow prowls round his front garden, sniffing the ground. The door is locked, but I'm running on adrenaline. It takes me just one attempt to shoulder it down. The hinges break with a sound like gunfire, but I don't care how much damage his property suffers if Noah's inside. I search each room with Shadow at my heels, until I hear the rapping sound under my feet, like before. I wrench open a door under the stairs, but the light's not working, forcing me to use my torch.

Damp air rises from Lanner's cellar. The back of my neck prickles when I spot mould on the ceiling and condensation on the walls. It's the type of place where the dead girl was held captive, yet it's empty now, apart from dozens of wine bottles in racks, lying in neat rows. I check every corner for a hidden entrance. The tapping noise is coming from the old-fashioned boiler, just as Lanner claimed, but his behaviour still bothers me as I hurry back upstairs. Shadow's disturbed too, scratching at the door to get back outside.

Light is coming from the house next door. Lanner owns that

property too, and I bet it hasn't been searched properly. His politeness disarms people, convincing them he's innocent. I yell his name when I try the front door, which only opens by a fraction, until I give it a hard shove. A bare lightbulb illuminates the hallway, and I see into an old-fashioned kitchen ahead. The living room contains a fireplace and a settee, but little else. The place is much too quiet, convincing me that something's wrong.

When Lanner appears in the hallway Shadow goes into attack mode. He's barking at top volume, leaping up to snap at Lanner, until he yells at me to call him off. My dog seems to have decided he's guilty. When I grab his collar, he continues barking. His aggression has affected the composer's confidence. He's standing with his back against the wall. His designer gear has been replaced by paint-spattered overalls and a torn sweatshirt. The man's face looks broken under the overhead light; the panic in his eyes is unmistakeable.

'You should muzzle that dog. Why are you here? You almost gave me a heart attack.'

'My son. Where is he, Mark?'

He blinks at me. 'You're not making sense.'

'Show me your basement, please. Give me a guided tour.'

'Why? There's nothing down there.'

He must see the anger on my face, because he soon complies, keeping his distance from Shadow. When I follow him down some narrow stairs, the cellar has pristine white walls. Lanner must be replacing the floor too, as boards are piled against the wall. Shadow's attention has shifted from Lanner to the room he's decorating. He's sniffing everything in sight, hoping for a trace of Noah's scent.

I swing round to face Lanner. 'What happened to those kids on Deadman's Pool, exactly? Give me the true version this time.'

'You already know.' His gaze is wary. 'They were picked up by your boss, after my call.'

'But you kept two girls for yourself, so you wouldn't be alone.

You got one pregnant, then killed the other. Maybe you've been doing it for years, helping the traffickers. Is that what you do with that telescope? Spend your hours watching for their boats?'

'That's a disgusting accusation.' He recoils from me, his face hardening with anger. His voice is bitter when he speaks again. 'All I've done is believe my own fantasies. That's pathetic, I know, but it's not a crime.'

'Your DNA will give us the truth. You can't hide anything.' I spot another doorway. 'What's through there?'

Lanner's face is blank when he opens it. He's fitted a lock, which convinces me it's served as a dungeon. But the room is just another blank white space, containing only the sharp reek of fresh paint.

'Stop playing games, for fuck's sake,' I hiss at him.

He appears to be enjoying my wild-goose chase. The rooms are so clean, it looks like they've been dipped in bleach. Lanner is smart enough to guess that we'd come looking for him eventually, and hide vital evidence behind layers of paint. He may have killed the girl already.

It's possible Noah is dead too. Anger floods through me, impossible to ignore.

I grab his shoulders, then slam him against the wall. 'Give me my son.'

I shake him like a rag doll, until Lanner's face pales, and my common sense returns. I can't afford to lose control. It's tempting to beat him to a pulp, but I leave him locked in his sterile basement instead. It's so brightly lit the space resembles an operating theatre. At least he can't do any more damage if Noah's hidden elsewhere. Lanner will stay there until I release him, but my heart's pounding, and fear is contagious. Shadow releases a piercing howl as he races outside. His call is like a rallying cry, calling every islander to join our search.

42

Mai feeds the baby a carton of pulped fruit from the supplies the man left. He eats greedily, sucking food from her fingers. When she tries to put him down, he cries, as though he's used to being held all day. But the time to act has come at last. The man sounded desperate when he threatened suicide, too proud to accept the punishment he deserves. She believes he will murder her and the baby, too, if she makes a single mistake.

'I'll keep you safe,' she whispers to the baby, as he drifts into sleep.

Moonlight beams through the window overhead. The room illuminates for a second, then darkness returns, thicker than ever. The baby startles awake and begins to wail, suddenly inconsolable. Mai sings him a Vietnamese lullaby, about fish swimming out to sea in winter, then filling the rivers again, each spring. The music works its magic, sending the boy back to sleep.

When Mai looks up again, a torch beam sweeps the window. She catches sight of the girl's face like before, pale and beautiful in the glare. But this time she doesn't disappear. This time the girl is staring straight at her. Mai should cry out to her, but she's too afraid. What if the man hears her? The girl is gesturing to her, beckoning her to the window. It's a struggle to focus, but the girl's voice, muffled by the glass, cuts through her exhaustion.

'Climb through the window,' she says. 'Quick. It's your only way out.'

'It's too high.'

'Try, please. I can't reach you down there.' The girl suddenly backs away.

'Come back. Don't leave us.'

'I will, I promise, but watch out. He's not far away.'

Mai hears her running away, footsteps sprinting over gravel. But she still feels elated. The girl knows she's trapped and has promised to help. Now she must do her part.

She's trembling as she climbs onto the table. The garden outside is empty, and her responsibility feels too heavy to carry. She takes the knife from her pocket, to gouge more plaster from the wall. When she glances back at the baby, his small form is relaxed, arms thrown back, above his head. She is his only protector.

'Kien.' She mutters the word under her breath.

Mai hears her father's voice as she works, giving her courage. One of the glass panes fractures: a shard cuts her skin as the pieces shatter on the floor. She keeps going despite the pain, blood oozing down her wrist. Winter air funnels through the opening now. As she works, she tells herself that she can shelter the baby from every threat, including the cold breeze.

43

Shadow stays close while I search Mark Lanner's garden. It's possible that he's built a shelter below ground. Overgrown plants trip me up while I thrash through branches in the dark, hunting for a concealed opening. I have to ignore the panic rising in my chest, knowing it will slow me down. My hopes revive when I enter the shed at the bottom of the garden. There's a trap door, which could reveal the hiding place. But when I wrench it open, it only contains a cache of logs.

I check the messages on my phone. The first is from Eddie, reporting that the hunt for Noah on Bryher is under way. St Martin's and St Agnes are being searched by community volunteers, led by Isla. Reality hits me again. The killer may already have buried my son's body. But I'll never stop looking. The next voicemail is from Nina. Her words are raw with panic, begging for news. She's the strongest woman I know, but even she has limits. Losing Noah would break her in two.

'Where are you, for Christ's sake?' I yell the words at the night air, but only Shadow responds, with a wild howl.

Lawrie Deane calls me before I can decide where to look next. There's been a sighting in the north of St Mary's of a man running down a lane, holding a baby, half an hour ago. I tell Deane to get there fast on the motorbike and search the area, inch by inch.

Shadow seems to know we've got evidence at last. He's running down the lane, back to my boat, leading the way. There's no point in staying here. If Lanner is involved in some way, he has no intention of telling me the truth, but at least he can't do any more harm, locked in that basement. I've bought myself time to search St Mary's. It's still possible that I'm wrong about Lanner, and the killer is acting alone, hiding from us in the dark, on Scilly's biggest island.

My dog leaps back onto my boat then stands on the prow,

sniffing the air, still focussed on finding Noah. The ocean has never felt emptier than tonight. There are no freighters on the horizon, and only dim starlight to guide our way.

44

Mai clears away spikes of glass, ignoring the pain from her wound. Minutes pass before she pulls herself level with the opening. The strain exhausts her, but this time she must succeed.

The child is crying hard, only falling silent again when she gives him a rusk to bite on from the package of food. He's so much bigger than Lao, his weight feels strange in her arms, but calmness enters her mind as she holds him on her lap. She's missed this intimacy so much, yet it brings sadness too. She prays that another woman is showing Lao the same kindness, if he's still alive.

Mai gets to her feet once the baby falls quiet. He doesn't make a sound when she lays him on the bed, peaceful, as his gaze follows her. She practises hauling herself up to the opening in the wall once more, then tears the sleeves off one of her thin summer dresses to make a harness. The baby's weight feels too heavy on her back. It will be much harder to escape with him weighing her down, but she can't leave him behind. She's still weak from the virus, but she can't abandon him.

She heaves in a deep breath then hauls herself onto the ledge. She eases the baby through the gap, then it takes all her strength to ram her shoulders through the opening, and finally squirm free. After so long underground, the outside world feels unreal. Maybe she'll wake up back in the basement, breathing the same dirty air?

Mai is still checking the baby's unharmed when she spots a light ahead, above a hedgerow. An engine's noise pierces the night's stillness. There's a juddering sound as a vehicle bumps closer, over rutted ground. She hides under some bushes, with the baby on her back. Fear floods her system again when the engine cuts out, leaving silence behind. Moments pass before she hears the man's heavy footsteps trudging across the gravel, getting closer all the time.

45

The station is empty on St Mary's, just when I need a dozen highly trained search-and-rescue officers. Lawrie Deane is following my order to scour the island's north, looking for the man seen there an hour ago, holding a baby. Eddie's still on Bryher, but he and Isla will sail here soon. Zoe has left me a message too. News has reached her at the hospital about Noah going missing. She sounds desperate to help, but it's best she stays with the baby, keeping him safe from harm. The new lead has changed everything. Instinct tells me to rush outside, to search for the bastard who's taken Noah, but I must check the evidence first.

Shadow has his own agenda. He's found one of Noah's jumpers in the team room, abandoned last time Nina brought him here. My dog buries his muzzle in the woollen fabric, inhaling my son's essence again. His pale-grey eyes stare me out, like he knows something I'm too blind to see.

I scan the list of searched properties on my phone. The team have been systematic, logging the date and time of each visit, yet the killer kept two young girls and a baby hidden from view with ease. It's a miracle they haven't been discovered in a place where most properties stand in huddles, protecting each other from Atlantic gales. The killer will be feeling smug about taking Noah, but I'm praying he'll want to savour the moment before acting again. He must have known that the quickest way to derail the investigation was to steal the thing I value above all.

I rack my brains, trying to think of anyone Nina and I have clashed with over the years, yet no one comes to mind. Forensic evidence could still expose the killer, but Liz Gannick's voice is shrill with tension when she answers my call.

'The carpet fibres are your best chance. I'm checking the ones from the school now for a match.' Her voice tails into silence, for once. 'Are you doing okay, Ben?'

'No, to be honest.'

'Keep going. I'll ring once there's news.'

She hangs up immediately, no doubt swinging back to her microscope. Lawrie Deane answers his phone after two rings. He's checking the road from Pendrathen Quay, and I can hear waves hitting the shore in the background. It sounds like the wind is gathering pace on the island's exposed north coast. Sympathy echoes in Deane's voice when he promises to check the whole area fast. I'm about to ring off when he says that Ginny Tremayne called earlier. Madron left hospital an hour ago, without being discharged. Our boss must be blundering round the island again, with a head wound that could kill him. Yet the news barely registers. I don't care, so long as he keeps out of my way.

I scan the list again, noticing that a few derelict properties haven't been searched. My gaze lands on the abandoned house near Telegraph Hill, next to Pete Harcourt's. I can see why it was forgotten – the place is condemned, and the walls contain asbestos. It's only when I spot the owner's name that my breath catches in my chest. Alan Madron. He bought it thirty years ago, and it's stood empty ever since. His name on the deeds and the building's derelict state could explain why no one has bothered to check inside.

I call Deane back immediately. 'Meet me by Pete Harcourt's place, can you, Lawrie? I need your help.'

'One more property then I'll be there, boss.' He sounds more upbeat, like we're getting somewhere at last.

'Let's go,' I call to Shadow.

Noah's jumper is still clamped between his jaws, but he drops it on the threshold. Then barks at top volume until I stuff it in my pocket. We set off in the van. Madron's words return to me from the day of his fall. He mentioned buying a house for his son that was never occupied. An odd thought enters my head: my boss could be involved in the girls' abduction. He never fully explained his early-morning trip to St Helen's. His story about trying to catch smugglers seems unlikely, and he may have been the first to reach the abandoned children, on Deadman's Pool six years ago. It's possible he kept them in the derelict house all this time. But the idea seems too far-fetched.

I keep my gaze focussed on the lane as I leave Hugh Town, driving into total darkness. My headlights are the only thing guiding my way.

46

Mai crouches in the bushes. She's terrified the baby will cry out and reveal their hiding place. She can no longer see light from the man's torch, yet he must be waiting for her to break cover. Her eyes slowly adjust to the darkness. When stars emerge from behind the clouds, the garden is visible, at last. It's surrounded by shrubs, with no clear exit.

'Stay quiet, little one,' Mai whispers to the child.

She's about to stand up when leaves rustle, then there's a phone's shrill ring. It's silenced fast, but she doesn't move. She clutches the knife in her pocket. Blood from her wounded hand has saturated her sleeve, but it's the least of her worries.

Mai listens hard to the night's sounds. A gull shrieks as it wings inland, and the ocean breeze is rising. She sets off at a run, with the baby on her back, praying the man won't follow.

47

The police van picks the wrong time to misbehave. The engine's labouring as I drive up Telegraph Hill, then it stutters to a halt. I've kept sane by focussing on my search, but this new disaster tests my limits. I'm forced to pull over, cursing. All I can do is leave the keys in the ignition then continue on foot, with Shadow at my heels.

Deane arrives on the police motorbike as I finish my journey. His eyes glitter with concern when he takes off his helmet and gives me an update.

'Mary Corden from Watermill Farm saw a bloke running down the coast road from her window, holding a baby. She couldn't identify him in the dark. God knows where he's gone. There's no sign of him up there, boss.'

'Maybe he's in there.' I nod at the derelict house.

'No one's been inside for years, boss. I don't even know who owns it.'

'Madron; his name's on the deeds.'

'Seriously?' He looks stunned. 'Why would he let it go to ruin?'

'Let's just focus on finding Noah.'

'It won't take us long.' He touches my shoulder, and I hear the conviction in his voice.

Deane's support almost finishes me, but I hold it together, gritting my teeth. Shadow has disappeared from view as we circle the derelict building. I hear his call from nearby, high and keening, letting me know he's searching the grounds. Hope is the only thing keeping me going. If we can find where the girls were hidden, it could lead us to Noah.

We hunt for a way inside. The door is boarded up, and metal panels cover the windows. Deane helps me wrench one away. The sash window behind is splintering, and the lights don't work when we climb inside. My torch reveals cracks running through the ceiling overhead. The building was condemned for a reason, the floorboards squealing underfoot, like an animal in pain. But I see a new side to Deane's personality: he doesn't seem to care if the roof collapses on us. He marches upstairs, while I search the ground floor.

'Nothing up here, boss,' he calls out. 'Just empty rooms and pigeon shit.'

The bathroom stinks of mildew and only contains a cistern and old tin bath. The kitchen is a shell. This building would have been a farmhouse back in the day, with views across open fields, but now there's no sign of life.

'Someone's in the cellar,' Deane suddenly yells out.

He's standing in the hallway, tugging a door handle. When I make him stop for a moment, we both hear a dry, rustling sound. This must be the right place, yet it feels darker than ever, as our torch beams slice through the air. Deane stands back as I deliver a few hard kicks to the door, until the boards crack. A family of rats scuttle through the opening as we head down the steps. Two single mattresses lie side by side on the floor. The sisters could easily have been kept here, alongside rats that must enter through the vent in the wall. If Noah was kept here, he's already been moved. The sound we heard must have been vermin, exploring their empire. The ceiling is covered in mould, and we can't stay down here much longer. Lawrie is wheezing already, his asthma triggered by the polluted air.

'Only a psycho would leave kids in a place like this.' He chokes out the words.

'Gannick will find out, don't worry.'

'What now, boss?' he asks.

I don't have a quick reply. The truth is, I've got no answers. Shadow's shrill bark reaches me again, from outside, but it feels like we're running in circles.

48

Mai is heaving for breath when she drops behind a hedgerow, with the baby still in his sling. A soft voice reaches her as she recovers. The girl with the dark hair appears at her side, her hand outstretched, placating, her finger pressed to her lips, telling Mai to stay silent.

'Thank God you got out,' the girl whispers. 'Quick, follow me.'

Mai chases after her through the darkness, stumbling over fallen branches, until they squeeze through a gap in the fence. She's still so weak it feels like they've been running for hours when the girl finally bundles her into a shed, then closes the door. Mai is too shocked to ask questions. It's the first time she's spoken to anyone except the man since Tuyet was taken, but her helper is too busy gazing out of the window to notice her reactions.

'It's okay, no one followed us here.'

Mai is trembling when the girl finally turns round. The moonlight exposes cushions and blankets, piled in the corner. It's a relief to sit down, with the baby sprawled in her lap. The girl studies her with open curiosity, her head cocked to one side. She lays one of the blankets over the baby to keep him warm.

'That cut looks sore.' The girl undoes the scarf around her neck, then ties it round Mai's hand.

'Why are you helping me?'

The girl's smile wavers. 'Bad things are happening here, but no one cares, except my friends. We can't even trust the police. I'll tell them about you and your baby once it's safe. Okay?'

'He's not mine. Take him, please,' Mai begs. 'If the man comes, he'll kill us both.'

'He's safer with you for now.' The girl stoops in front of her. 'He'll hurt me too, if he knows what I did. I have to fetch help from someone we can trust.'

'Stay safe, please. I have no one but you.'

The girl touches her hand again. 'What's your name?'

'Mai. And yours?'

'Sinead. You can trust me, Mai, I promise, but you have to stay hidden. We can't let him find you.'

The girl fishes inside a canvas bag slung across her chest, then hands her a can of Coke, a chocolate bar, and a bag of crisps, before slipping outside.

Mai eats the crisps in handfuls, cramming them into her mouth, then studies her tiny hiding place. It's just two metres long, colder than the basement, but bright with moonlight. She's elated to be free at last. The shed contains gardening equipment, rakes and hoes, plus an old picnic table. Mai uses the biggest objects to block the door. When she peers outside the land looks tranquil. Open fields stretch to the dark horizon, with no cars or houses nearby, yet the isolation feels terrifying.

Mai's instinct tempts her to take the baby and run outside again, to get further away from the man, but she's too weak. She collapses on the cushions again, drifting into sleep, with the baby in her arms. The last sound she hears is a dog howling in a field nearby. The noise is high and desolate, like the creature can't find its way home.

49

Isla and Eddie are sailing over, leaving Ray to finish the search on Bryher. They've circled St Helen's by boat, making sure the killer hasn't returned to the original burial place. Deane looks disappointed when I instruct him to meet them at the harbour. I want him to search any boat he finds, then the ones anchored in coves further up the coast. We're running out of places on land to search, and whoever seized Noah could be planning to escape by sea. Deane grumbles briefly, then does as he's told. I'm painfully aware that time's passing much too fast. The whole evening has been wasted, chasing loose ends. When I check my watch, it's after 10.00 pm.

I only remember the van has broken down once Lawrie's gone. It feels like the islands are conspiring against me. They suddenly feel much too big, with acres of dark fields to search. I close my eyes and imagine the killer's next move. Their behaviour's been measured until now. I hope they'll hide Noah somewhere safe then hunker down, to avoid discovery and assess their options.

I set off on foot cross country, determined to search every barn and outbuilding I pass, with Shadow at my side. The landscape feels calm, despite my panic, after days of driving rain. The wind is holding its breath as I trace the boundaries of fields, passing turnstiles and drystone walls.

Shadow slows his pace as we reach Hugh Town. It's like he knows we'll only find Noah by staying calm. He falls into step as I head towards Phillip Warleggan's home one last time. The old man has played the respectable citizen for decades, but I saw his true colours today, and his fury about being under suspicion. It's possible he's working in tandem with his close friend, Steve Angarrack. Warleggan's home has been checked repeatedly, but not since Noah was taken.

The lights are out in his property. If he's guilty he must have nerves of steel, to keep a young girl captive right opposite the chief of police's home. But Madron could be in on it too. No one answers when I ring the doorbell. My tension's rising. Warleggan could have sailed over to Bryher in his boat, seized Noah, then escaped by sea.

His door is unlocked, like many properties in Scilly. All the beds are made, the rooms smelling of polish. Everything feels too clean and innocent. The man's law-abiding exterior may be a cover for the type of evil you see once in a decade. He'd be furious to find me poking around again. It's lucky he's not here to slow me down.

My dog's behaviour keeps changing. He's turning in circles, confused by the smell of air freshener in the hallway. Shadow only calms down again when he follows me out into the garden. I use my torch to hunt in Warleggan's shed for a chisel and crowbar, then use them to break into the old smuggler's cottage. I prop my torch on the floor and attack the nailed-up door inside with all my strength. Ancient plaster showers from the wall when it finally creaks open.

Shadow gives a piercing howl, but his warning comes too late. A hard kick to my back sends me hurtling through the doorway and headfirst down a flight of stairs. My ribs bump over each tread, then my shoulders hit the stone floor with an ugly crunching sound. I land in a heap, unable to move, until the door slams above me. Someone laughs in the distance. The sound is high and grating, like a violin out of tune.

50

Mai cradles the baby. He shifts position on her chest, his body heavy with sleep. She's afraid of waking him as she peers out of the window. A torch beam is raking across the field ahead. Maybe people are searching for her, but it could be the man, on her trail? She's longing for Sinead to return. When she listens hard, she hears a new sound. It's a shuffling noise, of boots on wet ground, too heavy for a young girl. It must be the man; he'll find her if the baby cries. She covers his mouth gently, muffling him, then she pulls a tarpaulin over them both, hoping the man won't look inside.

Mai's heart leaps into her mouth again when someone's weight thuds against the door. It creaks as they try to shunt it open, but it holds firm. The shed floods with light coming through the window. She keeps still under the tarpaulin, with the baby clutched tight, but he's sensed her fear. When he startles awake she has to cover his mouth again before he can make a sound.

It takes ages for the light to fade and the footsteps to trudge away. Was her decision right or wrong? It might have been another stranger wanting to help her, like Sinead. But it could have been the man, furious that she's escaped. She's convinced he'll kill her if she drops her guard. Mai takes the knife from inside her dress and keeps it in hand, as the baby starts to cry.

51

Everything hurts when I open my eyes. My shoulder's burning, the pain too intense to ignore. It felt the same when I dislocated it playing rugby. It takes me two attempts to stand up, and the cave-like space isn't helping. The cellar is pitch-black, smelling of coal, tar and alcohol. Smugglers would have hidden here, under the false floor, to cheat the customs men. I'm surprised they dug such a deep space, but it would have held plenty of looted cargo.

Pain shoots through my shoulder again, blinding me. I take a deep breath, bracing myself, and press my arm hard against the wall, shunting the bone back into joint. There's a starburst of pain so powerful I feel sick. But it's worked – my arm's moving freely again. It looks like being my only piece of good luck. My pockets are empty; everything scattered when I fell. I run my fingertips over the dark ground, hunting for my phone, but it's in pieces. Only my torch is working. I use it to search the place, aware that whoever put me here will come back soon. I can't prove it was Warleggan, but it's his property. He may have followed me straight here.

The cellar looks ghostly by torchlight. Furniture is stacked against the walls. There are wooden beer kegs too, piled high and thick with dust. Shadows flicker over piles of chairs, covered in dust, and a dressmaker's mannequin appears to be edging in my direction. If the lost girls were held in such a cramped space, their lives must have been hellish. I run back up the wooden stairs, then try to kick the door down, but it's made of solid oak, and the lock's heavy duty too. My best chance of escape is via another opening, if I can find one.

I'm checking the walls when a noise comes from the floor above. My hands bunch into fists instantly. 'Show yourself, you fucking coward,' I yell out.

Shadow barks in the distance. I bellow his name and the sound comes nearer, then fades. Even he won't be able to help me this time. My dog loves opening doors, but a lock and key are beyond any dog's abilities.

I'm hunting for a weapon when there's a sudden burst of light and something is thrown downstairs, with a clatter of metal hitting each step. I inhale the dry stink of petrol, then a light flickers, and the door above slams shut once more. Someone has lit a match, igniting a stream of paraffin. Flames cascade down the stairs, and panic silences me. The fire is already too powerful to quell without water. They plan to burn me alive, inside a room crammed with junk. I don't want to die like this, alone and terrified, without seeing my family again.

Fire snakes across the floor towards me, setting everything it touches alight. I shunt objects into its path, building a barricade from tea chests and old chairs, to buy myself time. I don't have long. The room is already filling with smoke, the fumes choking me.

52

Mai is just drifting into an exhausted sleep when Sinead says her name in a low whisper. When she opens the door, the cold is intense. It seems to have penetrated her bones, making them so brittle, they could snap like twigs. The baby cries in protest, even though he's swaddled in blankets. When moonlight enters the cramped space, Mai sees that Sinead is scared too, her lips set in a tight line.

'You're brave to help me,' Mai murmurs, her teeth chattering.

'It's okay, but we have to go somewhere safer, Mai.'

'I can't run anymore.'

'I'll help, don't worry. We should leave right now.'

The girl reaches for the baby, but Mai clutches him tighter. Her own child was stolen. It's her duty to protect this one with her life.

'Let me carry him for a bit, then you can move faster.' Sinead's voice is so gentle, Mai loosens her grip on the baby.

'Do your family know about me?' she whispers.

'No.' Misery crosses Sinead's face. 'My dad might be involved. He's been seen, sailing to St Helen's at night.'

Mai stares back at her. Could Sinead be the man's daughter? If it's true, she's risking everything to help her escape. She wants to ask questions, but Sinead is already leaving, with the baby in her arms. Mai bends low as she runs, hoping no one will spot them through the hedgerow, as the cold bites deeper.

53

I'm struggling to breathe, until I remember my fire training at the Met and drop to the floor. Smoke rises, so staying low is my best chance of surviving. It feels like my heart is trying to break its way out of my chest. I have to see Noah and Nina again. I close my eyes, suppressing the panic. I can't rely on anyone calling the fire brigade, and if they do, nothing happens fast in Scilly. By the time the tractor arrives, towing its water tank, I'll be embers. The flames are closing in on me now, their dry crackling noise rising as a barrel catches fire. The heat's so intense I can hardly breathe, and the smoke is thickening. The air's getting blacker all the time.

I know it's my last chance when I run my fingertips along the wall with shaky hands. A sudden breeze touches my skin, giving me a moment of hope. There must be an opening in the wall somewhere. The fire is so powerful, it illuminates the space, orange flames twisting upwards, spinning like dervishes. It's getting louder too. Wood cracks like bursts of gunshot, the fire churning, as beer kegs explode in the heat.

Shadow's bark suddenly reaches me again. When I listen hard, it's coming from behind some panels stacked against the wall. I stand up, choking for breath, and stack layers of wood in front of me. They provide a shield, but now I'm trapped in a corner. If I step sideways I'll be caught by the flames. Panic's almost conquering me, until I spot a circular opening directly above my head. The smugglers would have dropped goods through it, hiding them before the customs men came. And then I see Shadow at the top of the chute, staring down at me, his bark rising in pitch. It's just wide enough for me to squeeze through the vertical opening, but the sides are sheer. I've got no way of climbing up there as the flames edge closer.

My air supply is nearly gone. Smoke billows in circles as I leap for the opening again, knowing it's my last chance. I'll black out here, if the flames don't catch me first.

Suddenly a new sound reaches me. A man is calling my name. Then a length of rope drops through the opening. Fire laps at my heels as I haul myself up it, hand over hand. I fail at the first attempt, because dragging my bodyweight up the rope takes effort, and the chute's slick walls are unforgiving. I pause at the bottom for a moment, before gathering all my strength and trying again. The opening is so tight I have to squirm upwards like an eel, with no idea who's waiting at the top.

I'm coughing my guts up when I finally surface, into the night's clean air. I lie on my back while Shadow stands over me, whimpering and licking my face. I must have passed out for a second, because my head's groggy and my vision's blurred when my eyes open. Lawrie Deane is kneeling beside me as I cough my guts up, expelling smoke with each breath. He's still holding the rope he used to haul me up the chute.

'How did you find me, Lawrie?'

'Shadow fetched me from the harbour. He was going nuts, so I followed him. When I saw the smoke, I ran straight here.'

'The pair of you saved my life.'

'Only just. I almost fell down that bloody chute. You weigh a ton, boss. You should lose a few pounds.'

I choke out a laugh. I'm covered in soot, and smoke is belching from the concealed opening, but I've been given a second chance. When I glance back down the chute there's nothing left beneath me, except a cauldron of orange flames.

54

Mai feels dizzy when Sinead finally slows down. After so long in captivity, the outside world feels alien. There are too many stars overhead, the moon's brilliance hurting her eyes. Instinct makes her reach for the baby again. Sinead is gentle when she places him back in her arms. She's relieved to hold him again; it's her job to keep him safe.

Mai comes to a halt when she sees a male figure waiting under a tree. Panic grips her. It was like this when she was kidnapped. Men left her and the other children at new locations every few days, then another driver would force them back into the van. They were too terrified to scream as it bumped over broken tarmac. She's about to run away when Sinead grips her hand.

'He's a friend, Mai. His name's Fordie. He wants to help us.'

Sinead releases a low whistle and the figure approaches. Mai sees that he's a boy, not a man; tall, with a kind face. His gentle expression reduces Mai's panic. Sinead holds a whispered conversation with him. When the pair sets off, she follows.

A tower looms from the darkness, its stone walls round, the windows unlit. Mai has never seen a building like it in her life. She battles her panic with each step. Sinead waits for her to catch up, her face solemn in the moonlight. If she really is the man's daughter, why is she risking her own safety? Mai places one foot in front of the other, determined to follow, even if Sinead's actions make no sense. Whatever happens has to be better than the man's brutal attacks.

55

I rub soot from Shadow's fur, soothing his panic. He always finds a way to help, but the near miss has left him unsettled; he stays close, watching as my breathing eases. My shoulder's still burning, but the pain barely registers.

'Do you think Warleggan's got Noah, boss?' Deane asks.

'It looks like it. He's destroyed all the evidence – fire wipes out DNA.'

'I can't believe it; everyone trusts him here.'

'He fooled us all.' I wipe soot from my eyes. 'Give me your work phone, please, Lawrie. Mine's melted by now.'

Deane drops it into my hand without hesitation. 'I've got my personal phone on me too. You can call me on it.'

The fire team is arriving, but it will take more than one tank to stop the blaze. Smoke is still billowing from the chute, and flames are dancing behind the windows. It took just minutes for fire to consume the entire basement, then burn through the wooden floor.

I want to search the grounds again for Warleggan, in case he's still prowling around, then I need to check Madron's place too. He knows it's empty, so it would be a good place to hide. I send Deane back to the harbour to help search the boats moored there. Shadow chases after him when he sets off, which surprises me. He helped to save my life but he's transferred his affections. Maybe he just needs food. Deane always feeds him biscuits at the station, in exchange for tricks.

When I look downhill, there are pinpricks of light from Eddie and Isla's torches. Deane told me that they've split up, searching either side of the harbour. I pray they'll find Noah safe on Warleggan's boat as I hunt for the old man again.

56

Mai glances over her shoulder, but no one's in sight. All she can see up ahead are muddy fields and the round-walled tower, rearing into the night sky. Its black silhouette looks forbidding, but Fordie runs towards it with a loping stride. She watches him use a tool, like a needle, to open the lock. His smile's victorious when the handle twists, allowing them to rush inside.

'Where did you learn to do that?' Sinead asks.

He grins at her. 'At school, for a dare.'

Mai glances around. The room is circular and full of expensive furniture. Its opulence feels daunting. Her trainers will leave dirty marks on the carpet. She's never witnessed this much luxury. In the moonlight flooding through the window, she sees two long sofas, plush rugs on the floor and shelves full of books.

'Sleep here tonight,' Fordie says. 'By morning you'll be safe.'

'There's a network of bad people,' Sinead whispers. 'We need to expose them all, but that'll take time. We're going to tell people we trust, then come back for you soon. The door's self-locking, Mai. No one can get inside. Will you be okay on your own for a little while?'

'Please come back fast.'

'We will, I promise.'

She puts her arm round Mai's shoulders. The hug only lasts a few seconds, but it helps her to relax. No one has touched her like that since her sister disappeared, months ago. She's forgotten how kindness feels. The sensation revives emotions she believed were lost forever.

Mai's fear returns after Fordie and Sinead leave. She moves from window to window, checking the building's secure. There's no chance of rest until she's certain the place is safe. She climbs the stairs, feeling her way through the dark, right to the top of the building. Tall windows have been cut into its curved walls.

She can see in every direction from up here. Mai understands the landscape, at last. The dark sea unrolls into the distance, with islands littering its surface, beautiful and austere. She sits by the window, with the baby on her lap. He's fretful after too long in the cold, so she hums a lullaby under her breath. Her body's longing for rest, but her eyes stay focussed on the fields ahead, scanning for even the smallest movement.

57

Deane's phone rings in my pocket ten minutes later, when I'm still searching Warleggan's garden for signs of him. My hopes lift, but all I can hear is the sergeant's ragged breathing, and a dull moan of pain.

'Where are you, Lawrie?'

'By the quay...' His speech runs out.

'Answer me. Are you hurt?'

The quay is only five minutes away, so I can't blame a faulty signal when the line dies. I know he's in trouble. Maybe the whole police team is, now we're homing in on the killer. The streets are deserted when I run down to the harbour. It's 11.30 pm, and people will be going to bed, leaving the town empty. It's a network of tiny lanes, with old cottages clustered together. I can't see Deane anywhere, and Shadow's vanished too, just when I need him to sniff out danger.

Eddie hurries towards me across the sand. Moonlight is playing tricks with his face, making him look a decade older.

'Lawrie just rang,' I tell him. 'I think he's hurt. We need to find him.'

'I'll check the alley.'

Eddie appears too concerned to notice my soot-marked clothes and filthy skin. His torch beam reflects from the walls as he gathers pace. But it's Isla's shout that goes up a few moments later. She's found Deane curled on the ground behind The Ship pub. He's unconscious, but at least he's alive.

I can see that Deane has tried to escape his attacker, crawling between two industrial bins, making himself invisible. He's lying in a foetal position, unconscious, with his phone on the ground by his hand. The killer must have been here recently, but the bastard's great at disappearing like a conjuror.

Eddie did first-aid training recently, his movements confident when he lays Deane in the recovery position, using his jacket as a pillow. Some of my tension releases when Deane's arms jerk at his sides. There's an ugly bruise developing on his jaw, but least he's alive. His skin's pale when he tries to sit up, then collapses again.

'Lie still, Lawrie,' I tell him. 'You'll be fine. Can you say what happened?'

'Too dark to see much. He kicked me in the guts, then legged it.' His words are a dull whisper. 'Feels like my ribs are broken.'

'Want me to take him to the hospital, boss?' Eddie asks.

'No, I need you looking for Noah. Someone else can drive him.'

The Ship's landlord appears once I bang on his door. He was just locking up the pub when he heard the commotion from the street. He agrees to take Deane to hospital, then helps him into his car. My worries about Noah have drowned everything else out. It looks like the killer is trying to break my team, targeting each of us in turn.

When I look back up the hill, smoke is still rising from the burning cottage, but Warleggan is still out of reach.

58

The tower is so quiet, Mai slips into a dream. An hour ticks past, and the river of her childhood is rushing by, swollen with rain. The water is blood red as currents twist under the surface. Mai hears the river's voice grow louder. Suddenly the bank collapses under her feet, and the baby is washed from her arms. Guilt roars in her ears as the torrent swallows everything in its path, leaving only terror behind. She knows the boy is lost forever. Water never returns what it steals.

Mai's fingers dig into the armchair as she startles awake, her mouth dry with fear. She can't tell how much time has passed, but it's still dark outside, and the baby is still sleeping on her lap. Only a thin shaft of moonlight illuminates the room. There's no sound, yet she senses danger edging nearer. Someone has found a way inside. Or maybe she's imagining it? She hears a clock ticking and rain spitting against the window, then the dog she heard before howls in the distance. Now there's a scuffling noise. Someone is trying not to make a sound as they cross the floor below.

Mai springs to her feet, clutching the baby tighter. She has stood on the riverbank too long, watching the water race past. Now she must fight the tide, like her mother did, whatever it takes.

59

Warleggan's boat is beached on the sand. I hoped to find Noah there, but I was fooling myself. The man wouldn't get far on a small, converted fishing trawler, with basic GPS.

Eddie looks tired when I jump down from the deck. I can tell he's still shaken by Deane's attack, but he's not letting it slow him down. He's about to search the next boat when his phone rings. I hear Gannick on speakerphone from ten metres away, her tone strident, but I can't distinguish individual words.

'She's got a match for the carpet fibres,' Eddie says. 'They're from Pilot's Retreat.'

'Warleggan's house, you mean?'

'No, boss. They're from the floor of a built-in wardrobe in one of Madron's spare bedrooms. I took the sample myself: you told us to treat our own houses like all the rest, so I bagged it for Gannick to check. Maybe he left it there, out of sight, when the rest was taken up.'

I stare back at him. 'It's the wrong time for jokes, Eddie.'

'I'm serious, she says it's a direct match.'

We exchange a look of shock then set off at the same moment. I try to keep pace with Eddie as we run uphill, but it feels like my lungs are still burning, and my shoulder aches with every step. My thoughts are slow to catch up too. Madron is a church-going pillar of the community. He's been a thorn in my side, but I've never doubted his motives until now. Houses blur as I run past, my breathing laboured when we reach the cul-de-sac. If the DCI's really behind all this, there's a danger he'll take his own life. He's too proud to accept punishment. Madron wouldn't last long in jail, on a diet of insults and violence.

I'm not expecting him to be at home, and little has changed in the cul-de-sac. The fire wagon is still parked outside Warleggan's home, the air acrid with smoke. I let Eddie batter down the door when we reach Madron's bungalow, despite his smaller build, to avoid dislocating my shoulder again. My heart's skipping beats as I hit the light switch.

We move through the house fast, and find Madron slumped over the desk in his office, barely conscious.

'I'll deal with him. Bring Gannick here, Eddie. Let her scour the place.'

It takes all my willpower not to shake the truth out of Madron. He's white-faced and broken, no longer a threat to anyone. It's possible he was in Warleggan's property earlier and he pushed me downstairs, hoping to protect his reputation. Now his strength's gone. He's babbling nonsense, his gaze out of focus.

'What have you done, Alan? Carpet fibres from here were found at the murder scene.'

'Brain fog, headache.' He reaches for my arm. 'Not mine, carpet.'

'You're lying, I know it's yours. Where've you taken Noah?'

'No.' Madron's hand clutches my wrist. 'Die at home.'

'Maybe you wrapped that girl's body here, and the baby too. Who's been helping you?'

'Gift.' He shakes his head, exhausted. 'Carpet, no, old friend...'

His speech runs out, like he's fighting for breath. It strikes me suddenly that he may be trying to place the blame on his old pal Warleggan, and if he's guilty, others could be in the know. His wife may have been in on his secret dungeon for the two girls all along. Surely he couldn't have kept such a huge secret from her? If she turned a blind eye to his evil, she's equally guilty. I'll make sure the New Zealand force deals with her too.

'Phillip Warleggan's a mate of yours. Did you two put those girls in his basement together?'

Madron has slipped out of reach. I can't tell if it's an act, or he's genuinely losing consciousness, slumped over his desk. I call the duty manager at the hospital to collect him. This time, I want him kept under lock and key.

Gannick's arriving when I hurry outside. The determination on her face steadies me; she'll discover what Madron did. She's already barking out instructions to Eddie, telling him to search the grounds while she starts on the interior. Eddie gets to work immediately, inspecting Madron's garden, his expression puzzled.

'Gannick thinks there's a bricked-up doorway in the hall, boss. Maybe there's a cellar under here, with a concealed entrance.'

'I've seen a locked doorway too. Use bolt-cutters to remove the padlock, can you?'

'She's on it already, boss,' Eddie says.

Madron's obsessive neatness makes more sense now. He's hidden his true nature for years, behind that calm façade, going to church each Sunday, playing the Good Samaritan. No one would dream he'd ever do wrong. Nausea rises in my stomach as I scan the ground. The sickness comes from failing to protect my son, and swallowing Madron's lies, for all these years.

60

Mai hunts for the best place to hide, stumbling in the dark. Luck is with her for once. She finds a bathroom with a bolt on the door. Mai carries the baby inside, then crouches on the floor. The air smells of soap and luxury. She would love to run some hot water and wash properly, for the first time in years, but she keeps still, with all her senses alert. The baby wakes up, bawling, giving away their hiding place.

Light shines under the door and she hears the man's voice. His tone is sharp with anger.

'Come out, Mai, there's no time for games. We have to talk.'

Mai remains silent, unwilling to offer him a single word.

'Remember I've looked after you all these years. Doesn't that count for anything?' She still doesn't reply, so his voice rises to a shout. 'You little bitch. You never loved me, did you? It was all a lie.'

Mai hears the pain in his voice but doesn't flinch. She keeps her body braced against the door and pulls the knife from her pocket, clutching it in her fist. He pounds the door harder this time. It's only when he starts to kick out that her fear spirals. The bolt will break, if his onslaught continues. She hears him muttering curses, and can only pray that he's too weak to destroy her shelter.

61

I help Eddie set up lights in Madron's garden, because the locked internal door gave us nothing; it was just a cupboard packed with expensive bottles of wine. Outside is our best chance. If Noah's hidden underground here, Madron will have worked hard to conceal the entrance. We can't waste time collecting arc lamps from the station, so we use electric lanterns from his shed to light our search.

I'm staying focussed on the ground at my feet when my uncle calls from Bryher. The whole island has been scoured, with no sign of Noah, but Ray has worked out how he was taken. Someone moored a small boat below Shipman Head Down. Marks on the sand show that it was dragged across the beach, then back into the waves at low tide.

Madron couldn't have done that in his condition. It must be someone stronger, with access to a boat and knowledge of the local tides. It's rare for anyone to moor by Shipman Point because the beach is submerged at high tide, but it gave the killer ideal access to the pub. He could seize Noah, then scramble back down the rocks and sail away. Warleggan comes to mind again, as Madron's helper. He's still missing, but his boat is moored in Hugh Town quay. If it's him, he used another vessel to reach Bryher. It feels like suspects are vanishing before my eyes.

Sinead Harcourt's conspiracy theory about the islands' elite might have turned out to be true. I should have listened harder. If Madron and Warleggan have carried out the abductions, she was right all along, and more of the islands' elders could be involved. They've fooled us, by placing themselves above suspicion.

Gannick rushes towards me, hand outstretched. 'I found this in his cabinet,' she says.

Another jade good-luck charm lies on her palm. It's a replica of the lotus flower we've seen on the prayer shawls, with the same delicate petals. The sight of it leaves me floundering. I can't ignore the evidence that my boss is linked to the killing, yet it wasn't him that seized Noah from Bryher. I'm certain now that he has an accomplice.

When the island's ambulance arrives, Eddie and I lead Madron outside, then force him into the vehicle. The DCI protests in a dull scream at leaving his home. The sound is pitiful, yet I don't offer him comfort. If he's helped to kidnap Noah, sympathy is the last thing he deserves.

62

Mai drags in a breath. The man has stopped beating the door, for now, but she's still not safe. Maybe he's gathering his strength to try again. Sinead promised to return soon, but her advice to relax in this strange building hasn't worked. At least the baby remains calm. His weight feels warm and comforting, but Mai is more terrified for his safety than her own. The man's anger turns him into a monster, capable of destroying everything in his path.

She rises slowly to her feet. Mai has thought of a way to let Sinead know that she's in trouble. When she pulls the cord dangling from the ceiling, the overhead light flicks on, then off. It's her only way to communicate with the world outside. Anyone that looks up will see her signal, pulsing from the tower's top floor. Mai pulls the cord again. She's determined to keep sending out bursts of light, at five second intervals.

The silence feels ominous. The man may still be waiting outside, but she's praying her rescuers will come.

63

My head's full of competing theories. If Madron played a part in all this, he'll be no danger to anyone at the hospital. It's Warleggan we must find. I still believe he shoved me down the stairs, and he's managed to escape detection. A plume of smoke rises from the ruined building at the bottom of his garden, but his home is unaffected.

'Who are Warleggan's closest friends?' I ask Eddie.

'Most people like him.' He's still on his hands and knees, inspecting the ground. 'He goes to church with Madron and the Angarracks; maybe they socialise too.'

Eddie's point chimes with Warleggan's claim that he's close to the Angarrack family. He might even be comforting Steve, now that his wife has left him. We're only a few minutes away from the Angarracks' house, here in Hugh Town, so I leave Eddie and Gannick at work in Madron's bungalow. The floor is covered in plastic sheeting, and she's shining her luminol wand over the walls of the one bedroom with a yard of red carpet lining a built-in wardrobe. There's an avid look on Gannick's face as she uses her tools to hunt for bloodshed. The property looks like an action scene from CSI. Panic only bubbles in my throat again when I remember that Gannick is also searching for evidence that Noah's been hurt.

I bat the idea away and set off to visit Steve Angarrack, despite his threats earlier. Light glares from his property, even though it's well after midnight, and the front door hangs open. I yell Steve's name but get no answer. When I step inside, I catch myself in the hall mirror – covered in soot, from my narrow escape from the fire. My face is so tense with panic, it's like confronting a stranger.

Music is spilling down the hallway. It's a rock anthem from before I was born. It seems too upbeat for a man whose wife believes him capable of murder, but I have to know the truth about his late-night boat trips.

Angarrack is hunched over his kitchen table, halfway down a bottle of vodka. He doesn't seem to care when I flick the off button on his sound system, casting us into silence. The man looks broken.

'You again. Been having a bonfire?' he mutters, then brandishes the bottle in my direction. 'Have a drink with me.'

'No, thanks.' I drop onto the seat opposite. 'I need your help, Steve. My son's been taken.'

He fixes me with a drunken stare. 'How do you mean?'

'Someone grabbed Noah from his buggy on Bryher.' I keep my gaze on his face, unblinking. 'Tell me what you know, Steve. The islands' powerholders are behind it, and they're sticking together.'

'I was never one of them.' He takes another slug of vodka.

'Explain your night-time boat trips for me, can you?'

'Stupidity, on my part.' He shakes his head. 'I fell for someone, because she listened, and saw past my image. I'd have done anything for her, until I came to my senses.'

My thoughts suddenly slot into place. 'Denise Laramie?'

'Emma was kind, like her, at the start. Then work took over. We forgot that family matters more than status or money.' He gazes down at the table. 'I sailed over to Tresco to see Denise a few times, then ended it. But too late. Emma's in bits, thanks to me. She even thinks I helped to kill that girl.'

'Did you?'

'Of course not. She just wants to shame me, in public. I'll have to leave the islands and start over.'

Tears of self-pity leak from his eyes. Angarrack has committed adultery, but not cold-blooded murder. It explains why Denise reacted to him so powerfully at the school, like he was some kind of God. I feel almost certain he's been too busy destroying his marriage to hurt anyone else.

64

Mai peers out at the dark landscape. Nothing is moving, except tree branches below, shifting in the breeze. Sinead can't have seen the flashing light, or maybe the man's tracked her down too. Mai goes on pulling the cord, even though her hands are shaking. Surely another rescuer will see her signal flickering?

The building is silent now. All she can hear is an owl crying overhead as it hunts for prey. The baby sits on the floor with his back to the wall, chuntering happily to himself. He's dealing with the situation fine, but for how long? Mai wishes she could offer up a prayer to keep him safe, but she stopped believing in her parents' gods years ago, when they failed to set her free.

Mai pictures the lotus symbol instead, beautiful and familiar. She remembers the flowers that blossomed near the river, every day. They closed like a bunched fist at night, then reopened each morning, full of hope. Her body feels tight with fear, but maybe the sun will warm her skin again one day, and her muscles will relax, like petals.

Suddenly the door shudders in its frame, making the baby cry out in shock. The man's fists pound on the thin panel of wood that's keeping her safe. A rush of anger flares in Mai's chest.

'Leave us alone, you monster!' she yells.

Curses tear from Mai's throat like a dam breaking. It's the first time she's shown her true feelings, no longer paralysed by fear. Her pride is slowly returning. She won't cower from him anymore.

The onslaught stops, for the time being. She reaches for the cord again. Her signal flashes brightly, keeping her hopes alive.

65

Pete Harcourt calls me on Lawrie's phone as I leave the Angarracks' house. Sinead is missing. I remember the solemn look on her face when she claimed that senior members of the community were committing terrible crimes and trafficking children. The girl loves to investigate matters for herself, so I need to track her down. Her curiosity makes her vulnerable, but she may also have answers about where Noah's been taken.

I tell Harcourt to wait for me at home. Angarrack's door is still open, allowing me to go inside and seize his car keys from where I spotted them on the hall table. He's in no state to complain, or even care who borrows his high-end car. There's no sign of him objecting when I set off for the Harcourts' in his brand-new Audi.

The lanes are still wet from rainfall, forcing me to slow down. I can't skid into a ditch and lose my chance to find Noah. My heart's still beating at a frantic pace. Statistics from the Murder Squad are keeping me on edge. My chances of finding Noah are falling all the time. Hostages must be rescued before their captors lose patience. I still don't understand the killer's motive in taking Noah, after leaving another child on our doorstep. I still believe more than one person is involved, each with different motives.

The Harcourts' place has lights burning in the downstairs windows. The house is silent for once, with no classical music playing. The place appears to be empty. It looks like Harcourt has ignored my advice to remain at home and rushed outside, leaving the door open. There's no sign of Sinead either. What if she's paid the ultimate price for insisting that the island's elite are evil? I have to get hold of her, but I only have Lawrie's phone, full of his contacts instead of mine. I scroll through the names and spot Annie Ford's number. I remember her saying that Sinead has been her son's closest friend for years.

Annie's voice is loud with anger when she picks up.

'I need Sinead Harcourt's number, urgently, please, Annie.'

I hear her hiss out a few swear words before she rings off, but she doesn't let me down. Moments later she's texted the number to me. My breath catches when I call it and Sinead picks up instantly.

'I've been looking for you,' her voice falls to a low murmur. 'Mai's in danger; you have to help her.'

'What have you been doing, Sinead? Where is she?'

'I can't say. We don't trust any of them: not Phillip, or your boss, or my dad. Even he might be involved.' Her breath's ragged like she's holding back tears.

'Just tell me where Mai is.'

'Telegraph Tower. Go straight there. We'll meet you.'

She rings off before there's time to ask if she's seen Noah, but I try to stay focussed. I can see the tower in the distance when I exit the Harcourts' place. It's only a short hike away across the fields, but the ground's sodden, mud sticking to my boots like concrete, weighing me down. My bones are protesting as I move faster. It feels like my body and mind are held together by pure adrenaline, as I keep my gaze fixed on the tall building ahead. It used to be a look-out point for the coastguard, but now it resembles a beacon. I catch sight of a light from the top floor, then it comes again, and my spirits lift. Someone appears to be sending out an SOS from a top-floor window. Light pulses there every few seconds, the rhythm quick and anxious. The signal gives me a shred of hope that I'm getting somewhere at last, and Shadow has picked up on it too. He bounds towards me, out of the darkness, giving a series of low barks.

I can't just hang around working out where he's been. The flickering light in the tower is drawing me closer, like a moth to a flame.

66

'Come on, we don't have long.' The man's voice is gentle for once, echoing through the locked door. 'Let me say goodbye. You owe me that much at least.'

She doesn't react, remembering the pain he's caused.

'You loved me too, at the start. I saw it in your eyes. We're meant to be together, Mai. I'll die here without you. I've been alone all my life, until you saved me.'

The man's childlike tone puts Mai in control at last. The feeling is heady, like she's been drugged. It's a surprise when he falls silent, then his footsteps thud away, down the stairs. She relaxes, for a moment, too exhausted to think, with the baby clutched in her arms.

67

I arrive at the tower breathless, then a figure stumbles out of the darkness. It's Phillip Warleggan. Shadow hasn't forgiven him for almost burning me alive. My dog flies at him with jaws snapping.

Warleggan looks petrified. 'Call him off, for God's sake.'

I grab Shadow's collar, but he carries on barking at top volume, and I don't blame him. If Warleggan has laid a finger on Noah, he deserves every punishment going. I swallow a breath, to stop myself yelling.

'What are you doing here, Phillip?'

'Searching for Noah since the local radio raised the alarm. I thought finding him would clear my name, once and for all.' He stares up at the building. 'There's someone in the tower. I heard a man's voice, yelling, just now. He sounded furious.'

'Was it Pete Harcourt?'

'I'm not sure. I was about to call you. I'm not equipped to deal with violent attackers.' His eyes are coal black in the moonlight, glinting with resentment. 'You still see me as your enemy, don't you?'

'Was it you that pushed me down the stairs? I'd be ashes if Lawrie Deane hadn't rescued me.'

Warleggan stares at me like he's baffled, his mouth hanging open. 'Ashes? And what stairs? You're not making sense.'

He could be a gifted actor, or he genuinely doesn't know that his smugglers' hideaway has gone up in flames. But there's no time to waste on his excuses. The light above us is still flashing, like the beam from a lighthouse. I'm desperate to find out who's sending that signal. But when I approach the door it's locked; I don't have a prayer of getting inside without a sledgehammer.

I'm searching around for a rock to lob through a window, when Warleggan produces a key.

'I'm the building's custodian, Ben, authorised to take visitors on tours in summer.'

I snatch it from his hands. 'Helping me now, are you? You've always had too much power. I bet you've got access to loads of other hiding places, so you can move victims around.'

'I don't understand. I'm just trying to help you.'

'Keep out of my way, and guard the place. Don't let anyone else inside.'

I can't guess how Harcourt got inside, if it's his voice Warleggan heard. The old man agrees to wait by the entrance, but I don't trust him an inch. Shadow noses through the opening before me, sniffing the air.

The building is pitch-dark. Nothing happens when I touch a switch, even though light was flaring from the top floor. Someone must be playing games with the fuse box. My torch makes little impact in a room this big, only lighting the way directly ahead. When I yell Harcourt's name, there's no reply. All I can hear is Shadow's bark, loud and frantic, as he races upstairs.

68

Mai pulls the cord again, but the light has stopped working. It felt like this when the kidnappers left her and the other children adrift at sea, on a rising tide. There's no way of communicating with the outside world. She could die here, forgotten, yet her determination to survive is growing stronger all the time.

She can hear the dog barking, closer than before. It sounds like it's inside. The sound fills her with hope, because she loved feeding scraps to the strays that haunted her village. But how did it get in? She can only pray that more help will follow.

Mai peers out of the window, and spots a figure below. It's an old man, gazing up at her. Then she hears new footsteps, faster and more agile than the man's. Is it a rescuer, or another abuser?

Captivity has taught her not to trust anyone. She checks that the bolt is still secure, then waits in the darkness, with her eyes wide open.

69

I stumble in the dark, aware that the killer may have me in his sights. I shine my torch along rounded walls, until I spot the fuse-box over a doorway. The electricity may have been sabotaged. I breathe more easily once I throw the right switch and light is restored. It feels blinding after being in the dark too long, my eyes blinking in protection.

I follow the stairs again. They wind around the tower's circular walls in slow revolutions. The building seems an odd place for danger, with designer furniture and plush carpet, but we've been inside every other building. Noah might be here, and I have to find him alive. I can't go home without our son.

Shadow races past me to the top floor. I yell out to him, afraid the killer has set an ambush for us, but he's already vanished.

70

Mai trembles when she hears the dog whining outside and scratching the door. Instinct makes her open it by a fraction. The dog squeezes through the gap, and she slides the lock back into place. His barking is replaced by a soft whimper, more like a greeting than a threat. She's not afraid, even though he resembles a big grey wolf. He gazes up at the baby, motionless, like a statue. Then he rises onto his back legs to sniff the boy's face. When the baby reaches out to him, gurgling with pleasure, the dog's tail wags hard against the floor.

Mai feels calmer with him at her side. The dog makes no sound when she crouches down, burying her hand in his fur. She can feel his heart beating under her palm. The rhythm is strong and rapid, like he's run for miles to find her. She can read the name printed on his tag because the lights are working again, and many of the words she read in school have stayed in her memory.

'Keep us safe, Shadow,' Mai whispers.

The dog licks her hand. Someone is still moving around on the floor below. She still can't tell if they intend harm or kindness, but the dog is poised at her feet, alert to every sound.

71

I climb the next flight of stairs, but Shadow has stopped barking. I can only hope that he's keeping safe. He's wiped from my mind when I spot something familiar on the top landing. It's a scrap of red fabric. When I pick it up, my heart rate levels. It's one of the mittens Maggie knitted for Noah. After scouring the islands, I must finally be getting close. But my breathing quickens when the lights fail again, casting me into darkness.

The killer has given himself an advantage as I navigate blind through the unfamiliar building. He could have been hiding on the top floor all along, playing games with the circuitry. I flick on my torch, then everything changes. Someone thunders upstairs and barges into me, the force knocking me sideways.

I jump to my feet, but I can't see my attacker in the darkness. My torch has rolled away, across the floor. Someone's approaching again, and my fingers close round a table lamp that I wrench from the wall. The room flickers with torch beams. How many people are in here? It could be a handful of men from the network, like the school kids claim.

I hit out when a fierce light blinds me. I grab my assailant's wrist and wrestle the torch from their hand. When my vision clears, it's Sinead Harcourt, her expression terrified.

'Quick,' she hisses. 'You have to stop him!'

Before I can reply, there's a new sound, one that grabs my heart. An infant is wailing in protest. Is it Noah, or someone else's baby? It's the kind of sound Noah makes when he's tired, or afraid. My attention fixes on it like a laser. It's coming from a room a few steps away. I rush over and try the doorhandle, but it's locked.

'Step away from the door,' I yell out.

I throw my whole weight at it. Pain floods my body, but I don't care. I try it again, breaking the lock with my second attempt.

I step back instinctively, and see Shadow inside, guarding a young black-haired girl. She's emaciated, her form just skin and bone. Relief overwhelms me when I see Noah in her arms. He looks unharmed. But my fear returns when I see the knife clutched in her hand.

'It's okay. You must be Mai, and that's my son you're holding. His name's Noah.' I keep my voice low, fighting my instinct to enter the room and grab him. If I go in too fast, I can't guess what she'll do. 'You're safe now, I promise. Why not hand him to me?'

Someone shunts me aside suddenly, leaving me sprawling in the dark, and my attacker free to enter the bathroom. Now the broken door slams in my face.

I yell for Sinead, but there's no reply, and the truth dawns on me. If the killer was inside the tower waiting for us, Sinead may already be dead.

72

Mai faces the man at last. He stands over her, his face furious in the torchlight.

'You betrayed me, Mai,' he hisses. 'How could you, after everything I sacrificed to keep you safe?'

He lunges forwards suddenly, with hands outstretched, like he plans to strangle her. Mai's fear hardens into courage. She will never let him hurt her again. When she plunges the knife deep into his shoulder the man rears back, bellowing in pain, as she shields the baby. He would have to break her to reach him, and that can't happen.

Mai's tension eases when the man whimpers. He will learn how pain feels. He will learn how it hurts to suffer like she did, when she was longing for freedom and her family.

But before she can do anything else, the door is wrenched open again, and the man is hauled outside and thrown to the floor outside. The tall man stands on the threshold again.

'I'm from the police,' he says. 'Let me help you, please.'

She can only pray that he really is the baby's father, as he claimed.

73

'You're safe now. You can drop the knife,' I say, keeping my voice low.

I'm terrified she'll harm Noah, until the knife clatters onto the tiled floor. A man in black jeans and a hoody is spread-eagled, face down at my feet, where I shoved him to the ground. Right now I don't care who it is, even though blood is oozing from his shoulder, leaving a stain on the floor. My son is handling the situation better than me, his fist curled round the girl's fingers, like he's found a new mother. Sinead Harcourt emerges from the shadows. My panic drops away when I see her approaching the victim in the bathroom to offer comfort. Both girls are taking care of Noah, giving me time to deal with the man I pushed to the floor.

When I turn him over, the man's identity doesn't make sense. It's Lawrie Deane, his skin chalk white, apart from the purple bruise on his jaw.

'What's this?' I ask. 'You should be in hospital.'

Deane must have discharged himself to help us and been stabbed as a result.

'It's okay. We'll soon get that wound under control,' I reassure him.

I grab a towel from the bathroom and press down on his shoulder to stop the bleeding. He's breathing too fast, from panic or the pain of his injury. I'm still stanching Deane's wound when Warleggan's voice calls me from downstairs, and the lights switch on again. It's then that I remind myself the threat's still here. The killer must still be in the building.

But then I look up to check on Noah, and see the expression on Mai's face: she's watching Deane with a cold glare, full of hatred. It's clear she knows him.

For a second I'm frozen.

He holds her gaze, then reaches out his hand. 'Mai, please.'

Deane knows her name. He knows *her* ... My mind whirrs and I'm suddenly dizzy. I clutch at the wall for a moment. Truth wants to penetrate but my mind's refusing it entry.

The girl spits something at him in her own language, pent-up rage spilling from her mouth.

And then I see Deane change. I've known this man for years but never witnessed the monster he's become, until now. The look on his face is murderous.

'You traitor. I saved you and that sister of yours. You little bitch...'

My mind clears and the pieces of the puzzle click into place. The red carpet ... I remember Deane saying that Madron had given him items of furniture...

My hands turn freezing cold as shock takes over. I've trusted this man for years, and seen him as a force for good. All I can do is rock back on my heels and stare down at him. He cowers from the fury and disbelief on my face, but that won't save him. I'll make sure he gets locked away for the maximum time possible, and that he dies in jail.

'You sick bastard,' I mutter under my breath. 'You used your job to stay ahead of the game, so we'd never guess it was you.'

Deane's crimes have been disguised to perfection, thanks to his knowledge of policing. The man's whole existence has been a lie.

'You could have let me burn in that cellar, Lawrie. Why didn't you?'

'I wanted to know how you feel, just once. Everyone thinks you're a hero, but you stole the deputy's job from me. You never even apologised.'

'So it's my fault you kept two girls locked up for years, and got one of them pregnant? That won't play well in court.'

Deane leaps to his feet, despite his injury, swinging his fists. It's more than Shadow can take. His attitude has spun from affection to hatred in a matter of seconds. He leaps up to attack him, until

I grab his collar to prevent him from delivering a savage bite. Deane's courage soon falls away. His trembling is even worse than his victim's when he slumps back to the floor, covering his face with his hands.

74

Mai still feels afraid even though the man's spell is broken. Sinead tries to take the baby from her arms, but she clings to him, even though her friend reassures her that the tall policeman really is Noah's father. Mai's head is spinning with exhaustion. She drops onto a chair still clutching the baby. The dog settles at her feet, standing guard. It could be imaginary, but the creature seems to understand that she still needs his protection.

When the tall man approaches, he looks like a giant, with dirt on his face and black, untidy hair. She's afraid of him until his face softens into a smile.

'My dog likes you, I see.' His voice is gentle.

'He protected us.' She uses her free hand to stroke his fur.

'We've been looking everywhere for you, Mai.'

His words startle her. Have people really been looking for her, all this time?

'I'm Ben Kitto, local police.' He looks down at the baby. 'Thank you for caring for Noah and putting him first. Please let me look after you now, okay?'

'But other baby – where is he?' Mai struggles to find the English words. She points at the man who is crumpled on the floor. 'He took my baby. Lao. Where is he now? Is he...?'

The man smiles. 'Your baby is safe. Lao is in hospital. We'll take you there soon and you can see him.'

Mai's face crumples, the relief feels overwhelming, rushing over her like a tsunami. She will get to hold him again, to touch his skin.

But this good news makes her hungry for news of her sister.

'And Tuyet. Did she get free?' she asks with a small glimmer of hope.

The stricken look on Kitto's face reveals the truth. Mai understands at last that her sister is dead, just as she feared.

Tears roll down her cheeks from sadness and anger. Only two of them survived. Tuyet will never see Lao turning into a man.

Mai allows the policeman to take his baby, but feels hollow once her arms are empty. She is too overwhelmed to speak when her new friend Sinead leads her back down the winding stairs.

75

Saturday, 13th January

'He's safe and sound, Nina. I'm holding him now. You can stop worrying.'

There's a tearing sound on the phoneline, like fabric being ripped apart. I can hear Nina crying with relief that our son's been found, but she hardly says a word. I'm staring down at Lawrie Deane while I make the call. I'm forced to guard him until Isla and Eddie arrive, but I'd rather abandon him on the floor, like a piece of filth. He looks childlike now, with his knees pressed to his chest, still hiding his face from the world. He knows me well enough to realise that if he moves a muscle, I'll beat him black and blue.

'Bring Noah home.' Nina whispers the words, then my godmother Maggie's voice greets me next. Nina must have passed her the phone.

'Is he doing okay, Ben?'

'He's grubby and hungry, but otherwise fine.'

There's a peal of laughter. Many things amuse Maggie, but this time it sounds hysterical, like she's been pushed too far. She doesn't bother to ask who's responsible for keeping the islands in fear for days. When she speaks again, she just begs me to hurry back to Bryher, so Nina can relax.

'I will, I promise. Thank everyone for me, Maggie. Tell them we found the killer.'

I put my phone away as Eddie comes racing upstairs. The shock on his face is so profound when I explain that Deane is our killer, he stops functioning for a moment, rooted to the spot like he's been struck by lightning. I put my hand on his shoulder to steady him. I know how much he respected Deane's quiet devotion to the islands, and now his picture of the man is shattering. It takes a full minute for his expression to change from blank-eyed shock to disgust.

'Guard him, Eddie. Use your handcuffs, then bring him down, please. I need to make sure the girl's okay.'

When I get downstairs Mai is standing near the tower's front door, leaning on Sinead's arm. She's shaking, her black hair thin from years of poor nutrition and lack of sunlight. Mai can't be much more than sixteen, yet she could be thirty, her skin unnaturally pale. I can tell she's reluctant to go outside. It takes bravery to re-enter the world after such a long ordeal, yet something in her gaze makes me certain that although she's damaged, she's not broken. I watch Isla's car pull up, with Noah still draped across my shoulder, fast asleep. Mai doesn't complain as Sinead helps her into the car to go to hospital and be cared for. Ginny will decide if she's strong enough to be reunited with Lao, or she needs rest first. As they drive away Sinead remains silent, like she needs a moment to accept everything that's happened.

Phillip Warleggan is still standing guard, despite my accusations. When I apologise, he doesn't even seem angry.

'I should have realised the truth was much closer to home, Phillip. I'm sorry.'

'No one could have predicted this, Ben.'

'So you didn't know about the fire at your smugglers' cottage? Deane set it alight. I'm afraid it's burned to the ground.'

Warleggan looks startled, then there's a long pause before he speaks. 'It was insured, Ben, maybe it can even be rebuilt. We've lost some history, but no one was hurt. Your son's safe. That's what counts.'

'You've helped us enough tonight. We'll need a statement from you about everything you witnessed, but that can wait till tomorrow.'

Old truths are gradually surfacing, and my heartbeat's slowing down as I turn to face Sinead Harcourt. Her two friends Fordie and Lisa Angarrack have emerged from the shadows while I've been talking to Angarrack. The three of them are standing together with arms linked, their expressions victorious. I see now that they've been working as a team, doing their best to help Mai. I'm about to ask for their side of tonight's events when Sinead steps closer, with words babbling from her mouth, like she's held them back for weeks.

'I knew Lawrie was involved. I saw him going into the deserted house next to ours a few times: that's what made me suspicious. And we saw his boat at St Helen's more than all the rest. No one was listening to me. And it didn't feel safe to tell you, till tonight.'

'I still don't understand where the network idea comes from, Sinead.'

'Kim Durgan's a friend of mine. She told me recently that a man came and took her cousins away, when she was trafficked here. She's only just started to talk about what happened to a couple of people – friends she can really trust. When I heard that Alan Madron was first to reach their boat, I thought he might have abducted Mai and Tuyet, before coming back for the rest.'

Fordie looks embarrassed. 'Then we made some mistakes. We couldn't believe that just one man could keep two girls hidden for so many years, in a place this small. Alan Madron's close friends with Phillip, and Lisa's parents, so we started calling them the network.'

'The whole thing made us a bit paranoid,' Lisa Angarrack joins in, her voice cracking. 'And my dad's been an idiot. He kept on taking his boat out when he thought me and Mum were asleep. He wasn't trafficking kids, or doing anything evil, like we thought. He was having an affair and Mum's walked away.'

'I doubted my dad too,' says Sinead, visibly upset. 'Fordie saw him out on our boat one night. But he misses Mum, like me. He probably just wanted to feel close to her again.'

When her voice trails into silence Fordie puts his arm round both his friends' shoulders, offering comfort. The three of them appear inseparable. It looks like the Angarracks' attempts to divide them have made the three friends closer. I can imagine them all going to university and making new lives for themselves.

'So is that the reason you three have been sailing out to St Helen's at night? You wanted to stop something terrible, and thought my whole team was in on it?' I scan each of their faces in turn as they nod back at me. 'You've saved two lives tonight. I'll make sure everyone knows about it.'

When the three teenagers smile back at me, their exhaustion shows, but I can see months of fear slipping away. I've lost a colleague tonight, but the islands are safe again. Maybe it's just as well that Madron is too ill to understand that the sergeant he trusted for decades is evil to the core.

I remember Mark Lanner suddenly, locked up in his basement for no good reason. It only takes me a moment to call to his neighbour to set him free. I'll have to go round the islands apologising to everyone I doubted, or abused, but right now that's immaterial. I thank the three teenagers again for all their help, then send them home.

Ten more minutes pass before Eddie finally escorts Deane back downstairs. He must have summoned help in advance, because two cars have arrived, driven by volunteer stewards. It's a reminder that we live in a community where people sign up to help each other without complaint, even in the middle of the night. Evil like we've seen tonight is rare, thank God.

One of the guys from the lifeboat crew is ready to drive us back to the station, and the other walks straight to Eddie. He must have enlisted him, in case Deane turned violent, but his energy seems to have vanished. Now he's lost his power over Mai, it's like he's fallen apart. He's standing with head bowed, still too cowardly to make eye contact, hands cuffed in front of him.

Eddie's face is full of anger and confusion. I can tell he's been following procedure to the letter, to keep his feelings at bay.

'We're ready, sir.' His words are a low murmur, when he looks across at Deane. 'He's not denying it.'

When I ask him to bring Deane back to the station with me, he nods rapidly. Deane traipses behind him to the waiting vehicle. He doesn't protest when Eddie orders him onto the back seat. He's following instructions like a naughty child, caught in the act. We'll need days to process it all and understand Deane's crimes. I have a feeling we'll never fully accept the truth. How could a man who claims to love his grandsons commit such monstrous abuse?

Eddie seems reluctant to get into the car beside Deane. 'Those wounds on his face were self-inflicted,' he says. 'Even now he wanted people to see him as a hero, saving people from harm.'

'He must have lost his mind, Eddie,' I say. 'Let's get him back to the station, the rest can wait.'

I sit in the front seat of the car with Noah clasped to my chest, half asleep after his adventure. None of us speaks when our volunteer drives us back to Hugh Town as dawn arrives. Deane doesn't reply when I tell him that a nurse will come to the station to stitch and dress his wound. It occurs to me that his future will be full of punishments. Maybe he's contemplating them already. He'll be spending the day in one of the minute holding cells he's kept clean for years, with little to distract him.

Something lifts from my chest when Deane is finally locked away. I don't care about his excuses, whatever they may be. I just need to be sure Noah's unharmed, so I carry him to the toilets. My tension fades as I fill a sink with warm water, then bathe the grime from his skin. A few tears drop from my eyes when I see that he's unmarked, all his bones intact. Noah's smile brightens as he splashes water at me.

'I'll never let you out of my sight again,' I whisper.

It's only when I spot my reflection that my shock registers. The soot is easy to wash off, but tonight's panic lingers in my eyes, even though I try to ignore it. I find an emergency jar of baby food in the station's small kitchen, and Noah swallows it in greedy gulps, then promptly falls asleep.

Tension hits me again when I spot Deane's police cap, still

hanging by the door. I feel like burning it, but his legacy must be dealt with formally, starting tonight. He's under arrest for murder, and I feel guilty for believing Madron could have been involved in such evil acts. It's his generosity that made me doubt him. He must have given Deane some red carpet and he then used it to cover the floor of the damp basement under his garden that he used to keep his prisoners.

Eddie volunteers to guard our suspect for an hour or two, so I can take Noah home, then return to close the case. When I peer through the observation hatch into the holding cell, Deane is lying down. He's covered himself from head to toe with a grey blanket. It's the only comfort the bare room provides, but I feel no sympathy. He's about to receive a crash course in the captivity he inflicted on others. Deane will spend so long in prison, it's likely he'll die there, before his sentence ends.

76

It's 8.00 am by the time I get home. Nina is standing in the porch of our cottage, and Noah is draped over my shoulder, asleep. Her face is blank when she seizes him then carries him straight to the nursery. I can see she's forgotten my existence as she checks his sleeping form for signs of damage, just like I did. When she finds none, she lays him in his cot then backs away.

She remains silent when we reach the living room. The fire must have died a long time ago, the air cold. I'm not prepared when Nina suddenly reaches back, then slaps my face so hard, the noise echoes from the walls. My skin stings, but the misery in her gaze hurts me worse.

'I can't do this anymore,' she whispers.

'He's okay, Nina. You saw for yourself, just now.'

'Noah could have died today; so could you.'

'We're both okay, I promise.'

'I almost lost you both. Nothing's okay, you idiot. Can't you see?'

When I reach for her shoulders Nina fights me off at first. Her fists batter my chest, as last night's terror floods out of her. It's a relief when the tears come, and she slumps into my arms, finally letting go. All I can do is rub her back and let her cry it out. It's a shock to see her break down, when she's always so calm and controlled, but Shadow does a better job of comforting her. He remains at Nina's side, then shepherds her to the sofa to recover, pressing his muzzle into her hand.

Nina's reaction puts things in perspective. My family matters more than anything, even my job, and the islands themselves. Her calm returns sooner than mine. She wants to know exactly what happened last night, forcing me to relive being locked in the burning cellar, then my frantic chase around St Mary's, until the truth emerged about Lawrie Deane.

'He abducted the two sisters, then murdered Tuyet years later. When he got Mai pregnant he left the baby outside the station. Even that was a selfish act. I bet he couldn't bring himself to kill a child that carries half his DNA. But I still don't know why he tried to steal Noah from us.'

'He came to our wedding. We treated him like a friend.' Nina's voice is still flat with shock.

'Everyone did, he was so convincing. Lawrie seemed to enjoy helping people.'

'He must be a psychopath. Fooling people, all that play-acting, it's how they get their kicks.'

'It'll take Mai years to adjust to her new life, won't it?'

'She'll need a lot of support, but having Kim will help. At least she won't be alone.'

'I think she sees the baby as hers, not Deane's. She almost collapsed with relief when she found out he's alive.'

'Surprising, isn't it? Some rape victims choose to keep their babies and give them loving homes.'

'How can they be that forgiving?'

'Because it's never the baby's fault.' Nina looks back at me. 'They're always innocent.'

Deane doesn't fit my image of a stereotypical psychopath, with good looks and a dazzling intellect. He's just a plain-looking man with a subdued manner. I can't imagine how he normalised keeping two girls underground, in a dungeon we failed to discover. I'll have to wait until tomorrow to learn if it gave him sleepless nights, or whether he's actually emotionless, behind all that fake sympathy and warmth.

'Things need to change, Ben.' Nina's gaze meets mine suddenly with laser force. 'Me and Noah don't get enough of your time.'

'I know. I'm sorry.'

'No apologies. Just listen to me. You've worked for the police for twenty years, putting yourself in harm's way. And in your downtime, you're a bloody lifeboat volunteer.'

'It's how things work here, you know that. People look out for each other.'

'I won't let Noah lose his dad at sea, like you did. I've already buried one husband, remember?'

'If you're insisting, I'll drop my lifeboat duties, I promise.'

'Can I have that in writing?' Her gaze lingers on my face. 'And we need a holiday to get over all this. Noah should see the world and learn how it feels to get lost in a crowd.'

'Book it, we can fly anywhere.'

Nina's smile slowly widens. I don't usually let her walk all over me, but today she deserves the upper hand. 'I lost control back there, out of fear. I shouldn't have hit you, Ben.'

'No apologies. Just listen to me.' She gives a shaky laugh when I quote her earnest speech back at her. 'Are we okay now?'

'More or less. I'm getting there.'

She looks towards Noah's nursery, and we both remain silent for a moment.

'I'm worried about Zoe,' Nina says at last. 'She's been looking after that baby like he's her own, and now she'll have to hand him over.'

'We'll take care of her. And she's a strong one. She'll survive.'

'Intact, I hope.' She nods at me. 'I need to sleep while Noah's down. I haven't shut my eyes all night. Come with me?'

'I can't be long. The case needs tying up, on St Mary's, then I'll take time off.'

'Stay with us, please, just for an hour.'

'Okay, I'll call and let them know.'

She drops a kiss on my cheek then heads for our bedroom. When I look out of the window, the landscape is dazzling. The winter sun is turning gold, and the sea glitters like polished glass. I've spent the past week dealing with the worst type of evil, yet this place will always look blameless. Even Deane's ugly deeds won't stain it for long.

No other landscape draws me like these islands, washed clean each day by Atlantic tides. Resigning from the lifeboat crew will be a wrench, but it's the least I can do for Nina, for agreeing to stay here. I can't afford to scare her again, or we'll all suffer.

My body feels lax with tiredness as I walk to the bedroom, hoping a short sleep will stop my racing thoughts. My mind's still filing away information I'd rather forget. Soon I will have to interview Deane, and hear what he's done, if he chooses to speak. The prospect sickens me. I've always hated deceit, and the man's whole life has been built from excuses and lies.

77

Mai wakes up terrified. Sunlight is seeping through the curtains, onto her hospital bed, and when she checks the wall clock, hours have passed since a nurse left her here. She intended just to take a nap, but exhaustion conquered her. Her panic deepens when she gets to her feet. What if she's trapped here too? Maybe those people last night were evil, just like the man? But when she twists the doorknob, it opens first time. Pressure lifts from her shoulders when she understands that she's free to leave, even though the world outside feels much too big. She has nowhere to go.

Someone has left clean clothes on a chair by her bed. New underwear, jeans and a jumper, plus a pair of trainers. Her body aches, but Mai is fully dressed when another stranger enters the room. A doctor smiles down at her. She's middle-aged, wearing a white coat, her grey hair swept into an untidy bun.

'Hello, Mai. My name's Ginny.' Her voice is gentle. 'How are you doing? Did you get some sleep?'

Mai nods slowly. It's hard to meet the doctor's eye, it's been so long since she saw anyone except the man.

'I want to examine you later, to check you're well.' She glances at Mai's hands. 'And I can bandage that cut properly for you. We'll do it whenever you're ready.'

Suddenly Mai feels overwhelmed. Why are these people being so kind to a stranger from a distant country? There's nothing familiar to anchor her to this place, yet she doesn't pull away when the doctor edges closer. The woman's touch on her shoulder is so light, it hardly registers.

'Would you like a visitor? I've told her not to stay long. We mustn't tire you, until you're fully well.'

'My son. When can I see him?'

'Today, I promise.'

When the doctor steps back, a young woman with glossy dark hair enters. Mai doesn't recognise her at first, then emotions hit her as she stumbles to her feet. Kim was just eight years old when they were separated. Now her cousin is a beautiful teenager – but still with the same shy smile.

Mai can't speak until Kim whispers a greeting in Vietnamese. They fall into each other's arms. The two girls sit together on the bed, holding hands. The younger girl weeps with relief, then places something on Mai's lap. It's one of their prayer shawls, threadbare but intact, connecting them to the past. Mai is dry-eyed when she thanks her, even though emotions are rioting in her chest. She's had to hide her feelings for so long, it's second nature to suppress them, but she can feel her heart coming back to life. There's a warm sensation in her chest. It flutters, like a candle's flame.

Mai stiffens again when a tall blonde woman enters the room. She feels dizzy when she sees Lao in her arms. It's hard to breathe when the woman slowly places him in her lap.

'I'm Zoe. I've been looking after your baby. He's beautiful.'

'How do I thank you?' Mai whispers. 'He looks stronger, and you kept him safe.'

'He's been missing you, every minute.'

Mai doesn't notice the tears rolling down the blonde woman's face as she leaves. She's too busy caring for Lao and introducing him to Kim. Her son smells different, of soap and innocence, not the grime and dirt of their cell. But one thing hasn't changed: his gaze is still full of trust when their eyes meet. No matter what happens next, she can never let the three of them be separated again.

78

Sunday, 14th January

Isla and Eddie are both in the team room when I reach the station, two hours after I left Deane there. Shadow is by my side. I tried leaving him with Nina, but he's sticking to me like glue, even though the threat is over. My mind still can't accept what's happened, and Deane's betrayal of trust must be even worse for my two younger colleagues. He was their mentor, but they're both hard at work, answering calls, reassuring islanders that the killer has been found. It dawns on me that our boss may never return to work, like Deane, but for different reasons, our team decimated.

'Put your phones on silent for a minute, please,' I ask them.

The landline goes on ringing. People are clamouring for information about the threat that's hung over the islands for days. I ignore it and pass on information I've received in a text from Ginny.

'The DCI has been flown to Penzance Hospital for treatment this morning. So Deane's our biggest concern now. He'll be going to the mainland later today, escorted by the Cornish Constabulary. They'll deal with his arrest, to avoid conflict of interest. But we need a preliminary statement before he goes.'

Eddie shakes his head. 'We won't get it; he's refusing a lawyer.'

'And he'll only talk to you, sir,' Isla says. 'He says he just wants to explain, one officer to another, before he goes. He told me when I took him his breakfast. I can't even look at him, boss.' Isla's voice is crackling with strain. Out of all of us, she was closest to Deane, relying on his advice when she first arrived. It's yet more proof that the man fooled us all.

'We don't owe him anything, Isla, remember? He's not who he pretended to be.'

'I know, sir. It's so disgusting, that's all. I'll never accept it.'

When her head drops forwards, Eddie puts his arm round her shoulders.

'Take it easy today, both of you. We all need time to adjust.'

I've got no desire for Deane's company, when I leave Shadow in the team room then follow the corridor to the holding cell. Our conversation will hold no legal weight, without a solicitor present, because I'm no longer the SIO.

My stomach's churning when I slide back the observation hatch. Deane is sitting bolt upright, in the same blood-stained shirt as he wore last night. I assume he's refused to put on the grey cotton tracksuit we provided because he's unwilling to look like a prisoner. Deane gestures for me to enter, like he's the one in command.

The cell feels claustrophobic, but my desire to hurt him has gone. Personal anger burned away when I saw that Noah's unharmed. It's been replaced by a simple desire to know what triggered his acts of madness. I lower myself onto the bed, leaving a metre of clear air between us.

'I hear you've been asking for me, Lawrie. You've got five minutes; that's my limit. Then you're going to the mainland.'

'Please don't use that dismissive tone. I'm a human being, like you, remember?'

'Are you? Monsters commit crimes like yours, not ordinary people.'

I have to bite my lip. If I speak again it will be a torrent of abuse, for the lives he's damaged.

'Just reserve judgement, that's all I ask, and let me explain from the start.'

'Five minutes, like I said.'

He ignores my comment, keeping his diction slow. 'It was me that intercepted Mark Lanner's call about those kids, adrift on Deadman's Pool. I still don't know why I pretended to be Madron when we spoke. But that's how it began.'

'You're still lying. I bet you were working with the child

traffickers, putting money in some offshore account, planning a new life, one day. You borrowed other people's boats, like Phillip Warleggan's in case the coastguard spotted you.'

He shakes his head. 'I did that because those kids were following me.'

'That's why Sinead and her friends thought loads of powerful people were sailing out to St Helen's. You even made them doubt their own parents, when in fact it was just you, going over there in their boats, digging graves.'

Deane doesn't bother to deny it. I'm almost certain he's been a go-between, which could explain why smuggling activity has been increasing every year.

He takes a breath, then words spill out of him. 'I sailed there out of pity for those kids, and that's the truth. I was in the same position, you see. I'd been abandoned too. My wife had left me that year, and you'd stolen the job that was rightfully mine. When Mai looked into my eyes, something passed between us. We were meant to be together, just her and me. Nothing else mattered. But her sister clung on to her. I couldn't separate them, so I had to take them both. She was always in our way.'

The conviction on his face is baffling. The man seems to believe that romance could exist between him and a child forty years younger. My hands ball into fists at my sides, but I can't hit him. If I start, I may never stop.

'How come you waited so long to kill Tuyet?'

'It wasn't deliberate. I took her upstairs for some fresh air, but she fell backwards down the steps, hitting her head. I couldn't revive her.'

'I don't believe you. You wanted sex with her too, but she fought you, tooth and nail. That's the truth, isn't it?'

'No. No. I told you, I love Mai. Tuyet just lost her footing, that's all.'

'If you're aiming for a manslaughter charge, not murder, that won't convince a jury.'

'Can't you see I'm being honest?'

'You don't know the meaning of the word.' I shake my head. 'I bet you enjoyed yourself on St Helen's. You'd go over and dig for a while, then have a nice barbecue. But why leave your rubbish there? It's not like you to be sloppy.'

'Fordie's boat was sailing too close. I was afraid he'd see me, so I hid. I had no time to collect the rubbish. I thought Mai loved me until last night. I only wanted to protect her, but I let it go on too long. I was terrified of losing my job and hurting my kids.'

'How come you left Lao here, then took Noah? It doesn't make sense.'

His gaze drops to the floor. 'Mai needed a child to love, far more than I realised. I wanted to take her abroad, to be a family.'

'I think you planned to dump her body in the second grave, then sail away, alone, to escape punishment. Working here helped you stay one step ahead and see off any trouble, but you slipped up. Sinead Harcourt and her mates were on to you. I've got them to thank for keeping Mai and Noah safe tonight. Once you saw she'd escaped I bet you planned to kill her, for never loving you in the first place. You'd have killed my son too, just for the hell of it.'

'That's pure fabrication.'

'It's true, isn't it?'

He looks away. 'I regret my actions now.'

'Is that right? You're a coward, Lawrie. No one will forgive you.'

'I knew you'd react like this, with contempt. You've never shown me any respect.'

'Self-pity won't change anything. You'll never come back here. I'm afraid your son's taken it badly. Put it this way, don't expect many Christmas cards while you're inside.'

Deane's voice sounds broken. 'Just tell me how Mai's doing, before you go.'

'She's reunited with Kim and Lao. She's an amazing young woman. God knows how she can love that baby after years of abuse.'

'Go ahead and hit me. I can see you're dying to, so feel free.'

'I'll let the courts deal with you, and it won't be pretty. The team on the mainland already know there's cast-iron proof that you're an abductor, a rapist and a murderer.'

Deane shuts his eyes, then folds his arms tight across his chest, protecting himself from the truth. He doesn't bother to say goodbye when I leave.

Eddie looks more upbeat when I get back to the team room. 'Gannick called to say that she's found the entrance to Deane's hideaway, boss. Apparently, his bungalow stands on the foundations of an old smuggler's cottage, like the one in Warleggan's garden, but bigger. It's got a network of underground tunnels and small rooms. One of them is lined with red carpet, most likely from Madron's house. The cellars are accessible by steps, hidden in a flower bed. The room where Gannick thinks Mai was held even has a window almost hidden by brambles, just wide enough for her to escape, once she'd broken it.'

'I hope Gannick's cataloguing everything.'

'You know what she's like, sir,' Isla says. 'All the bags and boxes will be alphabetised. But there's more: she thinks the two girls were kept in the derelict house Madron owned for a while, then Deane moved them to his property.'

'It's the planning that's hard to accept. He knew exactly what he was doing.'

A wave of nausea hits me out of the blue. We'll get an influx of journalists when Deane's crimes emerge; he'll become a celebrity, which is sickening too. They'll be queuing up for photos of his lair. It will be our most important duty to protect Mai's privacy. The Durgan family have already offered her and the baby a home, for as long as they need it, in their wonderful, overcrowded house. The news has steadied me. Knowing that people like the Durgans exist dilutes some of the bitter taste Deane's crimes have left in my mouth.

'Are you okay, boss?' Eddie asks. 'You look a bit shaky.'

'I just need some fresh air. I'll be back soon.'

My head's still boiling with ugly images when I take the short walk to Town Beach, with Shadow running ahead to the point where the lifeboat house stands guard over the bay. I keep my back to the harbour wall, sheltered from the breeze as seagulls fly in slow spirals overhead, scouting for food.

My vision soon clears. The sky is crystalline blue, like it's rehearsing for summer. I keep my hands buried in my pockets, to keep them warm. The next few weeks will be hard, while we examine Deane's lair, and mop up the aftermath. Island life suits most people, but for some it's ruinous. Winter throws us back on our resources. The isolation can cause even the strongest folk to struggle, yet Deane's actions defy logic. I can tell he's justified them in his own mind, believing he's been wronged. It may even surprise him to be judged a monster by millions when the story finally breaks.

I look across the harbour, where the ferryboat is waiting to take passengers back to Bryher. A woman's tall figure is climbing on board, but she hasn't spotted me. It's Zoe, with her shock of blonde hair. My friend's body language looks different today. Her movements are lighter as she takes her seat in the bow, like a weight's been lifted from her shoulders. I thought she'd struggle to hand Lao back, but maybe caring for him has answered a long-held need. Either way, I'll call her tonight, and invite her round to ours. When I watch the ferry enter St Mary's Strait the water's so smooth, it seems like a different entity from the storm-bound sea that played havoc with the investigation.

My strength is slowly returning as the sun casts light on the shifting waves, as the tide turns. My own fortunes are shifting too. I love this landscape and always will. I'm not prepared to let one man's sick mind cast a shadow over it for another day.

My pace is slow as I head back to the station, to brief the mainland team in full about Deane's crimes and the raft of evidence they need to collect. The courts are unpredictable, but

I'm keeping my fingers crossed that Deane gets the whole-life sentence he deserves. I don't relish the idea of describing all the damage he's done, but today's duties will soon be over. The only thing that matters is that Nina's waiting for me at home, while our son keeps busy, preparing to take his very first steps.

79

Cornishnews.co.uk

Depraved killer policeman kept girls in dungeon

Sometimes truth is stranger than fiction. Who could predict that a police officer on the idyllic Isles of Scilly would kidnap two young girls, and lock them away for six years, then murder the youngest? Tuyet and Mai Huang were kidnapped by child traffickers in Vietnam, aged just eight and ten. Sergeant Lawrence Deane intercepted their abandoned dinghy off the Cornish coast, and kept the two girls locked in a cellar under his back garden. When sixteen-year-old Mai fell pregnant Deane left her to give birth alone, after killing Tuyet. He spent twenty-eight years in the police force before his crimes emerged. Now he's awaiting trial for murder in Dartmoor Prison.

The islands' teenagers knew something was wrong, before the case was exposed. One brave young woman, Sinead Harcourt, and her friends Thomas Ford and Lisa Angarrack will travel to Buckingham Palace next week to receive King's Gallantry Awards for their part in exposing the killer. They saw boats sailing to the deserted island of St Helen's before the victim's body was found there. They knew that child traffickers smuggle around 10,000 minors into the UK, via clandestine routes, and believed that the islands were a stop-off point for the illegal trade in human lives. The police are still investigating whether Lawrence Deane was part of a wider child-smuggling ring.

Inhabitants of the sleepy community of Hugh Town on St Mary's are still in shock. Emma Angarrack, the island mayor, said: 'The community's reeling, but our thoughts are with the surviving victim. She has shown incredible bravery to survive such a terrible ordeal for six years.'

Interim Chief of Police, DI Ben Kitto, has released the following statement: 'We ask people to reserve judgement until after the trial, and to respect the victim's need for privacy.'

No one yet understands how a serving police officer could escape detection for so long. Lawrence Deane didn't just get away with murder. He was also a churchgoer and a trusted school governor, putting him in direct contact with hundreds of children.

The case proves that monsters can thrive anywhere. Even beautiful landscapes, like the unspoiled Isles of Scilly, can hide the ugliest crimes.

Acknowledgements

Thanks as always to the people of Scilly, who answered all my questions about St Helen's, and have made me so welcome over the years. Thanks to Tregarthen's Hotel and everyone at The New Inn, Tresco, for putting up with me scribbling away, in a corner of the bar.

Thanks also to the excellent charity WaterAid, for inviting me to take part in their annual book name auction. I'm so glad it raised some funds for you! It was also a privilege to include Thomas Ford's name in the book, for his family, after they sadly lost him at just twenty-two years of age.

I'd like to say thank you to the whole team at Orenda, particularly Karen Sullivan and West Camel. Working with you has felt like a homecoming! I'm so happy that you love the characters in my series as much as I do. And Teresa Chris, my long-time agent and friend, thanks a million for all your sage advice. I definitely owe you at least one large cocktail, next time we meet!